Praise for *Six Ways to Sunday*

'An entertaining tale of a young woman in love, determined to do what she can to make a change ... *Six Ways to Sunday* reminds me why I love the writing of Karly Lane and leaves me waiting semi-patiently for her next release.' —Beauty and Lace

'This is a great piece of Australian rural fiction that touches on very real issue and has a lovely romance at its centre ... Karly Lane has an uncanny knack for truly capturing the spirit of rural communities in this novel ... She clearly has a love for rural Australia and *Six Ways to Sunday* is a great addition to her ever-growing catalogue of compelling Australian stories.' —Read the Write Act

'*Six Ways to Sunday* by Aussie author Karly Lane is a brilliant story of courage in the face of adversity, of fighting for what you believe is right, and the way some small rural communities are left behind and forgotten in the advancement of time ... ★★★★★' —Reading, Writing and Riesling

'I cannot rave enough about *Six Ways to Sunday* by Karly Lane, which is an easy fit in my top ten reads this year. It is a book that I could not put down and would go back and read again and again.' —Talking Books Blog

'It's always wonderful to have a book you can pick up and know that you're going to enjoy it, and *Six Ways to Sunday* definitely fits that bill ... This is the perfect summer read.' —The Noveltea Corner

'While city girl to farm wife is by no means a new premise for a novel, Karly Lane's clear passion for rural Australia, along with her intelligent interweaving of serious rural issues into the storyline, elevates *Six Ways to Sunday* into a class of its own.' —Theresa Smith Writes

'A fast paced, well-written read with an entertaining plot and likeable (and unlikeable!) characters that are convincing and spirited.' —*The Weekly Times*

T0373930

Karly Lane lives on the mid north coast of New South Wales. Proud mum to four beautiful children and wife of one very patient mechanic, she is lucky enough to spend her day doing the two things she loves most—being a mum and writing stories set in beautiful rural Australia.

ALSO BY KARLY LANE

North Star
Morgan's Law
Bridie's Choice
Poppy's Dilemma
Gemma's Bluff
Tallowood Bound
Second Chance Town
Third Time Lucky
If Wishes Were Horses
Someone Like You

Karly
LANE

Six Ways to Sunday

ALLEN&UNWIN
SYDNEY • MELBOURNE • AUCKLAND • LONDON

Allen & Unwin
83 Alexander Street
Crows Nest NSW 2065
Australia
Phone: (61 2) 8425 0100
Email: info@allenandunwin.com
Web: www.allenandunwin.com

A catalogue record for this
book is available from the
National Library of Australia

ISBN 978 1 76052 885 0

Set in Sabon LT Pro by Bookhouse, Sydney
Printed in Australia by SOS Print + Media

10 9 8 7 6 5 4 3 2

The paper in this book is FSC® certified.
FSC® promotes environmentally responsible,
socially beneficial and economically viable
management of the world's forests.

For Jan and Noel

For Ian and Noel

One

Rilee dropped her head to the steering wheel and swore under her breath. She couldn't deny her predicament any longer. She was bogged—well and truly stuck.

With a tired sigh, she opened the door of the bulky Land Rover and took a look at the damage.

The tyres were half submerged and the mud was almost level with the bottom of the door. This was not good. Dan wasn't going to be happy . . . again. As if she'd conjured him with her thoughts, his voice came over the UHF radio attached to the dash, making her jump.

'Rilee, are you on your way with that fuel filter?'

Maybe she could ignore his call. She looked back down at the mud swallowing the vehicle and reluctantly reached for the handset.

'Not exactly.'

'What do you mean, not exactly . . . exactly,' he asked and she heard the fatalistic tone in the deep voice she loved so much.

'Well, I was on my way, but I seem to be a little bit stuck.'

There was an uncomfortable silence and Rilee pictured her husband of barely three weeks wondering how the hell he had ended up with a moron for a wife.

In all fairness, Dan was an incredibly patient man and had been nothing if not considerate of her citified ways, but today was just the latest in a long line of disasters that had all involved her in one form or another.

This particular disaster had started early that morning when she'd volunteered to help out around the place. Dan had asked her to water the cattle they'd brought in the previous day and put into the small holding paddock closest to the house. It was so hot, she'd gone back to sit in the ute, to get out of the sun and make a few phone calls, only to realise when she looked up that the trough was overflowing, almost emptying the tank and causing a mini flood in the paddock.

When she'd gone back to the house to explain to her father-in-law what had happened, she must have forgotten to latch the gate properly and when she'd followed him back up to inspect the damage, they'd found cattle roaming all along the laneway and happily grazing in her mother-in-law's beautifully manicured garden.

'Dan, Mick here,' the radio cut in abruptly. 'I've just delivered some papers out to your dad, so I'll track down your wayward bride if you want, mate.'

Rilee frowned down at the radio. Mick who? Wayward bride?

'Thanks, Mick. I can't go anywhere until I get that filter,' Dan answered. 'Rilee, whereabouts are you?'

'Umm, let me just check this street sign up ahead,' she muttered as she glanced around at her surroundings miserably: nothing but miles and miles of open flat land as far as the eye could see.

Dan's sigh came across the airwaves and she could tell he was trying to stay patient. Immediately she felt repentant. He'd been working long hours since they got back from their week-long honeymoon and really didn't deserve her sarcasm; after all, it was her own inadequacy that had gotten her into each and every mess since arriving at Thumb Creek Station.

'Look for a landmark and tell me what you see.'

'A landmark? All I see is paddocks, cows and more bloody paddocks.'

'Right. Mick, she's over towards the north paddocks, probably bogged just off the track at the old mailbox corner. That's where it usually gets boggy after rain.'

'Righto, be there in a few.'

'How the hell did you work that out?' she demanded.

'Because that's where the cows are. Don't leave the four-wheel drive until Mick gets there.'

Rilee bit back a weary sigh. A few could mean anything from minutes to hours out here.

With only the low, mournful cry of a crow for company, Rilee wound back the seat and shut her eyes.

Three weeks.

She'd been a married woman now for three weeks and so far, other than the first week spent on the Gold Coast, she'd barely had time to adjust to her new husband without his entire family looking on.

They'd only known each other three months, but it was long enough to fall head over heels in love with the tall, laidback man who'd walked into the bar that night.

The Spotted Dick was an institution. A small rather dilapidated pub in the backstreets of Paddington, what it lacked in visual appeal it more than made up for in great food and cheap alcohol. It had paid Rilee's rent and student fees while she'd put herself through uni. Over those years she'd developed a close relationship with her bosses, Janice and Sid Brown, expats from England who had become more like family than employers. Despite the fact that she was now a qualified naturopath with a full-time job in a busy inner-city clinic and no longer needed to work in the pub in order to pay her rent, she enjoyed the atmosphere of the place and often worked a shift when the Browns were short-staffed. Sad as it was to admit it, working at the Spotted Dick was the extent of her social life.

That evening there was a bucks night booked as well as the overflow from a busy annual horseracing carnival which saw the main bar packed to capacity each year. Rilee had been handed the bucks party in the function room out the back and serving the rowdy crew kept her busy the entire shift. She was pretty sure she'd never seen so many hats and denim in one place. As she moved through the room, collecting empty glasses and handing around platters of food, she managed to piece together that the groom had grown up in some place out west and studied at an agricultural college before moving to the city. The majority of the guests seemed to be old schoolfriends.

As she circled the room with a tray of drinks, one of the guests gave a shout out for a bit of quiet and a few hilarious speeches followed. Then the groom stood up to thank everyone for coming. 'After tomorrow there'll only be two eligible bachelors left, Jacko and Dan,' he said and a cheer rose from the men. Rilee glanced around to see who Jacko and Dan were and saw two men being slapped on the back up the front of the room. One was taller than the other and looked a little intimidating, with short hair and stubble on his chin. The other man was obviously enjoying the spotlight, and going by the crude remarks he was making about the kind of woman he was holding out for, it was safe to say he would probably remain single for a long time to come.

Rilee left the room to get more drinks from the bar and smiled as she passed Janice. Her boss had once been a pin-up girl in London with hopes of making it to the big screen, until she met her husband, an up-and-coming boxer, who'd swept her off her feet. Everything about her was loud, from the provocative clothing she wore to the huge hoop earrings and neck-breaking stilettos, but underneath all that was a heart of gold and Rilee loved the woman to death.

'How's things going in there?' Janice asked.

'Running like clockwork.'

'Saw a few of them going in earlier,' the older woman said, lowering her voice suggestively. 'Tell ya what, if I was a few years younger, I'd be giving some of those cowboys a ride they wouldn't soon forget.'

'Janice!' Rilee said with mock outrage; for all the bottle-blonde's bravado, she knew she was still very much in love with her husband.

'Get out there and flaunt what you got,' she told Rilee as she refilled the tray of drinks. 'Use it before you lose it,' she added with a pointed stare.

'Thanks a lot,' Rilee grumbled under her breath as she walked back into the function room. There was something decidedly sleazy about flirting with patrons while she was working and there was nothing overly attractive about a man who'd been drinking most of the evening.

Rilee had just collected a full tray of used beer glasses and was about to turn around when she found herself trapped against the table by a stocky man in denim jeans and a cowboy hat. 'You wanna go someplace when you knock off?' the blurry-eyed man said as he slid a hand from her arm to her hip suggestively. Oh great, she thought wearily, it was eligible bachelor number one.

Rilee gritted her teeth but held a professional smile in place. 'No, thank you. If you'll excuse me, I need to get these glasses back to the bar.'

'Come on, sweetheart,' he said and his hand moved from her hip to her backside. 'I bet you've never been with a country fella. We're not like these poncy suit-wearin' fellas around here.'

'I'm not interested. Please remove your hand and get out of my way.'

The man opened his mouth, no doubt to inform her of a few more sterling qualities country boys possessed, but before he could utter a word a large hand fastened onto his shoulder and spun him around.

'Knock it off, Jacko,' growled a tall man with a very grim expression.

'Fuck off, Kincaid. No one asked you to butt in.'

Rilee held her breath. There was clearly no love lost between these two men, and she was trapped against the table, unable to escape.

'Watch your mouth in front of the lady.'

Jacko was sufficiently fortified with false bravado to let off a tirade of foul language just to get his point across to this Kincaid fella. He barely managed to slur out three more profanities before a large fist snapped his head back and Jacko slumped forwards. Kincaid caught him under the arms, sitting him down in a chair and readjusting Jacko's hat; the man looked for all the world like he'd passed out with his head resting on the tabletop.

'Is he still alive?' Rilee murmured, placing the tray on the table and putting her fingers to Jacko's neck where she was relieved to find a steady pulse.

'He's fine. A head that thick would take more than a tap to put a dent in,' the taller man muttered in disgust.

Around them the party continued unabated, everyone else oblivious to what had just happened.

'Are you okay?' her gruff rescuer asked.

Now she could see him clearly, Rilee recognised him as the other bachelor from the groom's speech. Up close, he was rather good-looking, in an RM Williams kind of way. He wasn't wearing a wide-brimmed hat like Jacko and a few other men in the room wore, but had on a jacket over a striped dress shirt and moleskins that hugged a pair of muscular thighs. She had to admit he was sexy in a rugged, macho sort of way—if she was into that kind of thing, *which she wasn't*, she hastily reminded herself.

'I'm perfectly fine,' she said when she realised he was waiting for an answer. 'And I'm quite capable of taking care of a man with roaming hands. Was that really necessary?'

He seemed a little taken back at her anger, but then shrugged his broad shoulders. 'Probably not, but I've wanted to knock that little jerk on his arse for a while now. Seemed like the perfect opportunity,' he said with a crooked grin that made Rilee catch her breath. No way. She did not just act like someone out of a romance novel. No one in real life went weak at the knees at a smile.

'You're lucky the publican didn't see it or he'd have you thrown out. We have a strict no-violence rule here.'

'But they don't mind if their employees get felt up by the patrons?'

'Of course they do. But I had it under control.'

'Not from where I was standing you didn't. Anyway. You're welcome,' he said.

8

Rilee gave an annoyed groan under her breath as he turned away. 'Wait.' He turned back with a raised eyebrow. She hated that she sounded ungrateful when he had clearly been trying to help. 'Thank you.'

'No worries,' he said lightly before walking away.

Rilee mentally shook herself when she realised she was following his departure with a little too much interest. The man sure knew how to wear a pair of moleskins. *Get a grip, girl.* She dated now and again, but usually safe, nonthreatening kind of men. Not men like . . . him, she thought, giving him another quick glance. He'd picked up a glass of beer from a table nearby and joined the small group of men standing around talking. She watched as he lifted the glass to his mouth to take a long swallow. Rilee followed the length of tanned skin at his neck before looking back up and catching his eye as he lowered the glass. She looked away quickly, embarrassed to have been caught staring at him. This was ridiculous. He was so not her type. He was dangerous and it had nothing to do with knocking out Jacko. He was dangerous to her peace of mind. She liked men who didn't complicate her life. Nice, friendly men who didn't make her pulse race.

Eventually most of the party had decided to move on to another venue and Rilee was free to clear away the tables and start packing up. As she returned from the bar with an empty tray, she scanned the room for those broad shoulders and sexy moleskins, but there were only a few stragglers, none of whom made her knees give out. She told herself she wasn't disappointed that he'd gone. It wasn't like she'd expected him to come and say goodbye or anything. Why would he? She reached for another glass and turned, almost crashing into a solid wall of chest.

Two hands immediately went to her arms to steady her. She stared up and ignored the frantic drumming of her pulse as her gaze connected with a set of deep blue eyes the colour of denim. 'I thought you'd left,' she heard herself babble and silently groaned. Could she sound any more pathetic?

'I had to help put Jacko into a taxi. He never could handle his grog.' He dropped his hands from her arms and hooked his thumbs into the side pockets of his pants.

'I thought you didn't like each other?'

'He's a tosser, but I couldn't leave the stupid idiot to wander around the city alone in his condition, could I?' he shrugged.

Rilee liked that. He was responsible and a decent human being . . . who had earlier punched the very man he had just helped, she reminded herself to keep from weakening.

'We didn't get around to introductions,' he said, breaking the silence which followed. 'Dan Kincaid,' he offered.

'Rilee Summers,' she replied after a brief hesitation.

'It was nice to meet you, Rilee,' he said, holding out a hand. For a moment she stared at it warily, before she moved the tray to her other hand and accepted his handshake. She glanced down at his hand and frowned, before turning it to get a better look. 'Did you do this tonight?' she asked, nodding at the graze on his knuckles.

He gave a brief shrug. 'Just a scratch.'

'Actually,' she said, sliding the tray onto the table beside her and taking a closer look, 'it looks more like a tooth mark.'

'Probably,' he agreed, seemingly unperturbed.

Rilee sent him an exasperated glare. 'This needs to be cleaned up. Do you have any idea how much bacteria the human mouth contains?'

'Nope, but considering it's Jacko's mouth, I reckon we could safely double the number.'

'It's nothing to joke about. You could get a serious infection from this. Follow me,' she said, picking up her tray and heading for the door to the kitchen.

At this time of the night it was empty, the kitchen having already packed up, leaving only the bar staff and a few regulars out in the main bar.

Rilee went to the storeroom and pulled down a large first-aid box and carried it to a nearby benchtop. 'Sit,' she ordered over her shoulder.

Dan seated himself at the bench without complaint, watching her with lazy amusement. 'You provide first aid to your patrons often?' he asked.

'I have been known to on occasion,' she said, tipping a splash of disinfectant into a small plastic container and adding some water from the kitchen tap. 'Although not many people are silly enough to fight when Sid's around. He's an old bare-fist fighter from Liverpool.'

'So what was he doing leaving a female employee alone with a room full of blokes then?'

'Most people are presumed to be civilised,' she said acerbically.

'I wouldn't lump us all in with the likes of Jacko.'

Rilee glanced up briefly. 'So where is it that you come from?' she asked, taking his hand to clean the small gash.

'Pallaburra.'

'Where's that?'

'About eight hours west from here. Have you ever been out that way?'

'No,' she said. 'I lived overseas for a while, so I haven't really done much travelling around Australia.'

'Where did you live?'

'The UK.' She patted his hand dry before reaching for the butterfly strips. 'Any deeper and this would have needed stitches,' she told him.

'You're pretty good at this.'

Rilee shrugged. 'I studied natural medicine.'

'You're a doctor?'

'Naturopath.'

'So what are you doing working in a pub?'

'It's a good second income.'

He made a small grunt of surprise and continued to watch her work.

'What do you do for a living?' she asked to break the silence and the heavy weight of his gaze, which was making her a little self-conscious.

'I'm a farmer.'

'What do you grow?'

His eyes crinkled around the edges a little as he grinned. 'We raise cattle mostly, but we have some crops as well.'

'Is it a big place?'

'Fairly big.'

'There you go,' Rilee said as she finished attending to his cut and began to clear away her mess.

'Thanks.'

'Least I could do since you were hurt coming to my rescue,' she said dryly.

'If I knew you were going to patch me up I would have made a better job of getting hurt,' he grinned.

'Try to stay out of trouble for the rest of your visit,' she said after putting the first-aid box back where it belonged and leading him out to the bar.

'I'll do my best.'

'Well, nice meeting you,' Rilee said when they found themselves standing in the foyer.

'Yeah. You too, Rilee. I guess I'll see you around.'

She smiled as he walked out the door, and then released a long breath. What on earth was that? She didn't let men affect her. She didn't do distractions in her life nowadays. She did focus and determination. Dan Kincaid just needed to disappear back to Pallaburra so she could get back to concentrating on her plan.

Two

The next week was busy with back-to-back patient appointments and Rilee was surprised when the weekend came around again so soon. She arrived home Friday afternoon, dumping her armload of files and textbooks on the coffee table, which was exactly four steps from the front door of her tiny flat above a Chinese restaurant. It wasn't much, in fact it was pretty awful, but it was reasonably cheap for Paddington and it was close to work. Anyway, it wasn't as though she'd had the luxury of spending much time at home over the last four years for her less than appealing accommodation to be an issue; she'd spent most of her time at uni or working in the pub before graduating and working full-time at the clinic, so she was barely ever home.

Her mobile sounded from the depths of her handbag and Rilee rummaged through the contents to answer it. She saw the name of the pub flash across the screen and gave a small groan. It had been a long week and she wasn't rostered on for work at the pub this weekend. She almost didn't answer. But she knew she'd feel bad for the rest of the night if she didn't, so she pressed the answer button and forced a cheerfulness to her tone she was far from feeling.

To her surprise and relief, it wasn't a call to come in to work. 'Do you remember that bucks night you worked last week?' Sid started.

Remember? How could she forget those blue eyes and that sexy grin? 'Yes. Why?'

'There's a guy here looking for you. Wanted to know if you were working tonight.'

'What's he look like?' Rilee asked, suddenly realising she was gripping the phone rather tightly. *Please don't be Jacko.*

'Big guy. Short hair.'

From the background she heard Janice add in, 'Cute butt.'

'What does he want?' Rilee asked nervously.

'He didn't say. You want me to give him your number or not?' Sid said in his heavy cockney accent.

Did she? She wasn't sure. Why would he come back to see her? What if he was a weirdo and she couldn't get rid of him? Maybe she could just go down and see him at the pub, but then she'd have to talk to him . . . Did she want to talk to him?

'I ain't got all night, sunshine,' Sid said on the other end of the line.

'Oh. Right. Sorry. Umm, yeah, sure, give him my number.' *Oh God.*

'Right you are,' Sid said. 'Don't meet this guy at home. You can't be too careful these days,' he added gruffly and Rilee was touched by his concern.

'I won't, thanks, Sid. Sorry about this.'

'Yeah, well maybe you need to start getting out there a bit more instead of working and studying all the time. Might do you some good.'

'And who'd come and help you out then?' she teased.

'Life's not all about working.' An image of her bald, somewhat stout boss, with his slightly crooked nose from years of fighting, flashed before her eyes. Sid could look intimidating, like a man who could handle a bit of trouble, but really he was a teddy bear. 'Besides,' he said, clearing his throat quickly, 'you're not getting any younger, you know.'

'Thanks for that. I'll keep it in mind,' Rilee said dryly.

He hung up and Rilee sat the phone down on the coffee table, eyeing it nervously. 'Get a grip,' she told herself firmly. 'You're a mature adult, you can handle a phone call, for goodness sake!' But her hands felt clammy and her stomach was a jumble of nerves.

He probably wouldn't even call, she thought dismissively. Maybe he'd just been walking past and it was a spur of the minute thought to drop in and say hi.

The phone beeped and Rilee jumped, her fingers digging into the edge of the lounge chair as she stared at the unfamiliar number flashing across the screen. *Pick it up, pick it up!* a frantic little voice screamed inside her head.

'Hello?' she was trying for cool, calm and collected, but the slight squeak at the end may have given away how nervous she was.

'Ah, yeah. Hi. It's Dan Kincaid. From the bucks party last Friday night,' he added.

It was the same deep voice she remembered and it was just as lethal over the phone as it had been in person. 'Hi. How's your hand?'

He gave a low chuckle and Rilee tried her best to ignore the small shiver of awareness it triggered. 'Actually, I was hoping you might take a look at it.'

Rilee sat up straight. 'Why? What's wrong with it?'

'Nothing,' he said. 'I'm back in town for the weekend. I was wondering if you'd like to catch up while I'm here?'

'Catch up?' she repeated dumbly, her mind still reeling from the fact she was suddenly speaking to the man she'd been thinking about all week.

'It's okay if you're busy tonight, I just thought maybe if you were free over the weekend sometime.'

'I'm not busy tonight,' she found herself blurting.

'Great. Do you want me to come and pick you up?'

'No, that's okay, I can meet you. Where and when?'

They settled on a restaurant not too far away from the pub and only a few minutes' walk from her flat.

She dithered over what to wear for far too long before finally settling on a pair of good jeans, low heels and a glittery black halter top she'd bought on impulse months ago and had yet to wear. Twisting her hair up into a messy bun at the back of her head, she secured it with bobby pins and quickly touched up her makeup. She kept it at a bare minimum for work, with just a touch of eye shadow and some lip gloss; after all, her patients were more interested in her ability to heal them than her looks.

She spotted Dan as she neared the restaurant and nerves began a renewed assault. He was dressed a little more casually tonight in jeans and a shirt and gleaming boots. She'd almost hoped that seeing him tonight would be a disappointment. Unfortunately, he was just as good-looking as she remembered. Damn it.

'Where did you park?' he asked looking up the street behind her.

'I walked.'

'Alone?' he asked, lifting an eyebrow.

'Yes. Why?'

'This is the city. You shouldn't be walking around at night alone.'

Rilee bit back a laugh, then realised he was serious. 'It's okay, I don't live very far from here.' She'd also lived alone in London for years and managed to survive. She was pretty sure she could handle downtown Paddington.

'Still,' he said, glancing around as though expecting a gang of thugs to be lurking in a dark alleyway. 'You can't be too careful.'

Apparently you could. Example, exhibit A: tall, good-looking country boy.

'I wasn't expecting to see you again,' she said after they were seated at a table, waiting for their drinks.

'I wasn't sure how to find you. I remember you said the pub was your second job, so I took a gamble that you might be there.'

'Do you have another bucks night to attend?' she asked, only half joking. Why else would he be back in the city so soon?

'Nope.'

When he didn't elaborate, Rilee searched for something else to talk about. 'I bet you're sick of driving by now.'

'I flew.'

'Oh. Well, that makes more sense, I guess. Where do you fly from?' She may or may not have googled Pallaburra purely out of curiosity. It hadn't looked big enough to have an airport.

'I fly my own plane.'

'Really?'

'You sound surprised.'

'I guess I am. I just thought you were a . . .'

'Farmer,' he supplied dryly.

'I didn't mean it like that,' she hurried to apologise. 'How long have you been flying for?'

'Since I was sixteen. It's a way of life for a lot of land-holders. Makes life easier if you can cut through distance and isolation.'

'I can imagine. So you come to the city often then?'

'When I have to. I prefer not to if I can.'

'Ah, I see.'

'What do you see?' he asked, his eyes smiling a little as he looked across the table at her.

19

'You're a country snob.'

'I wouldn't say that. I like the city just fine . . . it has its good points,' he shrugged, 'but I don't think I could ever live here. What about you? Have you always lived in the city?'

'No, not always.'

'Where did you grow up?'

Rilee no longer hated this question as much as she used to. Once she would have hidden the truth behind a flippant remark or changed the subject, but as she grew older she realised she wasn't as ashamed of her upbringing as she had been as a self-centred teenager. 'I had a bit of an alternative lifestyle as a kid.'

'Alternative?'

'I lived with my parents in a commune until I was eighteen and ran away to the city,' she said, smiling dryly.

'Yeah?'

'Now you sound surprised,' she said, glancing up to thank the waiter who delivered their drinks.

'You don't look anything like I'd imagine a . . .'

'Hippie to look?' she supplied.

'I guess so,' he grinned.

'At the time I hated it. We moved from the city when I was eleven and I was filled with pre-teen angst, thinking the world was supposed to revolve around me,' she said. 'I look back now and realise my parents were going through their own problems. My dad had been made redundant and we couldn't afford to live in the city any more, so my parents decided to make a clean break and create a simpler way of life. All I could see at the time was that I was being forced to live on a farm with no electricity and I had to give up my friends and the home I loved,' she said with a twist of her lips.

'It must have been a shock to the system,' he said, reaching for his beer. 'Do your parents still live there?'

'Not on the commune. Same area though. They run their own business now.'

The topic changed and Rilee found herself enjoying their varied conversation throughout the meal and on through coffee, stretching the evening out for as long as they could until finally the staff were discreetly packing up around them.

'I'll walk you home,' Dan said as they stepped out into the night.

'You don't have to do that. It's not far.'

'I wasn't asking,' he said abruptly. 'You might be a big tough city girl, but where I come from you don't let women walk home alone at night.'

'Where you come from sounds scarier than the city,' she pointed out. 'Women shouldn't walk by themselves in the dark, they shouldn't be left to work in a room full of men alone ...'

He gave a small grunt at that. 'It's not a crime to have been brought up to take care of women, is it?'

'It just seems a little old-fashioned, I guess. I've been taking care of myself for a long time; I don't need a big strong man to step in and do it for me.'

He went quiet at that and she wondered if she'd offended him.

'I'm not going to apologise for stepping in with Jacko the other night. That's just who I am,' he said. 'However, the reason I won't let you walk home alone tonight doesn't have as much to do with my upbringing as it does with the fact I don't want to say goodnight yet.'

'Oh.' Her reply seemed woefully inadequate, but for the life of her she couldn't seem to make her tongue work. The truth was, she didn't want the night to end either.

'What made you come back from the UK?' he asked, breaking the silence that had fallen between them.

As a rule, Rilee tried not to talk much about that part of her life. The end had tainted all the happier times, but for some reason, here with Dan, it felt different. 'I got homesick,' she said lightly.

'Were you over there long?'

'About three years.'

'What did you do over there for all that time?'

'The usual. I backpacked for a while. I worked in pubs to save up enough money to travel around.'

'Did you go over there with friends?'

'No, well, I mean I made friends while I was over there, but I kind of liked being able to do my own thing.'

'That was a long time to be on your own.'

'I lived with someone briefly, but that didn't work out.'

'Ah. I knew it.'

'Knew what?' she asked, glancing across at him.

'There was a guy in your past who hurt you.'

'How could you know that?'

'Just a feeling. You seem so . . . self-sufficient.'

'So because I can take care of myself I must have been hurt by a guy in my past?'

'Something like that. You're different to most women I know. There's just something about you that I can't put my finger on. Like part of you is out-of-bounds.'

His assessment caught her off guard. 'And you came to this conclusion after a whole five minutes of knowing me?'

He didn't seem put off by her abrasive tone. 'Surprised the hell out of me too,' he grinned. They walked on and Rilee found herself distracted by the nearness of him. 'So what did he do? This jerk who hurt you?'

'The novelty apparently wore off and he decided he needed a little bit more variety in his life.'

'Then he was an idiot as well as a jerk.'

Rilee looked fixedly at a window display they were passing. 'It was my own fault, really. I knew deep down it was too good to be true. I let myself get sucked into a world I didn't belong in.'

When she felt him watching her, waiting for an explanation, she sighed. 'I don't know why I'm telling you any of this; it's not a part of my life I'm particularly proud of.'

'Why?'

Rilee shook her head slightly, almost as though trying to hold off the memories that were beginning to come tumbling back into her mind.

Dan stopped walking and reached out to take her arm gently, stopping her. 'I want to know everything about you, Rilee. Good or bad, I want to know it all.'

Rilee stared up at him and found herself confused by the battle raging inside her. Why wasn't this man scaring her when over the years anyone wanting to know any of this would have made her run a mile in the other direction? But a feeling of safety wrapped itself around her and made her want to tell him everything she'd rather forget.

Three

'I left home wanting this big adventure,' she said, deciding to start from the beginning. 'I'd always wanted to be a model and I couldn't wait to leave home. I was a horrible teen,' she gave a sad smile. 'I resented my parents for forcing their lifestyle upon me. I was so angry. I couldn't understand why we'd go from living a *normal* life to moving to some hippie place with no TV and none of my friends. I left the minute I was able to and swore I'd never look back. God, I was so young and naive,' she said, shaking her head.

'So you just packed up and went overseas? How old were you?'

'Eighteen.' She nodded at his doubtful look. 'I know, I think back now and wonder what the hell I was thinking.'

'So you're eighteen and find yourself in the UK?' he prompted when they'd walked a little way without talking.

'I landed in London and I guess I expected to meet with an agency and get a contract straight away,' she said with a sarcastic snort. 'That was my first slap in the face by reality. Within a week I'd used up most of my savings. I'd been rejected by every modelling agency I went to and pretty much lost all confidence after being told I was either too fat or not blonde enough, I didn't have *the look* they were after. It was a rude awakening, let me tell you,' she said dryly. 'For two years I worked in just about every kind of mundane job you could think of: I was a kitchenhand, cloakroom attendant, motel housekeeper. There was no way I was running home with my tail between my legs. I pretty much had to find any job that was going, which is how I eventually fell into bar work and met Sally.' She smiled fondly as she remembered the vivacious red-headed Scot.

'Sally had a connection to a guy who designed high-end jewellery. He was looking for models to do a photo shoot and Sally and I ended up getting a regular gig with him. Occasionally we'd model the jewellery at the races and fashion shows, and one night we were invited to model at the opening of an exclusive nightclub.'

The evening had been a jaw-dropping experience. Everywhere she'd looked in the nightclub were women in expensive glittering dresses, paparazzi crawling over one another to snap photos of the rich and famous. It was the kind of affair she'd only ever dreamed of as she was growing up and imagining a different, exciting life some place far away.

'We were *so* out of our league,' she said with a wry smile, 'but we didn't care. We were young and wild and up for any adventure that came our way.'

And when it arrived, it came with a jolt when Rilee, quite literally, ran into him. Alexis Savakis was the only son of a multimillionaire Greek businessman. He was devastatingly handsome and bored with life. It was a dangerous combination. Rilee apologised profusely as she tried to wipe her spilled champagne from the pants of the amused, dark-haired man dressed in what Rilee could tell was a suit worth more than she could dream of earning in an entire year of bar work. He somehow found her lack of sophistication refreshing, and she was mesmerised by his sexy Mediterranean good looks; she had no hope of resisting that lethal smile and sleepy-eyed sexuality.

'I knew I was completely out of my depth with Alexis, but he swept me off my feet. His friends couldn't understand what he saw in this wide-eyed Australian girl he insisted on bringing everywhere he went. I guess I knew deep down that it couldn't work—I mean, we had nothing in common,' she said throwing her hands outwards. *Except sex,* she added silently. That had been amazing, and probably the only thing that had kept him interested in her for as long as he had. But while their relationship lasted, he showered her with expensive gifts and clothes, seeming to take great pleasure in transforming her into the image of a woman who belonged in his world. 'But I went along with it,' she told Dan. 'I let him buy me.'

She felt a wave of disgust wash over her as she remembered. At first she hadn't wanted to admit it to herself; she'd wrapped it up in a pretty romantic package and pretended that it was love, but deep down she knew it wasn't. 'He took me to places I would never in a million years be able to afford.' They partied on islands, stayed in resorts that overlooked the ocean, dined in the most expensive restaurants in exotic places, flew in his private jet and sailed on his father's enormous luxury yacht in Monaco. It was a whirlwind twelve months. Rilee gave a harsh snort. 'And then when he got sick of me, he handed me a fistful of cash to take myself anywhere I wanted to go.'

As long as it was away from him.

The heartless way he could turn from lover to indifferent stranger had shocked her. She'd allowed herself to believe the fantasy he'd created. She'd ignored the little voice that whispered warnings to her and let him seduce her with his fake love and shallow promises.

'I couldn't face anyone I knew back in London—they all knew what had happened and I felt like an idiot.' She'd felt worse than an idiot, she'd felt dirty and used. 'So I decided it was time to take my wounded pride and broken heart home,' she said, trying to lessen the bitterness of her tone with a smile.

For a long time Dan didn't speak, and the sickening sense of shame washed back over her.

Then she felt his hands on her arms as he turned her to face him. 'That guy had no idea what he was throwing away, and it serves himself right for losing the best thing that would have ever happened to him.'

His words were said with such gentle sincerity that for a moment Rilee could only stare at him and blink back the unexpected sting of tears. When she'd recovered her composure she swallowed hard and forced a smile to her lips. 'I'm sure he kicks himself daily while he's riding his jetski around St Tropez.'

'I'm serious,' Dan said, ducking his head to make her look at him. He wasn't smiling, his expression intent. 'I reckon it was you who had a lucky escape.'

This time when Rilee smiled it was genuine. He was right. Had she not come home to lick her wounds and re-evaluate her life, she may never had reconnected with her parents and realised how deeply naturopathy ran in her veins.

As they neared a hotel further along the street, music pumped through the open doors and windows and people spilled out onto the footpath. Dan stepped closer and took her hand. As they moved away from the hotel, he didn't let go and she relaxed a little, enjoying being close to him. She felt comfortable around this man. He made her feel safe. She'd never experienced that before.

'This is me,' she said, coming to a stop in front of her apartment building.

She saw him look suspiciously over the Chinese restaurant and laundromat next door, and smiled as she stepped forward and inserted her key into the glossy green door situated between the two storefront windows. 'Did you want to come up?' she asked as nerves rushed in to push away the contentment she'd been feeling earlier.

'You're not sick of me yet?' he asked, throwing it back into her court.

'No, not yet.' She sounded more surprised than she'd intended.

'Great. Lead the way.'

Rilee turned and started the long climb up the narrow timber staircase. Her mind raced ahead, frantically wishing she hadn't left in such a hurry and had made sure everything was tidy. At the top, she unlocked another door and stepped inside, switching on the lights as she moved into the living area, which included a tiny kitchenette and dining table. She gathered the papers and files off the small square table she used as a desk more than a place to eat and put them inside the linen cupboard, shutting the door quickly so nothing fell out.

'Take a seat.' She waved her hand towards the lounge or the dining table and left him to decide where they should sit. 'Coffee?' she asked.

'Thanks,' he answered, still looking around the apartment with curiosity.

Rilee busied herself switching on the coffee maker and getting down two mugs from the open shelf above.

'How long have you lived here for?' he asked.

'Bit over four years,' she told him, looking over her shoulder. 'I don't need much room.'

'Apparently,' he agreed sending a bemused grin her way.

'Do you want a guided tour?'

'I don't know . . . I might get lost,' he told her dryly.

'You don't even have to move. That door on the left is the bedroom, and the door on the right is the bathroom. This is the kitchen and that's the living room.'

'It's nice,' he said finally, and she would have believed him if he hadn't had that slightly concerned expression on his face.

'It's pretty small even for the most hardened inner-city dweller,' she conceded, 'but it suits me. I'm rarely here, so I don't mind too much.'

He glanced around the room and his gaze fall on the large textbook on the coffee table. '*Principles and Practices of Naturopathic Botanical Medicine: Botanical Medicine Monographs*,' he read out, before looking up at her. 'A bit of light reading?'

Rilee chuckled and shook her head. 'It's a lot more interesting than it sounds.'

'So your real job is a naturopath, but you moonlight as a barmaid?'

'Working at the pub helped pay my rent while I got my degree,' she shrugged.

'How long have you been doing naturopathy for?'

'I've been qualified now for almost a year. I work in a large practice alongside other allied health professionals.'

'And you obviously enjoy it?'

'I do. It's fascinating. I'm hoping to go out in my own practice soon.'

'Yeah?'

'Yep. I wanted to get some experience under my belt and work with my mentor for a while before I branched out on my own, but I've been using the time to plan, and working shifts in the bar to save for the business.'

'Impressive,' he said, thumbing through the big book idly before putting it back down on the table.

She made the coffee and carried the two cups over to the sofa. Her two-seater lounge had always seemed plenty big enough, but clearly that wasn't the case when a broad-shouldered, long-legged man in denim was seated on it. As she settled back into the soft cushions she felt the solid warmth of Dan's thigh against her own and had to concentrate hard not to spill her coffee as she took a sip.

He leaned back, draping one arm along the top of the lounge, his mug cradled in a large hand resting on his knee. Rilee found it hard to relax seated so close to this man who sent her nerve endings into a meltdown with the slightest movement of his body.

'Maybe I should put some music on,' she said, ready to jump up, but he touched her shoulder with his hand and said, 'The quiet's nice.'

'Oh. Okay.' The quiet was actually a little unnerving. Without the distraction of conversation or noise she was acutely aware of every movement he made. She could feel the flex of his thigh muscles as he leaned forward and placed his cup on the coffee table. She felt the brush of his fingers in her hair and the weight of his stare upon her, silently asking her to look at him. Rilee lifted her gaze to meet his.

It was pointless to resist the pull of attraction between them, she'd felt it from the very first moment she'd set eyes on him last week and it had been building all evening. Slowly she leaned into him and felt his warm lips touch hers. He deepened the kiss and a shot of desire ran the length of her body at the touch of his tongue against her own.

When they broke apart they were both breathing heavily and Rilee felt flushed.

'I've been thinking about that since last Friday night,' Dan said softly, his fingers gently brushing a lock of hair from the side of her face.

'You have?' she murmured, still feeling a little dazed.

'Yep. I wanted to do it the moment I saw you.'

'So I guess we have Jacko to thank for bringing me to your attention.'

'I was watching you a long time before Jacko made his stupid move.'

'You were?'

'Not in a weird, stalker-like way,' he added quickly.

She had to grin at that; somehow she didn't think Dan was capable of being anything other than to the point. If he saw something he wanted, clearly he went after it.

'I was in the process of working out how to come and say hello when Jacko started mauling you,' he growled. 'It went a little different to how I had it planned.' His gaze caressed her face and settled on her mouth and Rilee felt her pulse increase. 'Are you busy for the rest of the weekend?'

Rilee blinked to clear away the haze of sexual tension. 'Busy? Umm, no. Not really. Why?'

'Because I want to spend it with you.'

'You do?' She really needed to start sounding like the intelligent woman she was, but instead she stared at him in a stupor.

'If you didn't already have any other plans.'

'I'm not doing anything special.'

'Good,' he smiled, and stood up, leaving her to blink in surprise. 'I better go.'

She knew it was late but she couldn't help but feel a little disappointed that he was leaving. 'Thank you for dinner. I had a nice time.'

'I wasn't sure you'd agree to see me again.'

The fact she had was still a bit of a surprise even to her. 'I'm glad you had to come back to the city,' She paused, tilting her head a little. 'What *did* you have to come back here for? Will you have enough time to do what you need to do?'

Rilee watched, her curiosity growing as he shifted uneasily and avoided her gaze. 'Ah, actually, I may have slightly misled you about that.'

'What do you mean?'

'I didn't actually have business meetings. I came back to ask you out to dinner.'

'You came all the way here just to ask me out to dinner?' The sheepish grin on his face made her stare in disbelief.

'Like I said, I haven't been able to stop thinking about you all week.'

'What if you couldn't find me?'

34

His eyes crinkled a little in the corner as he gave her a ghost of a smile. 'I would have looked harder until I did. I don't give up that easy.' He leaned down and kissed her and the jumble of confused emotions swirling inside her disappeared.

The kiss deepened and Rilee no longer knew where she ended and he began.

She felt the wall behind her back and the solid warmth of Dan in front, his chest pressed against her own, hands caressing, one in her hair the other moving along her torso. Her hips arched towards his, and she groaned when he slipped one thigh in between her own. The tantalising pressure sent her desire into overdrive. He caught her surprised intake of breath, his mouth hungrily demanding, as his hand slid beneath the hem of her top and found bare skin.

His hand moved across her ribcage, his fingers brushing the underside of her breasts, making her arch further, needing something more but frustrated by the barrier of clothing still between them.

Dan pulled his mouth away and dropped his forehead against hers, his breathing sounding as harsh as her own.

'I'll bring breakfast in the morning,' he said, slowly easing away from her.

Breakfast! She couldn't think of breakfast while her body was demanding more of what he'd just given her a taste of.

'I didn't come back here for a one-night stand,' he told her softly, his gaze probing her glassy eyes earnestly. 'I want you to know that.'

Right about now a one-night stand sounds pretty damn good. The wayward thought did little to help find her composure. 'What *did* you come back for?' she asked.

'I don't know. But it wasn't just to do this. I've never felt this way about anyone, Rilee. I've never had a woman drive me to the point of distraction before.' He tenderly tucked a strand of hair behind her ear. 'I had to come back and find out if I was losing my mind or not.'

'And if you find out you're not?'

'Then we'll figure out where to go from there.'

What was she doing? How on earth would a relationship with a man who lived out in the middle of woop-woop work? Her life was here. She was starting her own practice, for goodness sake.

'I'll see you in the morning,' he said, lowering his head once more to kiss her before dragging his mouth away with a soft groan and opening the door.

Rilee watched him descend the stairs until he'd vanished out into the street then sagged against the closed door. What. The. Hell?

∽

Rilee was awake and ready well before she heard the knock on her door the next morning—she'd hardly managed to sleep after Dan's departure. The man had stirred up more than her libido. He'd triggered a whole array of conflicting emotions and raised far too many questions she had no answers for.

'I wasn't sure what you wanted for breakfast, so I got a bit of everything,' he said as she gaped at the multitude of plastic shopping bags he carried.

'Did you leave *any* food on the shelves?'

He flashed her a grin and Rilee silently rolled her eyes at the pathetic belly flip it caused. She'd given herself a stern lecture—this time there were to be no funny feelings, no weak knees and definitely *no butterflies* in the stomach. So much for that.

They cooked breakfast together and drank coffee, and despite Rilee's best intentions she found herself weakening. Every lopsided grin, every accidental brush against his body, every lingering gaze found her falling further under his spell. It was lust. Pure and simple. He was ruggedly good-looking and the complete opposite of any man she'd ever been attracted to before. It was just a novelty. She really tried to believe it. She even set out to prove it. After spending the day together, playing tourist and showing him the sights, Rilee asked him back to her flat with the sole intention of seducing him. Her plan was simple. Once the mystery was gone, once they'd realised this was just a spontaneous crazy moment of weakness, they'd both go back to their respective lives, with fond memories of a great weekend.

That had been the plan. What she hadn't factored in, though, was the fact that being with Dan was unlike any other experience she'd ever had before. He took his time undressing her slowly and looking at her as though she was the most amazing thing he'd ever seen. While Rilee wasn't embarrassed by her body, she'd never thought of it as particularly sexy, but as she watched the look in Dan's eyes she felt a confidence unfurl inside her, blossoming under his gentle, almost reverent caress. The experience left her more confused than ever. Instead of feeling as though he was out of her system, she wanted him even more. How was that possible? This was not how it was supposed to go. The second and third time also left no dent in her desire. In fact, they spent most of Sunday in bed—and nothing. No sudden loss of appeal, no drastic need for space or time alone. In fact, her feelings for the man intensified.

Late on the Sunday afternoon, with only the sounds of the traffic outside, Dan held her close and ran his hand up and down her arm lightly. 'I'll have to get ready to leave soon.'

Her heart sank at the words before she forced herself to swallow the disappointment. 'I can't believe the weekend's almost gone.'

'If I didn't have anything on tomorrow I could have stayed a bit longer.'

'I've got work tomorrow anyway.' And a life to get back to.

'I'll see how busy things get over the next week or so and try to come back for a few days.'

Rilee bit back the initial leap of excitement. *The plan! Remember the plan?* 'I'm not sure how busy I'm going to be . . . There's a few parties booked in at the pub, I might be working a lot.'

'So . . . that would be a thanks but no thanks for another visit?' he asked slowly, his touch stilling on her arm.

Rilee closed her eyes, before easing out of his arms to brace herself on her elbows and look over at him. 'That's not what I meant. But it is what I think needs to be said. This thing,' she said, unsure how to address what it was between them, 'it's not going to go anywhere, Dan. It can't. And sure we could hook up whenever you're back in the city, but I'm not sure that's a good idea, either.'

'Why?'

Because every minute I'm with you, I feel like I'm falling deeper into something that I can't explain. 'Because it's a long way to fly just for the odd one-night stand,' she said instead.

'I told you before, that's not what I want.'

'I don't see what else it could be.'

'You don't feel whatever this thing is between us?' he asked bluntly, catching her off guard. 'I already feel like I've known you forever. I've never had that with anyone else before. Tell me you don't feel that too.'

It was ridiculous, completely insane, but damned if he wasn't right. She'd never told anyone, let alone a man she'd just met, half the things she'd told Dan. She did feel as though she'd known him a long time; it was incredible to realise it had only been two days. Her common sense scoffed, but that didn't change the fact she had an undeniable connection to this man. 'It doesn't matter what I feel. The point is that there's no future in this. My life is here. My business is going to be here. Unless you're thinking about moving to the city, I just don't understand how you can think this can be anything more than a weekend fling.'

Dan studied her silently for a long time and Rilee held his gaze with a regretful look of her own.

'I'm not giving up,' he said finally. 'I'll keep coming back as many times as I have to until we figure this out.'

Truth be told, Rilee wasn't sure she'd see him again after that day, but true to his word, Dan spent the next few months flying back and forth whenever he had a chance.

Each time he left, Rilee found herself distracted and miserable. She tried everything: booking in more patients, working extra shifts at the pub to keep her mind from wandering. She even made a point of visualising her clinic, seeing her name on the front door and fixing it firmly in her mind, only to find herself picturing Dan's face and conjuring up the feel of his rough work hands running over her skin. They sent text messages through the day; she always woke up at some ungodly hour to a *Good morning, beautiful* text message before he headed out to work for the day, and they talked on the phone late into the night. She missed him when he wasn't there and craved his arrival like a drug. Sometimes he'd only have a day in town, other times he'd squeeze in three or four days, and with each visit her resolve to remain objective and strong crumbled just a little bit more.

Three months after they met, Dan proposed. There was no warning. They were sitting on a headland, basking in the late afternoon sun, when he withdrew a small box from his pocket and asked her to marry him. It would have been the perfect story to tell their grandchildren one day . . . except that she didn't say yes. Instead she burst into tears.

Why couldn't he understand? She had dreams she'd been working towards for years, she couldn't just throw all that away. She'd put too much work into them.

Dan took her back to her flat and she asked him to leave. It almost killed her. She cried herself to sleep and refused to answer her phone. She couldn't talk to him. She couldn't make it any clearer. Yes, she loved him; she hadn't wanted to fall in love, but she'd had no control over it. She loved him. More than she'd ever thought it possible to love someone. But he was asking her to give up *everything* in order to be with him. Hadn't she learned her lesson with Alexis? Dan lived in a completely different world to her; how could she possibly expect to fit into his life even if she wanted to give up everything she'd worked so hard for? And yet . . . it wasn't the same as with Alexis.

A few days later she turned down a shift at the pub and, despite her best attempt to make up a plausible excuse, clearly Janice hadn't bought it, arriving on her doorstep moments after they'd hung up. She'd taken one look at her limp hair and the dark circles under her eyes and demanded to know what was going on.

'Dan asked me to marry him,' she said miserably.

'I'm guessing this is somehow a problem,' Janice said wryly.

'Of course it's a problem!'

'How?'

'He lives in the middle of nowhere. On a farm. I'd have to move there.'

'So?'

Rilee opened her mouth and closed it again a few times, feeling like a goldfish. 'What do you mean *so*? What about my business?'

'Do you love him?'

'Yes.' Rilee's groan turned into a sob.

'Can your business give you back the love that Dan can give you? Will it be there beside you every night? Would being away from it make you as miserable as you are now? Would it make you stop eating and showering until you look like a zombie?'

Rilee dropped her head onto the table and shut her eyes tightly. Yes, she would be incredibly disappointed if she had to give up her dream of opening her own business. Yes, she'd probably even cry . . . a lot. But Janice had a point. The thought of Dan not being in her life was too painful to contemplate. Even though she'd said no to him, she hadn't really considered the possibility that they would no longer be together. The realisation made her cry harder.

'You think about it a bit, but not too much longer. Either way, you can't stay hidden inside here all day. You need to make a choice.'

Her phone beeped later that morning and Rilee listlessly dragged it across the table to read it. She had a fleeting moment of joy when she saw that it was from Dan, until reality once more sank in.

I'm staying at the Regency. Can we talk?

She stared at the text and took a shaky breath. She needed to end this now. A few hours later she was showered, dressed and standing at the reception desk of his hotel. The elevator ride seemed to take a millennium to arrive at his floor, and her heart thudded in her chest as she scanned the door numbers. When she reached his room, she didn't even get the chance to knock before the door opened and Dan stood there, looking as tired and wrung out as Rilee felt.

'Dan . . . I'm so sorry . . .' Rilee said quietly.

She saw him close his eyes tightly and shake his head, disappointment flowing through him.

'I'm sorry for putting you through all this. I needed time to think . . .'

He opened his eyes and cut her off. 'I know you have to think of your practice. And I know how much it means to you, Ri. But every time I leave you behind, I feel like a little piece of me gets ripped away. I can't concentrate while I'm working. I can't sleep, I'm snapping everyone's head off. I miss you so goddamn much I don't know what to do. I don't want you to give up your business, but I can't stand the thought of a future without you. I love you.'

'I love you too,' she said, rushing on before she lost her nerve. 'I'm not giving up on my dream to open my own practice,' she said and saw him hang his head in defeat. 'But it doesn't mean I can't open it somewhere else.'

She saw him eye her hopefully, as though trying to interpret what she was telling him.

'Yes. I'll marry you,' she said softly.

'You will?' His voice was husky with emotion.

Rilee nodded through her tears. 'Yes.'

Everything was about to change. She wasn't sure if she was ready for it, but she knew it was coming, ready or not.

Four

Looking back, she knew it seemed rash, and she could understand his friends and family having doubts—after all, she'd snared the most eligible bachelor in the district in only three short months of meeting the man.

Apparently people had taken out bets on how long Dan Kincaid would remain a bachelor. It seemed twenty-seven was getting on in these parts. Although, in her defence, she hadn't been aware that he was such an eligible bachelor—she'd no idea when he said he lived on a bit of land that it had been Thumb Creek Station, the biggest parcel of prime grazing and crop land in the area, and she certainly hadn't realised that his parents would be so vocal in their disappointment at the marriage.

A distant hum snagged her attention, gradually growing louder until it became the distinct sound of an approaching vehicle. Steeling herself against the smug grin she anticipated, it was a relief when Mick, the stock agent, if the sign on his door was anything to go by, pulled up and gave a cheery wave.

'Well, you certainly don't do things by halves, do you?' he announced when he had finished walking around the four-wheel drive to inspect the damage.

'No, I like to do a job properly,' she agreed dryly.

'Sit tight and I'll hook up the winch and have you outta here in a jiffy.'

True to his word, Mick busied himself attaching the winch from the front of his truck to her vehicle and gradually the bulky vehicle she was in found traction and slid forward out of the deep mud it had been bogged in.

'So you're the new Mrs Kincaid then?'

'That's me.'

'Mick Honeywell,' he introduced himself, reaching forward and extending a thick paw of a hand for her to shake. He wore the obligatory stockman's hat, only his was in a lot better condition than the dirty, faded one that Dan was rarely without. Mick's face was tanned and leathered and he had an easy smile.

'Thanks for coming to my rescue. If you hadn't I'm pretty sure the general consensus would have been to leave me here.'

Mick gave a deep chuckle but didn't deny the statement, and Rilee gave a small disheartened sigh. 'How about I show you where you need to go,' he said. 'I think Dan will be looking for that part right about now.'

'Are you sure you have time?'

'Yeah, I'm the boss, so it's not likely anyone's going to fire me, is it?'

Rilee gave the man a brief smile before climbing back into the farm vehicle, now liberally coated in sticky brown mud, and followed along the multitude of dirt tracks still slick and muddy from the recent rain.

After they had been driving for close to twenty minutes, Mick pulled over and Rilee came to a stop beside him. 'You can see Dan now. Just continue along this road and you'll find a gate a few ks along. Go through that and you'll end up right alongside him.'

'Thank you, Mick, I don't know what I'd have done without you.'

'You'll be right once you get the hang of things out here.' His grin flashed and Rilee wished there were more Mick Honeywells out here and fewer Kincaids who seemed quick to criticise and make her feel inadequate.

She watched him do a U-turn and waved as he passed by. Putting the big vehicle in first gear, she set off towards the middle of the paddock and the speck that was her husband.

Rolling to a stop, Rilee watched Dan cautiously as he approached, wiping his oil-smudged hands on a piece of rag. He looked impressive in his worn jeans and T-shirt—even streaked with grease and dirt as they were. The brim of his Akubra was low on his forehead, shading his eyes and making it difficult for Rilee to gauge his level of irritability.

'I brought you some lunch, but it's probably a bit late now.'

'Thanks, I'm starving.' He tossed the oily rag in the toolbox behind him and Rilee eased open the door to slide out.

'I'm sorry.'

'It's okay, Ri. I just have to get this tractor fixed before it gets too dark to see what I'm doing. You better stay here and follow me back.'

She watched as he bit into the first sandwich, chewing and working at the same time, and stood by feeling useless as he fitted the filter she'd delivered.

When Dan had told her his family worked a property out west, she wasn't sure what she'd imagined; maybe a homey-looking house with a wide saggy verandah and two hardworking, salt of the earth parents who spent their lives working the land beside their son. What she discovered upon landing at Thumb Creek Station was something entirely different.

Dan had flown them home in his Piper, a small fixed-wing aircraft he'd had since he was sixteen years old. Upon arrival at Thumb Creek Station she'd discovered that inside the massive hangar was a second plane, a slightly larger one, that his parents used for regular trips to the city and visiting his two older sisters who lived in other states. It was at this point she realised her original assumptions about life on Thumb Creek had been somewhat inaccurate.

It was just on dark when they landed, so Rilee didn't get a very good look at the property from above, but the house was lit up like a Christmas tree. The grand two-storey stone structure was nothing like the homey place she'd been imagining. Being greeted at the massive front door by the housekeeper was yet another indication that perhaps her husband had been playing down his family's financial situation.

However, it was his parents' stunned expressions after he introduced Rilee as his wife that really stole the show. In the awkward moments they spent alone in the family room while his parents went to attend to something—code, Rilee decided, for going to have a minor breakdown in private—she turned to Dan and glared at him. 'You said you'd tell them!'

'Rilee, once you get to know my parents you'll understand why I didn't.'

'You can't just turn up and introduce me as your wife, Dan!' she whispered harshly, not wanting his parents to overhear should they be on their way back in.

'I'm a grown man, I don't need their permission to get married, Ri.'

'They're your parents!'

'We decided to elope, remember?'

'Yes, but that doesn't mean you don't at least mention to your family that you're getting married.' She understood that they'd rushed through the normal relationship milestones like meeting the parents and, sure, his parents had been overseas for a good portion of their courtship but, still, Dan was making unnecessary ripples for her to navigate here. They were going to blame her for their son's secretive behaviour, she was certain of it.

'So Rilee,' Mrs Kincaid said when they were seated at the dining table, 'were your parents as surprised by this news as we are?'

'Very little surprises my parents any more,' she said, trying for a bit of light relief.

'I see,' Mrs Kincaid frowned. 'And what do your parents do? What industry are they in?'

'Well, they're also farmers ... of sorts,' she added. At least the herbs they grew nowadays were all of the legal kind, which was a vast improvement.

'Oh?' Mrs Kincaid asked.

'What do your parents run?' Mr Kincaid jumped in to ask.

'Run?' Rilee asked.

'Crops or livestock?'

'Oh. Well, crops, I guess,' she began, but he was already firing more questions.

'Broadacre or small crop?'

'Umm,' Rilee frowned.

'Where are they at?'

Finally, a question she could answer confidently. 'They're up around the Northern Rivers area, in a little place called Tippery Heights.'

He nodded his head thoughtfully. 'What's the country like up that way?'

'It's beautiful,' she started eagerly. 'Lots of mountains.'

'What's the rainfall like? Be pretty high?'

'Dad,' Dan cut in wearily.

'What? I'm interested,' he said, returning his gaze back to Rilee expectantly, as though waiting to measure up their rainfall against his own tally.

'Umm, I'm not really sure. A fair bit.'

'How big is their outfit?'

Rilee looked helplessly at Dan, waiting for a translation. 'How many hectares?' he supplied.

'Oh. I think it's about thirty.'

Rilee saw the older man do some silent calculations. 'So about seventy-odd acres.'

'Um, I guess so. They supply different herbs for the natural medicine market in Australia and overseas.'

Rilee was extremely proud of her parents for turning their passion into a rewarding career. In fact, seeing what they'd done had encouraged her to pursue a naturopathy degree at a time when she'd been feeling lost.

'Natural medicine, you say?' Jacob said curiously. 'Much money in that?'

'They do very nicely. But they don't do it for the money, they truly believe in the products they make.'

Surprisingly, Rilee had discovered when she'd returned home from London that her parents were beginning to build themselves a fairly lucrative business. In those few years she'd been away, she'd been forced to grow up. She no longer saw her parents through the eyes of a rebellious teenager. They may have left the modern world for a more basic lifestyle, but they were both very savvy people and they'd found a niche market for their herbs in a rapidly growing natural health market. Their business had expanded over the years and they now turned over an impressive profit. You'd never know it to look at them, though: they still dressed in second-hand clothes and grew all their own food. They loved their quiet lifestyle and Rilee was happy for them.

Jacob's small scoff brought her up sharply. 'Everyone does it for the money. Otherwise what's the point in putting in all that hard work? Money's what makes the world go round.'

An image of a cold smile flashed through her mind and she remembered the day Alexis had informed her that he'd grown tired of her. As he'd driven away in his Porsche, she'd stood there broken-hearted and angry at herself for ignoring what she'd known about him all along: that he was a spoilt playboy with far too much money and time on his hands. Money might make the world go around, but she was glad it was not the driving force in her life or her parents'.

'I'll be going to the service in the morning if you'd like to come along, Rilee,' Mrs Kincaid said as the meal came to an end and Rilee and Dan prepared to leave the table.

'Service?'

'Church service, dear.' Ellen looked at her as though she were a slow child.

'Oh. No. I mean, I . . . I've never been to a church service before.'

Her mother-in-law lifted one perfectly shaped eyebrow. 'You've never been to church? Ever?'

'My parents aren't very . . . churchy,' she explained, lifting her hands helplessly.

'Oh. I see.'

That *oh* held a wealth of disapproval and Rilee bit her lip anxiously. 'But thank you anyway . . . for the invitation,' she added awkwardly before Dan stepped up and took her hand, saying goodnight to his parents, before leading her out of the dining room and up to their bedroom.

'I should have just said I'd go,' Rilee said with a groan as she kicked off her shoes.

'Stop stressing. You don't have to go to church.'

'You did see your mother's face, didn't you?'

'She's used to living with a bunch of heathens,' he told her with a grin. 'She's never been able to get Dad to go to church, and she gave up on me after I reached high school.'

'You used to go to church?'

'Yeah, Mum took all of us kids to church on Sundays.'

'Ha,' Rilee said surprised, looking at her husband curiously.

'What?'

'Doesn't it bother you that we're still finding out all this stuff about each other and yet we're married and supposed to already know this?'

'Where's the fun in taking years to get to know every last detail about a person and then getting married?' he asked, pulling her up against him. 'It'd be boring.'

Dan braced his hands on the frame of the open car door, snapping her from her thoughts and back into the present.

'All right, that should do it,' he said, then hesitated briefly. 'Sorry if I was a bit short earlier. I know it's been hard for you, Ri. It's just really hectic right now.'

It wasn't as though he hadn't warned her. The reason they'd had to squeeze in such a short getaway for a honeymoon had been because he needed to get back for seeding and there wouldn't be another break for months after that. 'I know,' Rilee sighed. 'I just wish I could be more of a help and less of a problem.'

'You *are* a help,' he said, tugging her gently from the car as he linked his arms loosely around her hips and looked down at her.

She sent him a dry glance that told him just how much she *didn't* believe that and heard him chuckle.

'I love you, Ri,' he said, quietly. 'Things will get better. I promise.'

Rilee smiled gently back at the man before her. 'I love you too.' She truly did. In a few short months, this man had become as essential to her as breathing.

As she followed him home, Rilee spent the drive thinking positive thoughts and giving motivational pep talks to herself. By the time they arrived back at the house, she'd almost convinced herself she could face anything.

Then she remembered she still had to get through dinner with his parents.

Five

Dinner was an even more strained affair than usual that evening.

This had been by far the hardest thing to get used to since moving here. She'd known that they'd be staying in his parents' house until the renovations were finished on their own cottage, but she hadn't counted on spending quite this much time with them. She and Dan seemed to have hardly any space to themselves. She understood that working in a family business meant there was always something to discuss, but considering Dan went to work so early, by the time his parents finished with him of an evening, there was no time left to unwind together before bed. He was usually exhausted and asleep as soon as his head hit the pillow.

Tonight at dinner Dan was especially tired, and he said little. His father had been reeling off a list of jobs that hadn't been done, thanks to the delay earlier today, waiting on getting the tractor fixed, and Rilee could see the tension in Dan increase as the meal dragged on.

Jacob Kincaid was from a long line of cattlemen. He was a tough man, a hard worker, and even though he enjoyed the finer things in life, he had always been happiest outdoors working the same land his forefathers had farmed. Dan shared a great deal of his father's physique: the broad shoulders and height as well as the same facial features, but Jacob had become cold and remote over the years, making him a hard taskmaster.

'I'll be happy when Mark gets back,' Dan sighed.

'Who was the fool that said he could have three weeks off in the middle of planting season?' Jacob growled.

'He had an emergency he needed to deal with. It was hardly his fault about the timing.'

'Seems to me he's always having an emergency. How many days has he had off in the last year?'

'He's a good worker and I can trust him. He's put in the effort over the last few years for us—we owe him a bit of leeway.'

'He works for us, we pay him. That's all we owe him. Don't you go getting all soft on me, son.' Jacob snapped, sending Rilee a sideways glare as though it were her influence corrupting his son.

Rilee concentrated on moving the food around on her plate miserably. She'd lost her appetite, enduring the meal out of good manners and moral support for her husband.

'I thought we might have a party to introduce Rilee to our friends,' Ellen announced, changing the topic hastily. 'I spoke to the girls today and they're both eager to come home and meet their new sister-in-law,' she added, delicately buttering a dinner roll.

'It's not exactly a good time, Mum. We've got the sales coming up. Maybe we can do it down the track.'

Ellen placed her knife on the side plate and sent a sharp look at her son. 'Isn't it enough you've made us a laughing stock by eloping? We didn't have a wedding to invite all our friends to, so if you think you're going to deny us a reception you are sorely mistaken.'

'There's really no need, Mum,' Dan protested wearily. Clearly he knew he was fighting a losing battle. One look at his mother's set features was enough to warn Rilee to keep her head down and mouth shut.

'Do you have any idea how many phone calls I've fended off about your little surprise? People are laughing at us, Dan! Tell him, Jacob.'

Jacob Kincaid continued eating his meal, merely giving the grunt that was expected of him.

'I think with cattle prices the way they are at the moment, Mum, there isn't much laughing going on around the district. I'm sure something else will come along to get the tongues wagging in town soon enough.'

'We're having a party, Dan, and you will enjoy it.'

Rilee hid a smile at her big tough husband being told what to do by his mother like a little boy.

She'd never daydreamed about her wedding as a little girl. All she dreamed about was running away to the real world and doing what normal people did, so a traditional wedding was not something she cared about. They'd wanted something simple and no fuss, and although she had felt bad that they hadn't included family, now she understood why Dan didn't want to involve his parents in their wedding plans. They wouldn't have stood for a quickie wedding at a celebrant's house. Her parents wouldn't have cared either way, but they were both away on a retreat, and if they didn't take the date they'd booked with the celebrant, they were looking at a wait of months. The distance and commute had been killing both of them.

A small part of her worried about the speed at which it had all happened, but another part, the part that knew how in love she was with this man, overrode those niggling thoughts. She'd never felt this way about another person— never missed someone so much when he wasn't there. Maybe it was crazy, but it was also just . . . *right.*

'I'm sure Rilee would like a chance to meet our friends,' Ellen said, sliding her gaze across to her and smiling serenely.

'I don't mind, Dan. A party might be nice.' Rilee just wanted to escape the table and this discussion. 'And I'm really looking forward to meeting Megan and Natalie,' she added. The truth was she was terrified of meeting Dan's older sisters. From the little she'd heard about them, they were no less intimidating then his parents. Megan was thirteen years older than Dan and a lawyer with a large mining company based in Perth. From the photos scattered throughout the big, old house, Meg seemed to have inherited her mother's confidence. There were no carefree happy snaps of her, most were formal portraits. She had long, dark hair and favoured her mother in looks. Natalie was eleven years older than Dan and seemed to have more of the Kincaid genes, and although there were a lot more photos of her caught in natural poses, she was no less daunting with degrees in finance and a high-paying job in Melbourne. Would they like her? Dan assured her they would, but she was still nervous about meeting them.

'Whatever you like, Mum, but don't go overboard. We don't want it turning into a circus.'

'Really, Daniel, do give me a little more credit than that,' she sniffed. 'Besides, it will give Rilee and me a chance to work together. There seems very little I'm allowed to help with in the renovations.'

Rilee immediately put down her fork. 'I didn't mean to make you to feel that way, Ellen.'

'Mum, don't start. Rilee, it's all right,' Dan smoothed. 'All we've done is pick a new kitchen and bathroom and throw on a coat of paint. There was nothing for you to help with, Mum, it's our house. You know you would have gone overboard and had the entire place gutted and redesigned if we let you loose in there.'

'It needs it. I just don't understand why you'd only do half a job,' she clucked with disapproval.

It wasn't exactly half a job, Rilee thought. They'd been knee-deep in renovations for weeks now. The little cottage wasn't sprawling, but it had character. It had been used as an overseer's cottage originally and was more than a hundred years old. Through the years it had been extended here and there, but the original architecture still remained and Rilee loved the rustic look of the place. There was a narrow verandah on the front of the house, with a bullnosed awning and old-fashioned leadlight windows and doors. The bathroom and kitchen had been in dire need of attention and while they'd had to do a lot of demolition due to years of water damage and rot, she'd tried to keep a rustic, country feel to the new design and was happy with the developing result . . . She just wished it was moving a little faster.

'Because we want to move into our own place. You remember what it was like to be newlyweds, don't you, Mum?' Dan asked cheekily as he spread butter on his bread roll and grinned over at his parents.

'Really, Daniel,' his mother chastised. 'Besides, Rilee needs to start meeting people. How is she going to get involved in the community if nobody knows her?'

'It's probably a good idea. I can talk to a few people about starting my business, get the word out early,' Rilee mused.

'Well, I don't know about that—I'm not sure I want my guests pressured into trying alternative medicines.'

Rilee bit her tongue against the automatic defence of her profession. Before meeting the Kincaids she hadn't come up against quite so much antagonism towards natural medicine. It was accepted by most people nowadays so she was surprised when Dan's parents stared at her like she'd grown a second head when she'd told them what she did for a living.

'I wouldn't be pressuring anyone into anything, but as you said, it would be a good way of introducing myself.'

'Maybe Daniel has a point, it is a busy time of the year. Perhaps it can wait a few weeks.'

Dan sent her a wink across the table, obviously thinking she'd been trying a little reverse psychology on his mother and was happy that it'd worked. Unfortunately, she'd been completely serious.

'So how do you intend to start this business?' Jacob asked and Rilee's hopes lifted a little at this unexpected interest, before they took a nosedive once again as he continued. 'Where's the money coming from?'

'I have my own investments,' Rilee said calmly, trying not to bristle at his narrowed gaze. 'I've been planning this for quite some time.' Admittedly when she'd been busy planning she'd imagined opening her practice in the city, but that was before Dan had barged into her life. She'd had to readjust her plans a little, but there was no reason her dream couldn't work out here. She wanted to help people, and people here were entitled to just as much care as people in the city.

Jacob gave a short grunt but didn't seem entirely convinced he wasn't about to be asked for some kind of contribution to her start-up costs.

'How on earth did you manage to have investments being a student and working in a bar?' Ellen asked as she daintily sliced through her meat.

SixWaysto Sunday

There was no disguising the mild distaste in her mother-in-law's tone at the mention of her previous employment, and Rilee felt the familiar insecurity creeping back in. Despite graduating and having a degree to her name, despite working her butt off for four long years to become a naturopath, studying chemistry, human and plant biology, nutrition and much more; despite all that, as well as working part-time so she didn't have to touch her savings, Rilee would always be the barmaid Ellen's son went and married.

'Well, it's amazing what you can achieve if you want something badly enough.'

Ellen's sharp gaze pinned Rilee across the table, and she could almost read what the woman was thinking: once Rilee had set eyes on her son, she'd done whatever it took to make sure she got him. The reality couldn't have been further from the truth, but she suspected no amount of denying could convince Ellen that Rilee hadn't latched on to Dan because he was worth a small fortune.

It was almost funny really. The Kincaids might be well off out here, but Rilee knew from first-hand experience that there were people with fortunes so huge, the Kincaids' was a pittance in comparison. But as far as this family were concerned, Thumb Creek was the only world that mattered, and out here they were King and Queen pin.

'Tomorrow I'll take you out with me and we can go over a few more areas so you get familiar with the place, okay?' Dan said encouragingly.

'Sure.' *Whatever.* She was more than a little over the whole ordeal tonight.

'I still don't understand how you could have gotten lost,' Ellen murmured.

'Put me in the middle of the city and I can get anywhere, but it's a little difficult out here where nothing's signposted,' Rilee told them quietly. 'Maybe I could use a GPS?'

'No point. Half the time you can't get a signal and then you're no better off because you've trusted a piece of Jap-made technology instead of using common sense,' Jacob announced dismissively from the head of the table.

'I told you how to get there: you were supposed to go to the old water tank paddock and then through the gate and along the base of the ridge to the pump paddock and then through the fire break corridor and into the good pasture where he was seeding.' Ellen Kincaid seemed bamboozled as to how anyone could have gotten lost from such clear directions.

Rilee was so tired of having her stupidity constantly pointed out. 'I looked for the old water tank but I couldn't find it.'

'Well, that's because it fell down and rusted away years ago, dear,' Ellen explained as though to a simpleton.

'Of course, that should have been completely obvious!' Rilee threw a furious glare across the table at her husband and saw him hide a grin. Setting aside her cutlery, she stood from her seat and excused herself, too angry to continue eating and tired of being treated like an idiot.

The evening sun had all but set as Rilee hoisted herself onto the top rail of the stockyards a little way down the gravel driveway. It was so beautiful out here. The silence was not that silent really, with the low bellows of cattle as they checked on their calves, and the squawk and noisy chatter of birds as they settled in for the evening in the trees; but it was a very different noise to what she was used to. No sirens, no car horns, no trains or buses or people chatting on their mobiles. A sadness filled the hollow pit in her stomach as she realised how desperately she wanted to belong out here and how miserably inadequate she really was.

There was a crunch of heavy boots on the gravel behind her and she glanced over her shoulder to find Dan heading towards her slowly. Turning away from him, she let her gaze rest once more on the rusty red haze that flooded the landscape as the sun sank below the horizon. Breathtakingly beautiful, and yet leaving everything in a dark silhouette that held a definite threat of danger if you were out there lost.

'It's no big deal, Ri.'

'It is. Your parents think I'm an idiot.'

'No, they don't,' he lied, and when she turned her gaze on him sceptically, he grinned to soften the untruth a little. 'They don't mean anything by it, they just aren't used to anyone who hasn't been on a property before . . . It's not like they get a lot of strangers out here.'

'And that's all they'll ever see me as, isn't it, Dan? A stranger.'

'You're my wife, Rilee,' he said forcefully, then softened his voice. 'They'll get over it, just give it time. 'Come on, it's going to be okay, I promise.' He hoisted himself up and over the fence she was perched on and stood before her.

Rilee let her eyes drop to Dan's as he slid his arms around her waist and moved in between her thighs. His gaze, so steady and reliable, held hers, and despite her sadness, she couldn't stop the flood of warmth and love that filled her.

It happened every time: just when she began to question how crazy this whole marriage was, even when she was at her lowest point, as soon as Dan was nearby, everything made perfect sense. 'You must have been out of your mind wanting to marry me,' she whispered, tipping his wide-brimmed hat back a little on his head.

'The minute I set eyes on you I was out of my mind,' he shrugged, his gaze never leaving hers. 'Come on, let's go and see how far they got with the house today.'

Swinging her down off the top of the rails, Dan didn't immediately release her as her feet touched the ground. 'Don't give up on us, Ri. We'll get through this, okay?'

A lump formed in her throat at his solemn tone and the tinge of fear she detected tugged at her heartstrings. 'I'm not going anywhere. Besides, if I tried, I'd only get lost and you'd have to come and find me anyway,' she said.

Dan kissed her long and deeply, making her instantly forget the humiliation of the day's events and reminding her instead of everything that was right in her world. Breaking apart, they were both breathing heavily and they hurried over to inspect the progress on their house renovations. They'd bided their time waiting for them to be completed by christening all the rooms over the last few weeks, relishing the time away from the main house they were sharing with Dan's parents.

The cottage had been vacant for a few years, and while it was by no means derelict, it had been sadly neglected, having been used as a single man's quarters for far too long.

Rilee had wasted no time starting her herb garden. She spent the first few days choosing the perfect spot, then began planting out her herbs. As a young child she'd often helped her mother in her city garden. Shelly had always said that in a hectic world, spending time tending plants and getting her hands in dirt recharged her batteries and gave her peace. After they moved, Rilee helped tend the commune veggie patch and picked produce as part of chores the whole community participated in, but she'd grown to resent it. It represented the lifestyle she was rebelling against. It wasn't until she returned from overseas, heartbroken and weary, that she finally realised what her mother had been telling her all those years before. Growing something in the earth, caring and nurturing it, reignited her spark for life, and gradually her love of herbs and using them to heal became her passion.

Every morning she lovingly tended the cottage garden, watering and hovering over it until the first delicate shoots uncurled themselves and stretched towards the vast blue sky.

Ellen had dismissed her new project as a waste of time. 'There's plenty of weeding and gardening you can do in the house garden beds if you're that bored,' she'd informed Rilee the first morning she'd come inside hot and sweaty, her cheek smeared with dirt.

It was certainly true that Ellen had a green thumb—the established gardens were magnificent, colour-coordinated and well tended, but Rilee's garden wasn't there to make the place look pretty, it was a working garden. There were a lot of pre-packaged remedies she could source from suppliers but there were also a lot of formulas that needed fresh, often specific, hard to find ingredients. In the city this didn't present a problem as she had markets and suppliers close at hand; however, out here she wouldn't have access to fresh ingredients unless she grew them herself. By the time she had her business up and running, she hoped to have her herb garden well established.

'It won't be too much longer now and we'll have our own place,' Dan said, pulling her to him as they stood by the garden bed and inspected the seedlings sprouting to life.

'Dan, when are you going to broach the subject of the cattle with your father?'

She saw the tension in Dan return as it had at the beginning of dinner and regretted being the cause of it this time, but it was something she knew was weighing heavily on his mind. She'd listened to him talk long into the night about his dream of developing his own line of cross-bred cattle, but he'd yet to make it a reality.

'I already have and he's not interested, end of story.'

'How can he ignore the proof—did you give him the printouts to read?'

'He wouldn't even look at them.'

'Well, that's making informed choices.' Rilee shook her head in disgust. 'How can he be running a business if he won't even consider ways to improve the place?'

'He comes from an era that doesn't like change, Rilee. It's always been a struggle to get technology on the place. He'll come around eventually, but there's no point pushing him on it or he'll just get stubborn. I'll talk to him about it later, but for now we just go on running the place the way he wants to.'

'He'll *get* stubborn? So what is he being at the moment?'

'He's being *Dad*,' Dan said, sending her a resigned grin.

'You'd better not take after him, mister, or there'll be trouble,' Rilee warned, and she wasn't joking. How on earth Ellen put up with such an irritable old coot was beyond her, but she wasn't going to be treading on eggshells for the next forty years, that was for certain.

Dan tugged on her hand and they headed inside to check on the renovation progress for the day before making some progress of their own . . . discarding clothing.

Six

Driving down Pallaburra main street was like taking a stroll through another era. The shopfronts were shaded by wide bullnose verandahs and timber posts. For a small town, it certainly wasn't without the necessities, but if you wanted anything other than the basics, it meant an hour-long trip to the next town. There was a combined primary and high school, grocery store, farm co-op, bank and chemist. There was a small café and takeaway and the requisite pub. In fact, Pallaburra had two pubs, aptly named the top pub and the bottom pub. Rilee had eaten at the top pub on a few occasions since coming out to Pallaburra; apparently the bottom pub was for the more social aspect of the town, like the football team and workers' clubs, with a rowdier reputation and a less strict dress code.

Rilee parked the station ute, with the Thumb Creek Station logo sprayed across the door, next to a dusty four-wheel drive with an equally dusty cattle dog in the back and climbed out, closing the door with a thunk.

She turned and noticed a girl with a pram walking up the street towards her. There was something about her that drew Rilee's attention. She was walking slowly, watching the schoolyard across the road and a group of schoolgirls who looked around the same age as she did. The baby gave a cry and the girl immediately bent over to soothe the infant before going on her way. Rilee looked back across at the school playground filled with loud squeals and children's chatter. The group of teenage girls laughed and joked together, their whole demeanour carefree and youthful. Rilee followed the retreating form of the girl with the pram. It was almost as though her every step was a struggle, as though her feet were weighted down. The two scenarios were in stark contrast and Rilee felt sad for the young mother.

Inside the café, two women in matching aprons were laughing with an older man in a worn, faded hat.

The conversation died away as they watched Rilee enter and she fought the urge to turn around and walk back out again. Instead she plastered a smile on her face and sat down at the nearest table, taking her time to hang her bag over the back of the chair and fiddle with the salt and pepper shakers in the centre of the table. After a few moments she became aware of the lingering silence and glanced over at the three people staring openly at her from their position at the front counter.

'Did ya want something to eat?' called over the woman with grey hair in a tight bun.

Rilee straightened in her seat and sent a nervous smile towards the trio. 'When you're ready to take my order is fine.'

'We don't wait on tables around here. If ya want something to eat, ya gotta come over here and order it.'

'Oh.' Rilee got to her feet, bumping her hip on the table in her haste. Way to be cool and calm in front of the locals. 'Sorry, I just thought—'

'That we'd wait on ya hand and foot.'

'How silly of me. Guess I've got a few things to learn around here,' she said with an offhand shrug.

'You got that right,' the younger of the two women murmured beneath her breath.

Rilee would really have liked to forget all about the coffee but it was too late now. There was no way she could leave without seeming as though she were having a tantrum.

'I'm Rilee . . . Kincaid.' It was still strange saying her married name out loud.

'We know who you are,' the young woman said, her arched eyebrow making it clear she wasn't impressed by the fact.

'Clem Singleton,' the man said, obviously taking pity on her.

Rilee sent him a grateful smile. 'Hello, Clem.'

'And this here is Pru and Shaz.' He waved towards the two women still leaning on the counter.

'Hello.' Rilee puzzled over the women's cool reception; as far as she knew, she hadn't done anything to deserve it.

'So, do ya wanna order something?' Shaz, the younger woman, asked in a bored tone.

'I'll just have a coffee thanks . . . to go,' she added hastily.

'Good-o,' Pru said with a nod, and passed a styrofoam cup from under the counter to Shaz, then picked up a cloth and bustled around the bench to wipe down a nearby table. 'So you've moved up from the big smoke?'

'Yes,' said Rilee, not feeling in the mood to chat after her lukewarm reception.

'Why would you move from the city to *here*?' Shaz piped up as she frothed milk in a silver jug. At least they seemed to know their way around a coffee machine—Rilee could forgive almost anything if it meant she could have decent coffee.

'I got married.'

Sharon gave a less than dainty snort. 'No man would keep me out here if I had a chance to live in the city.'

'Well, it's not that far. If I have withdrawals, I can always go back to visit.'

'Yeah, now you're a Kincaid you can afford to do whatever you want.'

Shaz's envious remark didn't miss its mark; Rilee felt the mutual agreement that seemed to float through the air between the three. 'I don't know about that, I'm sure there's some limits to what even the Kincaids can do.' Another silence hung. 'So, is there anyone around the area who does naturopathy?' Rilee asked, hoping to turn the conversation away from her in-laws.

'Naturo-what?' Pru's frown crinkled her forehead and her eyebrows almost disappeared.

'Naturopathy, natural medicine?' Rilee elaborated, her gaze swinging from one face to another as she searched the confused expressions for a glimmer of recognition.

'Natural? Like hippie mumbo jumbo?' Clem asked.

'Natural, like herbal medicine and treating health problems with diet and herbs . . . and other things,' she trailed off when she realised she had lost her audience. 'I'll take that as a no then,' she mumbled under her breath.

'Why would you want one of them for?' Pru asked.

'I don't *want* one, I *am* one.'

'Didn't they used to burn witches for that kind of thing once?' Shaz asked as she handed over the coffee. 'Three-fifty, thanks.'

Rilee dug in her purse and handed over the coins as she accepted her coffee, eager to get out from under the three weighty stares. 'Well, it was nice to meet you all. I better keep moving. See you again next time.'

Never had the banging of the screen door behind her sounded so good.

Outside she took a careful sip of her coffee and sighed. Ah, caffeine, her one guilty pleasure. The caffeine itself wasn't the part she was guilty about, it was adding the milk and sugar that was the problem. She always got a chuckle out of the relief that washed across her clients' faces when they realised she wasn't going to ban them from drinking coffee as part of her overhaul of their diet to address different ailments.

She actually believed caffeine to be beneficial. Being a stimulant, it increased the activity of the cardiovascular and digestive systems, as well as stimulating the central nervous system, resulting in increased alertness. In moderation, coffee had positive effects on the body. Indulging once in a while in good coffee was not the end of the world. Rilee understood all too well that there were times when only coffee or chocolate could fix a situation . . . and right now was one of those times.

There was a lazy afternoon feel about the sleepy little town and not a single car driving along the main street. There were a few parked utes with dogs waiting patiently in the back for their owners to return, tongues lolling from the side of their mouths as they basked in the warm sunshine.

As Rilee walked towards the chemist, she had to jump back quickly to avoid having her toes run over by a pram that came barrelling out the doorway.

Rilee smiled at the rather flustered young girl pushing it. It was the girl she'd noticed earlier.

'Sorry,' she mumbled, and Rilee realised why she was so flustered—the baby was bawling.

'Such a shame. Poor little thing, what kind of life has it got, hey?'

Rilee turned her head to find a woman beside her in a bright pink skirt and faded yellow blouse. 'Pardon?'

The woman looked at Rilee before nodding her head after the girl. 'Kids having kids. No idea what they're doing.'

Rilee wasn't sure how to respond to that—after all, she didn't know anything about the girl, although she had to admit she did look rather young.

'What's the world coming to?' her new companion continued. The older woman tore her pessimistic gaze from the main street and looked back at Rilee. 'The new Kincaid addition, I believe.'

Rilee's friendly smile dropped slightly. 'How did you know?'

'Well, you're not from around here, and seeing as everyone's talking about Dan Kincaid eloping with some city woman, it doesn't take a genius to figure out who you are.'

'Oh.'

The woman's cherry red lipstick cracked a little as her mouth creased into a smile. 'I'm Edna, it's nice to meet you, love.'

'Hello, Edna.' Rilee breathed out a relieved sigh; finally someone who seemed welcoming.

'So how are you finding Pallaburra? Bit different to what you're used to, I guess.'

'Just a bit,' Rilee agreed. 'But I don't mind. Actually, I was just admiring the architecture. There's not a lot of towns that still have so many original buildings in such good condition.'

'Is that a nice way of saying it looks like we're stuck in the past?' Edna arched one silver eyebrow, but Rilee was reassured by her smile.

'Not at all, I think it's lovely.'

'Yes, I hear the younger ones complaining about it, but I think it's comforting to realise my great-grandparents would still recognise the town if they were to come back. I feel a connection to the place, you know?'

Rilee didn't know, not really. She hadn't been born and raised in the one town, but she could imagine that it would be nice to belong somewhere like that.

'Well, mustn't stop, lots of things to do and the day's getting away from me.' Edna reached out to pat Rilee's arm. 'Lovely to meet you, dear, welcome to Pallaburra.'

Rilee watched the woman toddle off up the street, dragging a small trolley behind her, then turned and walked into the pharmacy.

A woman dressed in a fitted blouse and knee-length skirt glanced up from dusting a selection of perfume bottles. Her dour expression changed as soon as Rilee introduced herself. 'Ellen's new daughter-in-law,' she gushed. 'We've been waiting to get a chance to meet you. Errol,' she shouted, turning back to Rilee with a grimace. 'Sorry, dear, he's half deaf. Errol!'

Rilee didn't have time to reply before a white-coated gentleman emerged from the back of the shop with a frown.

'What are you out here yelling about, woman?'

'Errol, dear,' she said with forced politeness. 'This is Ellen and Jacob's daughter-in-law, Rilee. This is my husband, Errol, and I'm Betty,' she added.

The man peered at Rilee over the top of his thick-rimmed black glasses and gave a short grunt. 'Good to meet you.

Haven't seen you in church,' he added without bothering to hide the disapproval.

Rilee sent a nervous glance across to his wife who stood with her head tilted like a curious owl. 'No, I . . . it's been pretty hectic with our house renovations and whatnot . . .' she heard herself saying weakly. Why she didn't just come out and say she didn't go to church? She had no idea, only that Errol had a rather intimidating air about him.

'So, what can we help you with, dear?' Betty asked in the uncomfortable silence that followed.

'Oh, nothing really, I just thought I'd come in and have a look around and introduce myself. I'm hoping to set up a naturopathy clinic sometime in the near future.'

'Naturopathy?' Errol repeated and Rilee watched in fascination as a large, grey, bushy eyebrow peeped over the top of his thick glasses.

'Yes,' Rilee said. 'Natural medicine.'

'I know what it is,' he said bluntly. 'I'm just not a believer in it.'

Rilee smiled politely. This wasn't the first professional she'd met who disapproved of natural therapies. 'Well, I guess that means we won't be stepping on each other's toes then,' she said lightly. Errol narrowed his gaze as she waved her hand at the sparse shelving. 'Since you don't seem to have a huge natural component to your store.'

'Like I said, I'm not a believer in it. Most of it's a waste of good money.' He turned and headed back through the doors at the rear of the store.

Betty flicked her duster over a nearby shelf and cleared her throat hastily. 'Well, do give my regards to Ellen, won't you.'

That went well, Rilee thought as she stepped outside and put her sunglasses back on. What was the saying? Pleasing *everyone* is impossible, but pissing them all off is a piece of cake?

Yep, it shouldn't be that difficult to get on the wrong side of pretty much the whole town by the day's end.

Seven

A few days later, Rilee was on the verandah reading when she heard the gate open and looked up to see Dan walking towards her. She loved the way he walked; his strides were long and confident, and there was an easy swagger to his movements she found incredibly sexy.

'Are you home for lunch?'

'Amongst other things.'

'Oh really?' she said, closing her book and smiling as he leaned across her chair, trapping her with his strong arms.

'Really.'

'It just so happens we have the house all to ourselves. Your mother went into town.'

'I know, I passed her on the way out,' he said with a roguish grin.

Later, as she watched Dan pulling on his boots, Rilee stretched in the tangle of sheets they'd created. 'I wonder when all this sex will wear off.'

'You got a problem with it?' he quizzed, sending her a grin over his broad shoulder.

Rilee's chuckle was a low murmur. 'No, but I figure it eventually gets old, unless your parents still have an afternoon quickie?'

'Never. Ever. Say those words out loud again,' he groaned, and gave a shiver of abhorrence.

Rilee raised an eyebrow. 'You think you were some kind of immaculate conception?' she asked drolly.

'I try very hard never to think of my parents and the word "conception" in the same sentence.'

'Your family is definitely on the conservative side. I guess that's just another thing we're opposites in,' Rilee said with a small grimace. 'My parents have always believed sex was a gift. They've never understood why most people treat it like some dirty little secret no one should talk about.' There had been times as a teenager when she'd wished her parents had been a little less forthright with their views on sex. It was just lucky she'd never had to worry about having friends over for it to be a major embarrassment.

Her childhood had been anything but normal. She'd grown up in a commune in the hills outside Nimbin in the far north of New South Wales, where everything they had was either grown or bartered for and the outside world barely existed. While it should have been an ideal world for a child to grow up in, with everything focused on nature and none of the stresses of modern-day life, for Rilee it was a prison. She missed her friends, she missed the city, she'd never even visited a farm before they moved there. She didn't fit in.

There had been many times she'd been ashamed of the lifestyle her family led. People used to look at them with disdain when they went into town to buy supplies; the general assumption was that there was far too much free love and drug-taking going on. In reality, life in the commune was relatively normal, just in a slightly unconventional way. They had school lessons throughout the day and chores to do, just like the rest of Australia; they just didn't go to school and there was very little modern technology.

There were about forty people in the community, mostly families with children. Rilee was one of the eldest kids, with most of the others much younger, which was difficult. She missed having someone her own age to talk to and often envied the younger ones who all played and formed sibling-like ties with each other. They made fun of the fact she was scared of the animals and hated getting dirty. They'd grown up in the community and didn't know anything except the life they were living. They didn't even seem to care that they'd never visited a city and had no interest in ever doing so. Rilee didn't understand that at all. Why would they want to stay in a place like this for the rest of their lives when there was so much more of the world to see?

Dan gave a hollow laugh. 'You're right, we did have opposite upbringings.'

She could imagine the type of childhood Dan would have had. He may have grown up with wealth, living on one of the biggest properties in the district, but Jacob Kincaid would have been a difficult father to please. It was hard enough watching him when he spoke to Dan as a fully grown man. Many times Rilee felt the urge to throw her arms around Dan to protect him from the hostility and disapproval in his father's voice. It must have been lonely for him with both his sisters having left home when he was still quite young.

She'd gathered from the few things Dan had said that his mother had had trouble conceiving after the two girls and had almost given up hope of ever having the male heir they'd been hoping for, then Dan had arrived. She'd never be game enough to bring the subject up with Ellen, who seemed such an intensely private woman, but Rilee knew trying to have children and no doubt having miscarried quite a few along the way had to have been a devastating experience for the poor woman.

After Dan went back to work, Rilee found herself feeling unusually melancholy. It was strange how as a child you saw things so differently. Her childhood really hadn't been so bad—the things she'd always thought so important, like money and expensive clothes, hadn't brought her happiness in the end. It had taken returning to Australia for her to realise she wanted to be a naturopath. It was in her blood. Her mother had been a naturopath without knowing it, learning from her own grandmother as a child, using natural remedies for everything from a cold to sunburn to treating wounds. The benefit of modern-day naturopathy was that with the help of science she could explain the mechanics of how herbal medicine worked. People were more inclined to trust something that could be explained scientifically rather than left in the realm of witches and hippies. She wasn't entirely reassured that Pallaburra was going to embrace her profession quite as much as she'd hoped. If Errol and the earlier café experience was anything to go by, she wasn't feeling exactly confident.

❧

Rilee rested her head on her arm as she lay on her side watching her husband the next morning.

'What's on the agenda today, Mrs Kincaid?' Dan asked as he pulled on his boots.

'I'm going into town to talk to the real estate agent. I want to see if they have anything suitable to rent for my rooms.' She saw Dan's smile waver slightly and frowned. 'What?'

'Nothing. That's great.'

'Why is it that I get the feeling you're not very supportive of this?'

'I am. I think it's great that you've got something to keep you occupied.'

'Like my career?' she said dryly.

'I just . . . I don't want you to be disappointed.'

'In what way?'

'This isn't the city. People here take a while to come around to . . . new things. I just don't want you to get all excited about your business and then see it fail.'

'You think I'll fail?'

'Not you. I know you're good at what you do, Ri. But I'm just not sure you're going to have the kind of success you might have had somewhere else.'

Rilee stared at him silently for a few moments as the hurt trickled into annoyance. 'Funny how you weren't being this open about my chances of starting my own clinic when we were discussing getting married.'

'I want you to do what makes you happy, Ri. I just don't want you to be disappointed if it doesn't work.'

'And I'm *not* going to sit around out here and become your mother. I'm not interested in being on every damn committee in town, or running off to the city to shop. This has been my dream, Dan.'

'I know, but would it hurt to leave it for a year or two?'

'A year or two? Do you have any idea how hard I've studied to get this far? Take a look at those bookshelves, Dan—do you see any Mills and Boon on there? No, you don't, and you know why? Because those big, fat chemistry, anatomy and pharmaceutical textbooks are taking up all the room!' she said, waving her hand at the shelves across from them. 'Do you have any idea what I gave up to come out here? I had a client base back in Sydney—I would have had full bookings seven days a week if I wanted to work that much. People respected what I do. I left all that behind to come to a place where people think what I do is mumbo jumbo, and I did that because I love you. Don't you dare stand there and dismiss what I do as though it's something insignificant. I gave up my life to be here with you and for that I deserve a hell of a lot more respect than you and everyone else out here have been giving me.'

'I do respect you. I know what you gave up to be here.' Dan reached out to touch the side of her face gently. 'I just don't want to see you get disappointed.'

'This is what I know. This is what I'm trained to do.'

He didn't reply straight away, but when he did his expression seemed intent. 'We could have a baby.'

Rilee held his hopeful gaze and blinked away the surprise. They'd spoken about having kids, but Rilee always assumed he would understand that she wanted to work first. Having her own business would give her the flexibility to work around having children, but surely he understood she'd need to build up her business before they could do that? 'I can't believe you can just shrug off everything I've worked so hard for like this.'

'I'm just saying that if things didn't go according to plan, we could always just go straight to starting a family. I want kids with you, Ri.'

Rilee was torn between the sweetness of his comment and the way he could dismiss her career so lightly. 'I do too, but I want my career first. I need to do this, Dan, and I'm going to, with or without your support.'

Dan studied her silently before nodding his head and kissing her forehead. 'You'll always have my support. I love you, Ri.'

She listened to his footsteps echo down the hallway before she went back to mentally organising her morning, but some of the earlier excitement had gone from the task.

Doubt lingered at the back of her mind. What if Dan was right? What if, despite all her hard work, her business failed? Could she be happy without her career? All this time she'd justified giving up her city clinic by thinking that people needed care no matter where they lived. But had she been living in denial about the whole thing in order not to feel as though she'd sold out her dream by moving here?

She'd thought hard about her decision, and it hadn't been made lightly. But when it came right down to it, she could not imagine life without Dan in it. She still believed she'd made the right choice, she'd just thought she'd be able to have a career as well as a husband. Now she wasn't so confident.

Rilee ran her hand along the majestic carved balustrade of the staircase as she walked downstairs. The house was nothing short of magnificent. It had been built by Dan's great-great-great-grandfather during the gold rush, thanks to a fortune made supplying the goldfields and townships which had sprung up all over the countryside in these parts. Rilee stopped and studied the various photos that lined the walls. She never grew tired of looking at them. Her favourite was the yellowing photo dated 1885 with people lining both the upstairs and lower verandahs. The family members were easily recognised by their clothing, the women wearing expensive-looking dresses with bonnets and the men wearing suits, complete with top hats. The rest of the people in the photo were staff, Rilee assumed, and it was astounding to see how many there were. There were women, young and old, in white aprons and frilly hats, stockmen with slouched hats and riding boots, and young stable boys and workers' children. There had to be at least forty people in the photo. Thumb Creek in its heyday. Nowadays only Dan, foreman Mark, Jacob and a few part-time labourers in busy times were needed to keep the farm running, thanks to modern technology and equipment, and Mrs Pike, the housekeeper.

'Impressive, isn't it?'

Rilee turned and saw Ellen at the bottom of the stairs watching her. 'It sure is. So much history,' she said, shaking her head.

'The Kincaids certainly have that.'

'It must be nice to live in a place built by the family's ancestors.'

'I've always found it . . . somewhat stifling.'

That surprised Rilee. Not only the fact Ellen had revealed something like that to her but that anyone could find a beautiful old building like this stifling.

'I've always preferred the city,' she said. 'Which is why I have my concerns about your marriage.'

Rilee tried to keep her expression neutral. 'Oh?'

'I came from the city, much like you, with little idea what I was getting myself into. It wasn't fair of Dan to marry someone like you.'

'Like me? How?'

'Dan explained that you were in the process of starting up a clinic in the city before he met you. I know what it's like to give up on your dreams for a man, and I can tell you, while it all seems romantic right now, a few years down the track you won't be thinking that.'

Rilee opened her mouth to protest but Ellen held up a hand, silencing her. 'I'm giving you some advice that I wish someone had given me a long time ago. If you have any doubts, you need to speak up now and leave. The longer you stay the deeper this place drags you in, until you can't leave, and one day you'll wake up and realise you've missed your chance.'

Rilee stared at her mother-in-law, taken aback by her candid revelation. On some level she knew she was being insulted, but all Rilee could hear was the bitter resentment of a woman who lived with great regret.

There was no hiding the fact that Dan's parents had their problems. They had separate bedrooms, for starters. She'd asked Dan about it, but he'd shaken his head and told her not to go nosing around in his parents' problems. 'Don't you care? Aren't you worried about them?' she'd asked, unable to hide the incredulity in her tone.

'Of course I care but, Ri,' he'd sighed and scratched the back of his neck, something he tended to do when he felt awkward, 'my parents are private people. They don't discuss their problems . . . with anyone. Not me and especially not someone they've just met,' he said pointedly.

'But it's not healthy.'

'That's the way it's always been. Mum does her thing, and Dad does his. Sometimes they avoid each other, sometimes they're okay. I gave up trying to work out their marriage years ago. We just don't discuss it.'

She held Ellen's gaze firmly, making it clear she wasn't backing down. 'I love Dan very much,' Rilee said. 'I wasn't expecting it, and it didn't come along at the best time, but it happened and I'll go wherever he goes.'

'I hope you don't think you'll ever convince Daniel to leave here. You'll be sadly disappointed if you do. This place runs through their veins.'

'I wasn't thinking that.' The thought had never crossed her mind. She'd realised right from the start that when he was in Sydney there was always a part of him wishing he were back home. 'Everything about our relationship has been a whirlwind, I know, and I'm sorry that you and I didn't have time to get to know each other beforehand, but what's done is done and I hope we can make up for lost time now.'

Ellen stared at her with a contemplative expression before giving a slight nod. 'I just felt someone should warn you,' she said and walked away without a further word.

Rilee turned back to the photo on the wall, and rubbed her arms briskly to ward off the distinctive chill left in the air.

Eight

The sound of clucking and squawking came from the chook pen as she headed towards the large fenced-off enclosure. Unlatching the timber-framed door covered in wire, she edged inside, holding the two buckets before her like a shield.

She eyed a few birds pecking at the ground across from her and gave them a wide berth, but as soon as they realised she was there, their interest picked up and they began to close in on her quickly. Rilee hated their evil little chook eyes, which at the moment were fixed firmly on her as they circled like feathered sharks, but what she hated even more was the rooster. Big Red was what she called him, amongst other things. He'd made her chore a living hell since the very first day. Rilee spotted him making a beeline for her at alarming speed.

One of the hens flapped her wings in the dust at her and Rilee yelped, throwing the contents of the bucket. She didn't care that half the kitchen scraps ended up on top of the closest of the chooks, she just made use of the distraction, hurrying inside the covered area where the laying boxes were found.

The pungent smell of chook manure was rather over-powering first thing in the morning as she gathered the eggs, some still warm, in the bucket, caring less about how careful she was being and more about getting out of the smelly chook pen alive. She kept an eye on the remainder of the pack ... herd ... brood ... she was past caring if she had the correct terminology. She wasn't sure how far up on the intelligence scale chooks were, surely nowhere near dolphins or elephants, but Red in particular seemed to harbour a vendetta against her, and Rilee was positive the look in his beady black eye was one of smugness as he paced back and forth in front of the doorway.

'I'm bigger than you, and I'm smarter than you—I have two degrees, for God's sake! I can do this!' she muttered fiercely.

With a deep breath she marched back into the pen. Within seconds the angry rooster ran towards her, lunging and trying to strike her with his sharp claws.

Rilee threw an egg at him and ran as fast as she could to the main gate, slamming it behind her as Red crowed and squawked loudly on the other side.

'Well, I hate you too, you stupid bird,' Rilee yelled. As far as she was concerned, chooks were something she'd much rather buy frozen from the supermarket!

'I've never seen him act like that before.'

Oh great, of all the people who could have witnessed her harassment by the rooster it had to be Ellen. 'I've never really gotten on with animals.'

'I wouldn't have thought that, having being raised in the country.'

'I wasn't very outdoorsy.'

'I see.'

Rilee fought the urge to grit her teeth. The woman had the most annoying habit of adding disapproval to the smallest word.

'Well, if collecting the eggs is too much of a challenge for you, you don't have to do it.'

'It's fine. I'll manage.' It wasn't like she had anything else to do. Steadfast Mrs Pike, with her severe bun and sensible shoes, had everything in the house under control, and really didn't seem to have much to do with anyone on a personal level. It was hard to determine the woman's age, somewhere in her fifties at a guess, but Rilee suspected that if she smiled more often she'd look at least ten years younger.

The relationship between the housekeeper and Ellen was interesting to observe. It was like something out of the Edwardian era. Ellen swanned about the house like some lady of the manor and Mrs Pike did everything except bob into a curtsy and say 'Yes ma'am' after each exchange. Rilee had tried on more than one occasion to engage the housekeeper in conversation, but she had never got very far, other than short, respectful replies. Dan didn't really see anything strange about it. 'Some people just aren't chatty, Ri,' he said with a shrug.

This was the reason she needed to start her practice up as soon as possible: she was going stir-crazy, becoming slightly obsessed with the minutiae of daily life on Thumb Creek Station.

❧

Rilee opened her eyes and listened carefully, wondering what had woken her. She tried to snuggle into the warm blankets and go back to sleep, but unfortunately her bladder was now awake as well.

Careful to ease out of bed without waking her husband, Rilee headed down the hall towards the lavishly appointed bathroom she and Dan used. As she reached the door, she jumped back in alarm when she heard the sound of a toilet flushing.

As the door opened, there was a surprised growl as her father-in-law stepped out into the hallway and caught sight of her. 'You scared the life out of me, girl.'

'Sorry,' she stammered. 'I wasn't expecting anyone to be up,' she managed as her heart slowly settled back into its normal rhythm. A small surge of annoyance fluttered to life as she heard the tsk of annoyance from her father-in-law as they tried to sidestep each other. For goodness sake, why was he using the bathroom up this end of the house anyway? It wasn't as though he was strapped for choice; there was an en suite and main bathroom up the other end of the monstrosity of a house. This wasn't the first time she'd been awoken by the sound of him getting up through the night. She'd been wanting to bring up the subject of his nocturnal wandering for a while, but Jacob wasn't the most approachable man. Still, this was something she was growing a little concerned about—professionally.

'Jacob,' she said quickly before she could acquiesce to the little voice inside that was warning her to keep her mouth shut. 'I'm sorry if this is a little personal, but I can't help but notice you get up a lot at night. I can give you something that can help with that and any other issues you might be having.'

'What issues? What the hell are you going on about?'

'Getting up a lot at night can be a symptom of a lot of things—things that can be treated. I handled a lot of male problems in the clinic in Sydney.'

'Well, you won't be *handling* anything of mine. I don't need any help.'

'You don't have to put up with things the way they are.'

'Things are fine,' he snapped.

Things were not fine. Not in the least. It was sad that two people who had been married for so long barely spoke civilly to one another. In her work as a practitioner, she knew that sometimes you had to play detective to work out underlying causes of patients' problems, and over the last few weeks she'd been observing, putting together pieces of the jigsaw that was this dysfunctional family's life.

'Really? Don't you miss . . . being with your wife?' she asked abruptly. She couldn't stand it. 'Is staying in a different bedroom because you're either too embarrassed or too stubborn to get help really worth making yourself and Ellen so miserable?'

He turned to glare at her. 'What would you know about anything?'

'I know I haven't been part of this family very long and maybe I am out of line bringing this up,' she said, rushing on as she saw his temper building, 'but you get up at night to urinate, frequently. I don't know if you're displaying any other symptoms, like erectile dysfunction, for instance, but you need to get things checked out before they get any worse.'

'I am *not* discussing this with you,' he snapped, 'This is none of your damn business.'

Rilee sighed as he stomped off down the corridor. She knew she'd probably just done more damage than good, but she was trying to help the damn man. Why couldn't he see that?

'Are you out of your mind?'

Rilee jumped at the voice from behind her, turning to find Dan, shirtless and blurry-eyed, gaping at her. 'Please tell me I'm dreaming and I didn't just hear the words "erection" and "dysfunction" used in the same sentence . . . *to my father.*'

'I've been wanting to speak with him, but I can never catch him alone to talk about it.'

'Rilee, you can't expect people to have a rational discussion about things like erectile dysfunction,' he said, lowering his voice. 'Around here, men don't talk about stuff like that. Not even to their doctor.'

'I'm not *having a discussion*,' she corrected. 'I'm trying to save his stupid life, and that's just . . . ridiculous. How on earth do they think doctors can treat them if they won't talk about symptoms?'

'They don't usually go to a doctor, and certainly not for things like that.'

They didn't go to the doctors? 'But . . . health checks and screenings are *vital* for catching diseases early. They save lives.'

'It's hard to change your ways when you've been brought up to get the job done no matter what. When you're a farmer you can't take sick days—there's too much to do. There's animals that rely on you to feed them, there's crops that need to be sown or harvested, and it's your yearly income that's riding on it. It takes time to change the mindset of people used to doing things a certain way.'

'You won't be able to look after your animals or harvest anything if you ignore symptoms that could be warning you of a serious illness.'

'All I'm saying is you need to figure out a different way of approaching people out here. You can't ambush them in a hallway in the middle of the night and expect them to open up to you.'

Rilee *had* found a different way to approach the subject—she'd been watching Jacob and decided that tackling the issue without beating around the bush was the only way to go about it. Sure, with other people she wouldn't have been quite so blunt, but Jacob was old school, and he wouldn't have reacted any better had she pussyfooted around the subject. 'Will you try to talk to him?'

'He's not going to listen to me,' Dan sighed. 'He never has before, I can't see him doing it now, and especially not if he thinks we've been talking about his . . . problem. He's a proud man, Ri.'

'And that pride might just be the death of him.'

'You think it's that serious?'

'I think it's sensible for a man of his age to get anything abnormal checked out by his doctor,' Rilee said quietly. 'It could be an infection or it could be something more serious. Either way, to leave it unchecked is just . . . irresponsible.'

Dan gave a sigh and reached out to pull her against him. 'Come back to bed. You can't do anything tonight.'

Rilee didn't protest. There was nothing she could do if Jacob didn't want her help, but it still didn't sit right with her to stand by and watch as he allowed his health to deteriorate.

As she lay next to Dan and listened to his deep, steady breathing, she was busy planning how she could change her approach and get through to men like Jacob.

Nine

Rilee looked up from the local paper as Ellen came into the kitchen. She noticed the tired expression even her impeccably applied makeup couldn't cover. 'Good morning.'

'Good morning, Rilee,' Ellen answered in the polite, neutral tone she seemed to reserve especially for her.

'How did you sleep?' Rilee asked as Ellen made a pot of tea.

'Fine, thank you. Although it's usually the host who asks the guest how they slept,' she said with a smile that didn't quite reach her eyes.

Pulled in line yet again. Rilee would have normally let the matter go at that point, but the woman's attitude was rubbing her the wrong way this morning. 'I only asked because you're looking a little tired this morning.'

'Yes, there's been quite a lot happening around here lately. I'm sure things will settle down eventually,' she dismissed, taking a tissue from the counter and turning away to pat lightly at her face. 'It's unseasonably warm this morning.'

Rilee was actually thinking there was a bit of a chill in the air. 'I see the show is coming up. Do you enter any of your flowers?'

'Yes, my roses usually do quite well.'

'I can't wait. It'll be my first time at a show.'

'You haven't been to an agricultural show before?'

'Nope,' she said.

'How . . . unusual.'

'That pretty much sums up my entire childhood,' she said with a lopsided smile.

'Speaking of which, when do we get to meet your parents?'

Rilee glanced up sharply at that. She and Dan had plans to head up to Tippery Heights as soon as there was a break in Dan's workload, but that wasn't going to be anytime soon. She'd tried her best to prepare him for meeting her parents. She knew he'd find some of their ideas a little out there, but she was pretty sure they'd get on. His parents, on the other hand . . . She could just imagine how Jacob would react when he found out her parents were permaculturists.

'I'm not sure. They're kept pretty busy.'

'They'll have to come to our party. You will invite them, won't you.' It was a statement, not a question.

'I'll let them know,' she said, more to keep the woman happy than with any real intention of doing so. 'You know,

I can mix you up some herbs and some chamomile tea to help you sleep at night, if you like,' Rilee said as she watched Ellen pour boiling water into her teapot.

'That's all right, I've never been a great sleeper.'

Rilee bit her lip for a moment as she decided the best way to approach the subject she wanted to bring up. 'It's funny, all the years I spent sleeping alone, but now I can't imagine not having Dan there beside me any more.'

Ellen stopped stirring her tea but didn't look up.

'I guess I can understand how sleeping in separate rooms would make sense. It would be a bit disruptive with Jacob getting up through the night all the time.'

'Excuse me?'

Rilee wrung her fingers together. Damn Dan and his lecture last night. She tackled sensitive, sometimes embarrassing issues every day with patients. Yes, she knew this wasn't a patient asking for a consultation, but she was so frustrated that these people treated her like an idiot because she didn't know about farming, when what she did know about would probably improve their lives enormously.

'I tried to speak to Jacob about his frequent bathroom trips through the night. I'm concerned that he should be seeing a doctor about his symptoms. I thought maybe he'd listen to you.'

Ellen glared at her, a look of utter horror on her angular features. 'I don't know who you think you are, but while you're under *my* roof you will kindly refrain from sticking your nose into other people's *private* business,' she said in a low hiss.

'I'm not trying to be nosey. I'm speaking as a health professional.'

'I don't see anything *professional* about this conversation.'

'Ellen, I'm sorry if you feel offended. I was only trying to help.'

'Well, nobody asked you to.'

Rilee listened to the angry sound of her heels marching up the hallway and sank back into her chair despondently. She knew she'd overstepped the mark, but she'd been hoping that maybe, as his wife, Ellen would be an ally in her push to get Jacob to seek help. Clearly that wasn't going to happen.

Her parting remark had stung more than she cared to admit. No one had asked for her help. No one asked her for anything. She didn't fit in and she didn't belong, that much was becoming abundantly clear.

∽

Rilee wiped her arm across her forehead and grimaced at the streaks of dirt and sweat that came away. She could only imagine the sight she made. 'Come and help out in the yards, he said. It'll be fun, he said,' she muttered as Dan grinned across the backs of disgruntled cattle being pushed through a race.

'Aww, come on, Ri. Think of it as bonding time.'

'Bonding? I'm thinking it's more like cheap labour.' It was hot, dusty and noisy in the yards and Rilee was fairly sure she wouldn't be agreeing to tag along for the day ever again. They were a man down and she'd initially thought it would be a good way to see a little more of what her husband did when he was gone all day. So far she was struggling to get her head around all the various components of farming. She was yet to experience harvest time, but she could only imagine it would mean as many long days and nights out in the paddocks as seeding had taken. Then there was the livestock side of things—cattle that needed moving to another paddock, drenching, tagging or marking—not to mention a never-ending cycle of maintenance—fences that needed fixing, all manner of vehicles that had to be kept running. She'd been trying her best to learn about this new and foreign life she'd been brought into, but it was a lot to take in at once.

For the most part everyone was being helpful. She'd stuck pretty close to Dan and he showed her what to do and explained why they were doing it. He was a very good teacher, and she admired the way he spoke and treated Mark, the station foreman and the younger worker. His father, on the other hand, was as grumpy as ever and she noticed the other men tried to steer clear of him where possible. He swore and yelled his way through most of the morning and by smoko Rilee had just about had enough.

She watched her father-in-law disappear around the corner of the shed as Dan handed her a mug of coffee poured from a thermos. 'That's no way to treat people, you know. How on earth has he managed to keep staff this long?'

'He's a cranky old bastard most of the time. It's just the way he is.'

Rilee didn't believe Jacob's bad mood was to be blamed entirely on an unfortunate personality.

Dan paused, eyeing her over his mug. 'I'm pretty sure I don't like whatever you're thinking.'

Rilee glanced over at her husband and patted his hand as she stood up. 'I'll be right back.'

'Ri,' Dan started to protest, but sighed as she lifted an eyebrow in silent challenge. 'Never mind.'

She picked her way across the hard-packed ground liberally dotted with dried cow poo and leaned against the rail fence near the rear of the shed where Jacob had gone a few moments earlier.

She saw his step falter a little when he looked up and saw her waiting as he came around the corner.

'Before you say anything, I just want to apologise for the other night. I didn't mean to overstep the boundaries but I am genuinely concerned about you, Jacob.'

She saw his face darken. 'I told you before, it's none of your damn business.'

'Why would you let something like this continue when it's clearly making you miserable? If you don't care about yourself then what about your wife?'

'What the hell would you know about anything?'

'A lot more than you, obviously, if I can see what's going on and you can't.'

Jacob gave a disgusted grunt and moved to walk past, but Rilee wasn't about to give up so easily.

'Have you been having regular prostate checks at your GP?'

'Bloody doctors. If you ask me, doctors are the reason this world is getting soft. They make money off scaring everyone into thinking they're dying.'

'All right, if you don't want to see your doctor, I can help you.'

'I don't think so,' he said coldly, moving past her and storming off across the clearing without looking back, leaving Rilee to stare after him in frustration. As they returned to work, Jacob's temper seemed even worse than before.

'What the hell did you say to him?' Dan growled as he came up beside her later.

'Nothing that made any difference apparently,' she said, looking across at the older man, who was wearing a deep scowl.

'Well, do everyone a favour next time and don't say anything at all. He's an even bigger pain in the arse than usual. The boys are ready to walk off the job.'

'I was trying to help,' she said quietly.

'You can't help someone who doesn't want to be helped. Just leave it be.'

That didn't make any sense. The healer in her found it hard to turn her back on someone who was obviously suffering, but she had no idea how to make Jacob understand that he needed to get help.

Ten

Two weeks later the cottage was finished and Rilee could barely contain her eagerness to move in. Armed with cleaning paraphernalia, she spent the day clearing away the builders' mess and unpacking the few things she'd wanted to keep when she left the city—mostly reference books and equipment. She couldn't wait to try the big claw-footed bathtub she'd had installed. Dan had protested that it was a waste of time, seeing as it would hold too much water to use more than a couple times a year, but it was the only thing she'd wanted in the entire renovation. She didn't mind compromising on any of the other items, but the bathtub she stood her ground on. It set off the rustic country feel to perfection.

Heavy boots on the steps outside alerted her to Dan's arrival, and she gave the bathtub one final wipe before dropping the cloth back into the bucket and turning to greet him.

'This is a nice surprise,' she said after he lifted his head from their kiss. 'It's a bit early for lunch, isn't it?'

'I'm not home for lunch . . . unfortunately. Just dropped in to pick up some paperwork. How's the unpacking going?'

'Almost done.'

'We'll have to go shopping for some more furniture one day soon,' he said, casting his eye around the lounge room as they walked back towards the kitchen.

'We've got the basics.'

Dan circled her waist and dragged her close. 'A bed and a fridge, that's all we really need,' he agreed, nuzzling her neck.

༄

Later, when she was working on her business plan, she heard a voice outside.

'Hello? Anyone home?'

Rilee looked up from the computer screen and called, 'Just a sec.' Who on earth was this? At the front door she saw someone hidden behind an enormous pot plant. 'Oh, here, let me get the door for you.' Rilee opened the screen and stood to one side as the pot plant with legs moved inside.

Having deposited the plant on the kitchen bench, a woman maybe a few years younger than herself turned and smiled a welcome at Rilee. 'Hi, I'm Shae Fuller. My husband is Mark, the station foreman.'

'Oh!' Rilee gave a gasp of recognition. 'Hi, yes, I've met Mark, and I was wondering when I'd get a chance to meet you.'

'I stayed on a bit longer to help out after my gran's funeral and just got back last night. I hope I'm not interrupting—I just wanted to pop over and introduce myself.'

'No, not at all. Would you like a cuppa?' Rilee busied herself making coffee, sending the massive plant on the bench a glance.

'I brought a housewarming gift. It's a fern.'

'That's very kind of you. I'm afraid I have a bad track record with indoor plants.'

'You won't be able to kill this one, trust me. I've had one for three years and it's still going strong.'

Rilee felt better after hearing that bit of news, but she still eyed the plant doubtfully. She was good with herbs but she usually managed to kill house plants. They took their coffee outside to sit on the verandah; the steps made a surprisingly comfortable seat.

'So how are you fitting in?'

Rilee glanced down into her coffee cup and gave a small grimace. 'Well, apart from becoming the laughing stock of the district, fine I guess.'

'That bad, huh?'

'Worse. I can't seem to do anything right around here.'

Shae gave a smile of commiseration. 'I think it would be a big adjustment coming out here fresh from the city.

Don't be too hard on yourself, everyone makes mistakes at first. You'll get the hang of it.'

'I hope so. I don't get trusted with much, but I look at how much work there is to do around the place every day and it's mind-boggling how it all gets done.'

'We've been away a few weeks, so it's made a bit of extra work for everyone, I guess. It's not usually this bad. I work from home in freelance marketing and communications, which keeps me busy but nowhere near as busy as some women living on the land. I always think back to what my gran's generation had to do,' she smiled dryly. 'She'd have to help pick beans before making breakfast and getting seven kids fed and ready for school, then go back out in the field until it was time to go in and make dinner, as well as take care of all the washing, cooking and kids . . .'

'Oh wow.' Rilee couldn't imagine that kind of life—she was struggling just trying to collect the eggs. 'So you come from a long line of farmers then?' She managed to disguise the disappointment after her brief moment of hope that she'd found a fellow non-farmer.

'My parents still work the original farm alongside my brothers and their families. Where did you grow up?'

'Originally Sydney before we moved to the far north coast of New South Wales.'

'Really? Whereabouts?'

'A small . . . community, on a farm.' *Of sorts.* Rilee hedged. She really didn't want to alienate this nice stranger on the first meeting as usually happened once people found out she'd been brought up in a hippie commune.

'So you were a country girl?'

'Yeah, I know. You'd think I'd be better at this whole rural thing, wouldn't you? My parents were vegans, so even though we had chooks, we didn't use any animal products ourselves—we sold the eggs for extra income.'

'What on earth did you eat?'

'Tofu and lentils . . . *lots* of lentils.'

'Are you still a vegan?'

'God no. I gave that up the minute I left home.'

'So do you remember the last lentil burger you ate? I'd imagine it's like an ex-smoker remembering the date of their last cigarette,' Shae grinned.

Rilee began to smile, until a memory resurfaced. 'On the train, the day I left for Sydney.' Her mother had packed her a bag of food for her big trip. She remembered thinking to herself how she was so glad she'd never have to eat another stupid lentil burger ever again. 'I threw it in the bin the minute I got on the train.' Rilee felt remorse settle upon her shoulders like a heavy shawl. 'My mum had made the effort to get up early and pack me a home-made lunch and I couldn't wait to throw it away the first chance I got,' she said sadly. It had been years since she'd thought about that day. How could she have been so ungrateful?

'Hey, you were a teenager, we all did horrible things to our parents. Go and give her a call and apologise, it'll make you feel better—I do it all the time to my mum. Half the time she doesn't even remember it, and then I realise I've been feeling guilty for nothing!'

Rilee smiled at the woman's attempt to make her feel better.

Shae gave a small grunt. 'I love my family to death and all, but even at twenty-nine and married, I still get phone calls asking me to explain myself and wanting to know when they can expect grandchildren.'

Rilee thought she detected a slight catch in the woman's tone, but Shae moved the conversation along before she had time to dwell on it. 'So I hear you're planning a new venture.'

'How did *you* hear about it?' Shae had been away for much of the time—surely news couldn't travel that fast?

'Dan talks a lot about you. From what Mark says it's hard to shut him up sometimes.'

'Oh.' Rilee couldn't help her surprised delight at that comment.

'He said the extra-long lunch breaks were great too. For some reason, Dan's very eager to get home for lunch nowadays,' she grinned.

Rilee did blush a little at that.

'So how's this business going?'

Rilee, grateful for the change in subject, said, 'I've got my business plan almost completed, and I've booked an appointment with the real estate agent to look at an office space to rent, so I guess we'll soon find out if I can get a business up and running.'

'It sounds very exciting.'

Rilee detected a small reservation though, despite her encouraging words. 'But . . .'

'I only just met you, and I really don't want to rain on your parade when you've put so much work into this, it's just that I have a feeling you might come up against a little bit of resistance with most people around here. Maybe it's something you should consider before you invest too much money into this business venture—I'd hate to see you lose all your money over this if it doesn't go the way you hope.'

'Did my husband put you up to this?'

'Up to what?' Shae frowned uncertainly.

'The caution about starting a business out here. It's almost word for word what he said the other day.'

'I haven't spoken to Dan; I just wanted you to be aware of what you might be up against.'

Rilee gave a small twist of her lips. 'Sorry. I guess I'm a bit sensitive about it all at the moment. I figure things will start out a little slow but once word starts to get around, I'm sure business will pick up.'

Shae shrugged lightly. 'Just so you're aware it could take a while.'

'I don't have anything else to do, so I'll have plenty of time on my hands.'

'What kinds of things can you help with?'

Rilee looked up at her new friend, trying to calculate the level of genuine interest in the question. 'All sorts of things. Fatigue, depression, allergies. Fertility problems, menopause, arthritis—lots of things.'

'Something for everyone in there,' she joked half-heartedly.

110

Rilee could sense something behind the woman's response but didn't want to push. Maybe once they got to know each other she'd open up a bit more.

'Well, I better get moving. There's heaps to catch up on since we've been away.'

'Thanks for the present, and for coming over to say hello. It'll be nice to have someone around here to have coffee with now and again.'

'I'm really glad you're here, Rilee,' Shae smiled, then headed back down the stairs and climbed into a ute, before leaving via the long dirt driveway.

Walking inside with the empty coffee cups, Rilee figured maybe it wouldn't be so bad here now that she'd made a friend, and her hopes began to lift a little at the thought.

Eleven

The sound of the front door opening distracted Rilee from her computer screen the next morning. 'I knew you couldn't resist that offer for a morning quickie,' she called, shutting the laptop as she heard footsteps heading up the hallway. 'Let's go, big boy—' Her mouth gaped as she discovered her mother-in-law frozen in the doorway, a hand fluttering around her throat anxiously. 'Ellen! I'm sorry, I thought you were—'

'Dan, yes . . . I gathered.'

Mortified, Rilee retied the sash of her silk dressing gown tightly around her waist and crossed her arms protectively across her chest. *Well, this was . . . awkward.* 'Newlyweds,' she laughed, hoping it didn't sound as hysterical as she feared.

'Yes. Well.'

'Was there something you needed, Ellen?'

'I was coming to ask if you'd like to have lunch in town today.'

The invitation caught Rilee off guard momentarily, but she recovered quickly. 'That would be lovely. I actually have to go to the post office, so that works in well.'

'I'll just let you get dressed then.'

'Oh, *now*?' She stole a glance at the watch on her wrist—it was barely nine.

'I have a ladies' church committee meeting before lunch. You can sit in—the meeting won't take long and it will be a good opportunity to introduce you to a few people in town.'

'Oh, okay, I'll just duck in and have a quick shower then. Help yourself to tea or coffee, make yourself at home.' *As though you haven't already.* Since when did people just walk into someone else's house without knocking? Irritated by her mother-in-law's proprietorial attitude, she slammed drawers as she searched for something suitable to wear. What the hell did one wear to a bloody ladies' church group meeting anyway? Conscious of her guest probably nosing around her house as she showered, Rilee made quick work of getting dry and dressed.

She hurried through her makeup routine and was pulling on a pair of small heels as she hopped down the hallway and out to the kitchen. Now that had to be some kind of record, she thought to herself and wished Dan had been here to witness it.

'Oh, you didn't need to hurry that much. You should have taken time to do your hair, dear.'

Gritting her teeth, she forced a smile to her lips. 'I did do my hair, it's supposed to look slightly tousled.'

'Oh. I see.'

Rilee saw the woman's eyebrow hitch slightly, and Ellen gave a doubtful smile as she stared at her finger-styled damp hair. There was nothing wrong with her hairstyle. She'd worn it like this plenty of times; it was cut like this on purpose. What was wrong with this woman? Surely it was permissible to wear your hair in something other than tied back in a ponytail once in a while?

'Well, if you're sure, dear. We've still got plenty of time if you'd like to finish getting ready.'

Irritation reared its ugly head once more, and Rilee fought her usual response, which would have been to keep the peace by going back to the bathroom and changing. Not today. 'Nope, I'm good. Let's get going.' She grabbed her handbag from the kitchen bench and headed out the front door, not bothering to see if Ellen was following or not.

It was going to be a long day.

❦

The meeting was held in the back room of the top pub, which was really quite lovely inside. The old pub dated back to 1870 and had been preserved beautifully, and although its original old-world charm had been retained, it had been given a new lease of life with lighter furnishings and white paint replacing the darker shades of reds and greens and velvet furnishings that would have been prominent in the pub's heyday. The conference room was decorated in shades of buttercup and white and there was plenty of sunshine filtering in through the large windows and French doors which opened out onto the wide timber verandah that surrounded the hotel.

The ladies had added their own little touches to the space, with fresh-cut flowers in vases on the front table and around the room, and a huge morning tea spread on a side table. Minutes from the last meeting were read out by a harried-looking secretary and Rilee tried not to let her attention drift too much, aware of the furtive glances being slid her way throughout the announcements.

Ellen, for her part, sat ramrod straight with her ankles crossed and put to the side, the very image of a June Dally-Watkins star pupil, not batting so much as an eyelid at the obvious interest in her new daughter-in-law's presence.

The secretary announced she was handing the proceedings over to the committee's president and Ellen gracefully stood and glided to the front of the room and the small platform where the podium stood.

Rilee stared after her mother-in-law in surprise; she didn't know Ellen was the president. Clearly she was in her element in this role. Grace and poise emanated from the woman. She still had that condescending tone that rubbed Rilee the wrong way, but here it suited her position. She ran the meeting with all the professionalism and smoothness of a seasoned presenter. The woman could easily pass for the managing director of a company.

'And so I'd like to introduce you to my daughter-in-law, Rilee.'

Immediately all sets of eyes in the room were on her as Rilee realised she had been lost in thought. She gave a nod of hello and sent an awkward smile around the meeting, wishing she'd been told beforehand to expect this mass introduction. Thankfully the meeting was declared over and it was time for morning tea.

Ellen made her way across to her, a long-legged blonde in tow. The woman was attractive, sleek like a thoroughbred, with elegant long nails and silky smooth hair that fell below her shoulders.

'Rilee, may I introduce you to Priscilla Montgomery, a dear friend of the family,' Ellen purred with a warm smile at the blonde beauty, the kind she had never given Rilee.

'Hello, Priscilla. Your parents were big Elvis fans I take it?'

Arctic blue eyes drilled into her and Rilee felt chilled to the bone. 'So this is the woman who finally captured Daniel's heart.'

Daniel? She'd asked Dan if he was ever called Daniel, and he'd said only his mother called him by his formal name, and usually when he was in trouble. Well, his mother . . . *and* Priscilla. 'Apparently so,' Rilee smiled.

'I hear you're into this new fad of herbal medicine.' Priscilla regarded her haughtily down her long nose and Rilee thought the thoroughbred comparison was just right.

'It's actually been around for thousands of years, so it's not exactly new.'

'Hardly a replacement for modern medicine, though. Surely people are wary of putting their health into the hands of people who replace medications with vitamins and herbs?'

'It's not supposed to replace modern medicine, it's used to complement it, and it's more than just herbs.'

'You're going to have a hard time convincing anyone around here to agree.'

'I'm surprised by that—it's quite accepted back in the city, not to mention all around the world. With so many new discoveries about the long-term effects of so-called safe drugs, most people want to make an informed decision about their health. I guess it's just taking a bit longer to reach out here.'

The smug smile disappeared. 'You might want to rein in your superiority complex, country people don't much like being told they're backward,' Priscilla told her coldly.

'I didn't say anyone was backward. I merely pointed out that most other places don't have the same fear of naturopathy that a lot people around here are showing. It seems strange.'

'It may help to keep in mind that *you* are the stranger here, not the other way around.'

Rilee counted to ten and held back the desire to snap at the woman, certain that her fate would be well and truly sealed if she made the mistake of alienating the entire committee in one morning. Forcing a smile to her lips, Rilee excused herself to go and get a cup of coffee. She could turn the other cheek with the best of them, and if that meant ignoring the stuck-up blonde with the horsey face, so be it.

'I see you met Priscilla,' said a voice beside her.

Rilee turned and met a familiar face. Finally, thought Rilee with a sigh, someone friendly. 'Hi, Edna. Yes, I've just had that particular pleasure.'

'Don't let her bother you. She's always been Ellen's favourite. Until you came along and upset the applecart, that is.'

'Her favourite?'

Edna lifted her eyes from the huge slice of chocolate cake she'd just loaded onto her plate and gave a mischievous grin. 'Priscilla was supposed to be the next Mrs Kincaid. You've swooped in and taken her promised husband.'

Twelve

On Sunday Dan surprised her by suggesting a picnic down by the creek that ran through part of the property. In some places it was no more than a narrow waterway carved through the paddock like a ditch; in other places it widened and timber bridges had been built in order for livestock and equipment to cross. But her favourite part was some distance from the homestead, where the tree line became denser and the creek formed a type of waterhole oasis. Either side of the waterhole the creek trickled over gravelly rock, making a babbling, gurgling background that was soothing. Large flat rocks edged the water and huge gum trees and other native species formed a shady, secluded escape from the real world. The thought of getting away alone with her husband was too tempting to resist. Even though their house wasn't next door to his parents', it was within view, and maybe it was her overactive imagination but she could swear it felt as though every move she made was being judged and notched up against her on some kind of tally sheet.

More than once she'd told herself she was becoming paranoid, but no matter how hard she tried to pretend she was leading her own life, the fact was that everything seemed to go through Jacob and Ellen first.

The sun felt warm on her skin as Dan gently traced circles across her back. They'd eaten their hastily thrown together lunch and now she was feeling drowsy and content.

'Are you happy here, Ri?'

His quiet words brought her wide awake and she rolled onto her back to look into Dan's face. He propped himself on one arm, so close she could feel his body heat. Staring up into his serious face, Rilee saw the strain in the small lines around his eyes as he tried to search her face for an answer to his question.

'I'm not unhappy,' she hedged, and she wasn't. She'd been in places far worse than this in her life. Working in a bar in order to put herself through her degree, disillusioned with pretty much everything, including men and relationships, had certainly been no stroll in the park.

'That's not an answer.'

Rilee raised her hand to the rough stubble that darkened his jaw in a sexy, rugged way. 'I'm happy wherever *you* are.'

He gave a ghost of a smile, but his eyes were still serious and far too perceptive for comfort. 'I've been thinking about what you said the other day. I don't want to turn you into my mother.'

'I didn't mean—' Rilee automatically began to protest, but Dan was shaking his head.

'My father brought her here as a young bride from the city. Sound familiar? She didn't like it at first. She still prefers to spend as much time as she can back in the city. She wanted Dad to sell up and move, but he never would. I don't want to force you to stay here if it's going to make you end up hating me.'

'That's not going to happen, Dan.'

'Sometimes I get the sense you feel like you've trapped yourself here.'

An uneasy feeling ran through her at his comment. There had been times since coming here that she had felt trapped, had wondered whether she'd made the right decision, but she didn't know he'd been aware of that. 'You better not let your father hear you trying your hand at psychology. I don't think he could handle two of us crossing to the dark side of mumbo jumbo,' she teased lightly.

He held her gaze steadily for a few more moments, then said with a touch of self-deprecation, 'Maybe I'll just stick to farming.'

They fell into an easy silence, but Rilee was troubled by his analysis. She loved him—there was no doubt in her mind at all that she'd made the right decision to marry him—but this lifestyle was nothing like she'd been expecting. She hadn't had the first clue what it would be like being the wife of a farmer. She wasn't sure exactly what it was she had been expecting, but the long hours Dan worked and the lonely days of trying to find something to do while he was out working, while trying to avoid her distinctly cold mother-in-law, had not been part of it. She'd have to work harder at keeping her concerns quiet—the last thing she wanted was for Dan to be worrying about her as well as the thousand other things he had to think about.

'I never did get around to asking you about the meeting you and Mum went to the other day. How did it go?'

Rilee gave a small groan. 'It was okay.' She rolled away and stared up at the cloudless blue of the sky above them. The smooth rocks of the creek bank were warm beneath her. 'I know I need to get involved with the community to fit in better, but I honestly don't know if I'm cut out to be church group material.'

'They raise money for worthy events and it keeps Mum out of my hair if she's bossing around the rest of the town.' She could hear the grin in Dan's voice.

'I shouldn't complain, but honestly, they're fundraising for all these places everywhere else. Aren't there things around *here* that they could be raising money for? I mean, look at Pallaburra. We don't have any doctors, the closest one is two and a half hours away. I asked your mother who her doctor was and she said she went to one in Sydney! *Sydney*, Dan.'

'We've always used Dr Morley. His father was Mum's doctor when she was a kid.'

'I know for a Kincaid with their own aircraft that's really no less inconvenient than most people having to drive two hours, but seriously, how are most *normal* people supposed to get their kids to a doctor that far away?'

'I'll try not to take offence at the normal people comment,' he said dryly.

'I just think there's more than a few things around this place they could be trying to improve.'

'So do something about it.'

Rilee turned her head at that and saw he was serious. 'I can't even convince people around here to believe I'm a trained professional, you *really* think they're going to listen to any of my suggestions?'

'You won't know if you don't try.'

For an insane moment she actually considered it, until Priscilla's smug smile came to mind. 'I met someone at the meeting who knew you.'

'Rilee, I was born here, everyone at that meeting knows me.'

'When were you going to mention Priscilla Montgomery?'

When he didn't answer, Rilee looked over at him and lifted an eyebrow in question.

'I didn't know she was back in town.'

'Well, she is, large as life. So how come you never told me you were practically married to her?'

'We weren't *practically* anything. We've known each other all our lives, but there was never going to be a marriage.'

'Someone forgot to mention that to Priscilla and your mother.'

'I never promised either one of them anything. In fact, I went out of my way to make it very clear I didn't intend to marry Priscilla. She went off to the city and I thought that was the end of it.' He seemed genuinely annoyed.

'Maybe they thought you'd change your mind.'

'There's nothing they can do about it now, is there, so forget about them.' He stood up and headed for the creek, wading in until waist deep and then diving beneath the water and vanishing from sight.

Rilee felt a tiny niggle of uncertainty at his abrupt behaviour. Something warned her that there was more to this story than he was telling her.

He emerged from the creek and shook the water from his head, reaching for a towel hanging on a nearby tree where they'd hung them after their earlier dip. Rilee watched him silently, content to let their previous conversation go if he didn't want to discuss it, but he surprised her when he sat down on the ground next to her and started talking.

'The Montgomerys and Kincaids have been friends for years. Priscilla and I grew up together. We had a brief teenage romance. I guess Mum always thought at some point it would rekindle. I told her not to hold her breath, but she was like a dog with a bone.'

'Can't believe that for a second,' Rilee said drolly.

'Anyway,' Dan continued after leaning back on his elbows, 'Mum was driving me nuts—more so than usual,' he said with a slanted grin, 'and she invites Priscilla over for a mini intervention. They were both there waiting for me when I walked in after a buying trip away. So they reveal this almighty marriage proposition, complete with guest list for the wedding, time frame of when an appropriate announcement should take place and a list of all the benefits a joint marriage between Thumb Creek and Little Bend would bring both families.'

Rilee could picture the scene exactly. 'What did you do?'

'I lost it. I told them to forget it, that if they couldn't take the polite hints I'd been giving then I'd make it real clear for them so there was no mistake.'

Rilee flinched, despite the small voice cheering on her husband for standing up to them. After all, she knew what rejection felt like from a man you thought you were in love with.

'I told them that when I got married—*if* I got married—it would be on *my* terms, with a woman of *my* choice, when *I* was ready.'

'That must have gone down well.'

Dan gave a snort. 'There were tears and tantrums and swearwords being thrown about that I'd never even heard before.'

'And that was just from your mother!' Rilee muttered.

Dan chuckled, but shook his head at the memory. 'It wasn't pretty.'

No wonder Ellen and Priscilla were so annoyed with her. They'd had everything worked out perfectly until Dan had decided to go and be difficult and marry some stranger from the city, no less. She didn't hold out much hope she was going to be winning over either woman anytime soon.

Thirteen

As Rilee rounded the aisle of the supermarket she noticed
a young girl at the far end and realised it was the same
young mother she'd bumped into at the chemist. She saw
the girl carefully select a lipstick from the wall display of
cheap makeup. Her hand hovered over the red plastic basket
balanced on top of the old pram with its faded navy fabric
before she quickly replaced the tube back on the shelf and
pushed the pram towards the checkout.

Rilee thought once again about the number of young
mothers in town, tied down with children before they'd
even had a chance to live their lives.

As she reached the end of the aisle, Rilee glanced at the
rectangular lipstick box that had been haphazardly placed
back on the shelf. Candy Pink. Rilee smiled sadly. The

teenager with a baby was still just a young girl who wanted the same thing every other girl her age—godawful bright pink lipstick. Rilee dropped the lipstick into her trolley, heading towards the cashier to line up behind the young girl as the last of her items were being tallied.

'Forty-seven eighty-two,' the cashier was saying to the girl as Rilee began unpacking her trolley.

There was a moment's silence as the girl rummaged through her purse.

The cashier shifted her weight to the other foot and waited impatiently with a deadpan stare. 'I already told your mum that there's no more store credit.'

'I don't want any credit,' the girl mumbled.

'If you don't have enough you'll have to put something back. What do you want to take out?' the woman asked briskly.

Rilee saw the girl bite her bottom lip as she tried to decide what she needed the least. From what Rilee could see there wasn't an easy choice, with only nappies, baby formula, a few bananas, milk and a small tray of minced beef on the counter before her.

This wasn't right, Rilee thought, feeling terrible for the young girl's plight. 'Here, let me,' she said, taking out her purse and handing the cashier a fifty-dollar note.

It was hard to say who looked more surprised, the cashier or the girl. 'Are you sure?' the cashier asked, staring at the cash doubtfully.

'I'm sure,' Rilee said.

'No,' the young girl said harshly. 'It's fine, I don't want any of it.'

'Please,' Rilee said quietly. 'You can't put any of that back, it all looks important. Do it for your baby.'

The poor kid looked torn between humiliation and desperation and Rilee sent a glare at the cashier. 'Take the money,' she said pointedly.

As she turned away to get the change, Rilee saw the girl hastily gather the plastic bags and hang them over the handles of the worn-looking pram, her eyes downcast before she hurried out of the store.

'I wouldn't make a habit of that around here,' the woman said gruffly.

Rilee took in the cashier's jowly neck and pallid complexion and thought she showed the signs of poor diet and too much alcohol. Rilee had to refrain from slipping the woman one of her business cards. 'No one ever died of showing a little kindness now and again.'

The woman gave an unimpressed grunt. 'I found out the hard way. They'll take advantage of your charity and they won't thank you for it.'

'Thanks,' Rilee said, handing over the cash for her own groceries and pushing her trolley outside to her car.

'I'm going to pay you back for this.'

Rilee turned at the comment and saw the young girl standing beside her. 'Great, but there's no rush.'

The girl rubbed her nose as she considered Rilee suspiciously. 'Why would you help me like that?'

Rilee began to pack her groceries into the back of the ute. 'I could see you were struggling and I wanted to help.'

'You don't even know me.'

'You're trying to do the right thing by your baby,' Rilee said, glancing down at the sleeping child. 'Here,' she handed over the lipstick from the bag she'd just put away. 'I saw you looking at it earlier.'

'No . . . thanks,' the girl tacked on, although she stared at the lipstick intently.

'Come on, take it. On a bad day, there is always lipstick,' Rilee said and smiled at the girl's confused look. 'I don't know who said it, but it's true.'

The girl reached out hesitantly. 'I'll add it onto what I owe you,' she said as she slipped the lipstick into her pocket. 'I better go.'

'Wait. I'm Rilee, what's your name?'

The girl seemed to be weighing up the wisdom of revealing her name, but after a few moments must have decided it couldn't hurt. 'Talissa.'

'It's nice to meet you, Talissa,' Rilee smiled.

Talissa ducked her head shyly before turning away to push the pram down the street.

Rilee watched her walk away as she hooked the loops of the ute's canvas cover to secure the contents in the tray. If today was any indication, the teenager was putting her child's welfare ahead of her own, and that showed a lot of maturity. Rilee was impressed.

∽

'Rilee?'

Rilee's head jerked up in alarm. Oh God, had she dozed off? With a quick look from the corner of her eye, she realised curious eyes were upon her and Ellen was waiting expectantly for some kind of answer. 'Um, sorry? I didn't quite hear the question.'

A cool smile touched her mother-in-law's precision-lined, peach-shaded lips. 'I asked if you would be able to commit to knitting a bag of squares for our woollen blanket appeal.'

'I . . . haven't knitted for years. I'm not very good at it.'

'I'm sure you'll remember once you get going again, dear. Now if there's nothing else to discuss, we might adjourn for morning tea.'

'Actually, Ellen,' Rilee stood up quickly, watching Ellen frown in irritation. 'I wondered if I could make a suggestion.'

'What kind of suggestion, Rilee?' It was hard to ignore the strained politeness in the tone.

'Well, I've just been curious why is it the group's supporting a project that's so far removed from our community?'

'I beg your pardon.'

'I'm not saying this knitting fundraiser isn't a great idea, but I just noticed there's nothing that supports local causes.'

'Local? Like what?'

'For instance, I've noticed there seems to be a high incident of teenage pregnancy in town. Maybe the group could look at some kind of education policy to get put into schools to introduce incentives for girls to stay in school, maybe some kind of scholarship towards university?'

'That might be a little bit too ambitious, don't you think? Besides, our group has always fundraised for the homeless and we will continue to do so.'

'I'm not suggesting you stop knitting your blankets, but surely there's also need closer to home?'

'I tell you what, at our next meeting, if you think you'd like to join the group, we can discuss it then.'

Rilee knew she'd just been dismissed and she heard the twitter of conversation flutter around the room after Ellen quickly declared the meeting over. She was only trying to fit in, like Ellen had wanted her to do. Well, she didn't have to put up with this crap, being talked down to like an idiot. Let them knit their damn squares.

A fleeting image of a young girl with a baby looking longingly at a group of schoolgirls made a small voice tsk in shame inside her head.

She tried her best to ignore the interest her little inter-action with Ellen had caused, squaring her shoulders as she plastered a polite smile on her face and wishing fervently that she'd driven herself in so she could go home. Unfortunately, as she'd come in with Ellen, she was going to be stuck here for quite some time to come.

She really only had herself to blame. She shouldn't have opened her mouth. Did she even want to join this group? If it was the only way to be in a position to make changes, to put forward ideas, then could she afford *not* to join?

When had life suddenly gotten this complicated? All she'd been planning to do was open a clinic, for goodness sake. She didn't have time to be taking on a new group and fundraising. It was crazy. This wasn't even her fight. And yet she couldn't forget that look of longing she'd witnessed on Talissa's face as she'd put that damn lipstick back on the shelf. How could she stand by and continue to let kids ruin their lives? How could she *not* try to find some way to break this cycle?

Fourteen

'We've been summonsed for dinner over at the house tonight,' Dan announced as he tossed his hat on the bench and crossed the kitchen to wash his hands.

'Why?'

'I don't know. Mum called me on the radio earlier. Thought you might have heard.'

'No, I've been outside all morning in the garden.' She'd thought that once they moved into their own place dinner with the in-laws would only happen on special occasions. She'd thought wrong. It was taking quite a lot of getting used to, all this family stuff.

'Have you done anything I should know about in advance? Pissed her off somehow?' Dan joked.

'Well, I've been breathing all day, so I guess that could be it.' Rilee flicked the coffee machine on and reached for two cups. 'Is there any way we can get out of it?'

'Don't look at me, I'm too attached to my testicles to risk losing them.'

'Chicken.'

'Speaking of which, how's it going with Big Red?'

'Still a stand-off.'

'You want me to deal with him?'

'No. Thanks.' She knew what that meant: Red would end up in the pot for dinner. 'I'm going to work that particular problem out on my own.'

'Okay,' he shrugged. 'But it's probably only delaying the inevitable.'

'I'm not going to have an animal sentenced to death just because I'm scared of it,' she frowned.

'It's just a chook,' Dan said, eyeing her strangely while accepting his coffee.

'I know. But I don't want you to fight all my battles for me. I can do this.'

'All right, soldier,' he said, after downing his coffee and leaning over to kiss her goodbye. 'I'll leave you to it.'

Rilee knew he wouldn't understand her logic—how could he? He'd been brought up in this world where everything had its place and was there for a reason. Cattle were bred to eat and sell; chooks were kept for eggs and meat. Dogs were not pets, they were workers; even the cats were only tolerated because they kept the mice and other rodents under control. There was no such thing as a freeloader at

Thumb Creek Station. Everything had its place . . . except her. She didn't really fit anywhere. She wasn't earning her keep; she felt redundant here.

Well, she was going to fix that. One way or another.

∽

After the church committee fiasco, things had been rather quiet over at the main house, but Ellen seemed in a particularly good mood as she greeted them and led the way into the dining room.

Rilee had never really cared for the decor in the room. The old-fashioned wallpaper and heavy, dark green velvet drapes that hung at the tall windows made the room feel oppressive and museum-like. A fireplace with an enormous marble mantelpiece dominated the far wall, and two huge oval portraits of the original Kincaids stared down with stern gazes that seemed to follow Rilee around the room in a most unsettling way.

Talk centred mainly on work and what needed doing the next day before Ellen finally cleared her throat and caught her husband's eye. 'We didn't invite these two across for dinner just to talk farm work,' she said pointedly.

'So what's the big occasion?' Dan asked half-heartedly, his attention focused on the plate that had just been placed in front of him.

'I've decided to go ahead with the party.'

'What party?' Dan asked, his fork poised between mouth and plate.

'Your post-wedding reception, of course. I refuse to put it off a moment longer.'

Rilee tried to keep a neutral expression on her face and hoped she hadn't just groaned out loud.

'I've told the girls and they've both put it in their diaries.'

Rilee's ears pricked up at this piece of news. Finally, she would get to meet Dan's two sisters.

'And when are we doing this?' Dan asked before shoving his fork in his mouth and chewing.

'The twenty-fourth, that gives us three weeks,' Ellen said, flicking her napkin with practised ease and spreading it across her lap. 'It's the only free weekend we have in the foreseeable future.' She picked up her cutlery and delicately cut her thinly sliced beef into smaller portions. 'If you can have a list of your guests to me within the next two days, Rilee, that would be lovely,' she said without lifting her gaze from the plate.

'I'll get right on it.' It wouldn't take long; there was really no one other than her parents and Shae. The Browns would be too busy and three weeks was too short notice for them to organise someone to take over supervising the pub for a weekend.

'So what have you been up to, dear? You've been rather scarce over the last few days.'

Rilee concentrated on sectioning her baked potato and meat ratios into equal portions. 'Oh, I've been keeping busy. Actually I have a meeting with the careers advisor at the high school tomorrow.'

'What for?' Dan asked, lifting his gaze from his meal to eye her curiously.

'To find out how we can implement some kind of program for at-risk girls. He seemed really interested in it.'

'So you're still determined to go through with it then?' Ellen said, raising her eyebrows slightly.

'Yes, Ellen,' Rilee said. 'I am. Someone has to try to make a change.'

'Another one of those,' Jacob muttered from the head of the table. 'Don't like the way something is, let's change it.'

'Not all change is bad, you know,' she said a little more sharply than she'd intended and saw Dan send her a sideways glance.

'Let me tell you something, girly,' Jacob started, pointing his knife at her. 'The problem with this damn world is that too many do-gooders have too much free time on their hands. Instead of going out and getting a job like everyone else, they decide to stay in university and think up ways of changing everything. If something's working, you don't mess with it. That's the way we did things in my day and in my father's day before me. You didn't see the world going crazy back then.'

Rilee stared at her father-in-law, unable to decide where to even start with a reply, but Dan's apprehensive expression changed her mind. She could see him bracing himself for confrontation. But there was no point getting into a debate with a man like Jacob. He was stubborn and arrogant, two qualities that didn't lend themselves to constructive discussion. There was no point arguing with a man who refused to accept anyone else's views on anything.

'So I'm thinking we'll have a rustic-chic theme to the reception. I'm thinking an outdoor garden setting with a pig on the spit and roasted vegetables and long tables that everyone can walk past and serve themselves. But with a touch of class—formal attire. What do you think, Dan?' Ellen cut in smoothly, changing the topic like a pro.

'Sure, Mum. Whatever you want.'

Rilee picked up her cutlery and went back to eating her meal. Once the Ellen train was in motion, there wasn't any way to derail it without being caught up in the wreck. For the rest of the meal Rilee kept her head down and mouth shut.

Later, as she and Dan walked back to their house, Rilee brought up a subject she'd been wondering about for a while. 'How does it work with your sisters and the farm? Do they have any input in the business?'

'No, they both left the place as soon as they could and headed for the city.'

'So will the place eventually get split between you all?'

'No, the farm goes to me.'

Rilee frowned. That seemed a little sexist.

'It's okay, Ri, they aren't going to be left high and dry. Mum and Dad have sorted out investments that'll go to the girls.'

'But what if they wanted part of the farm?'

'Trust me, they're getting the better part of the deal.'

'But surely Thumb Creek is worth quite a bit more than any investment could return?'

'Maybe on paper. The reality is, I may be inheriting a property, but I'm also inheriting its debt as well. The girls will have money and property, free and clear. We, on the other hand, will have quite a few generations' worth of debt hanging over our head.'

It was a sobering thought. 'Exactly how much debt are we talking about here?'

'You don't have to worry about it, Ri. It's all part of life on the land.'

But she did worry. Debt was not something she particularly liked the sound of, and after seeing the fuel bill the other day, she had a feeling it wasn't the kind of debt most people were used to. 'Dan, I really think we need to discuss this. I don't have any idea how all of this works.'

Dan stopped walking and turned her to look at him. 'I don't want you to worry about it, okay? It's under control. Besides, I thought you wanted to run your own business? You really think you're going to have time to work on two?'

He had point. But still, if she and Dan were going to be responsible for a hefty debt some day, she should take a bit of an interest in how it all worked.

Rilee was still thinking about it long after Dan fell asleep next to her. What she needed to do right now was focus on starting her clinic. With everything else that had been happening around here, the project to keep girls in school swirling around in her head, and now this damn party

Ellen had dragged her into, Rilee could feel herself losing sight of what she'd set out to achieve.

Well, it was time to refocus. As soon as this party was done, she'd get the ball rolling with her clinic. The sooner she was back in her own element, the easier it would be to settle in. She needed her career to give her back some much-needed confidence.

Fifteen

'Okay, Red, I didn't want to do this, but you've forced me into a corner,' she said, trying to sound assertive.

Earlier she'd taken out her box of Bach flower remedies and set about making a recipe to combat the hostile rooster. A drop of chicory, which worked well in animals for possessive and territorial issues. Some beech to tackle the rooster's intolerance towards people, and some water violet which was good for stand-offish animals with a dislike of affection. She figured that just about covered most of the rooster's unfavourable traits.

She could have added her potion to water, but she really needed to target Red, so she was going to have to be sneaky about it. She tipped the contents of the small bottle onto the piece of bread she'd brought along with her. Red eyed her with his beady stare, and Rilee swallowed back a rush of fear. 'It's only a bird,' she muttered to herself firmly. She tossed the bread to the feathered fiend and watched as he greedily gobbled it up, beating the other chooks to it as she was hoping he would, before looking back at her expectantly for another piece.

When Rilee returned to the pen half an hour later, she tossed the feed as a distraction and edged around the frenzy of chooks diving for the corn and pellets, making a beeline for the feeding dishes to fill with the remainder of the food. Much to her relief, Red was too busy pecking at the feed to even glance at her.

She made the rounds of the laying boxes and collected the eggs, all the while keeping check on Red's location. While he didn't seem completely docile, he also wasn't intent on chasing her either. When she'd finished collecting the eggs and was ready to leave the relative safety of the laying pen, Red wasn't doing his usual patrol back and forwards, waiting to attack her ankles. She searched the yard and found him happily pecking along with the other chooks, seemingly oblivious to her presence.

Rilee couldn't help the satisfied grin that crossed her face as she placed the basket of eggs on the kitchen counter in the main house.

Ellen looked up from the recipe book she had been browsing through and lifted one manicured eyebrow.

Rilee didn't say a word. Small as it was, it was still a victory, and as she made her way back to the house she felt a tiny bud of optimism inside her begin to unfurl. It was a start.

⁂

'You *drugged* the rooster?'

'I didn't drug it,' Rilee hedged as she sipped her coffee and watched Shae across the kitchen table. 'He just needed a hormone realignment.'

'Clearly,' Shae said dryly. 'I don't know why more people don't call a naturopath to give their poultry hormone rebalances.'

'You know, that's not a bad idea.' After her success with Red, Rilee had actually been thinking about introducing some of her treatments to animals.

'I was joking,' Shae said, staring at Rilee incredulously.

'I wasn't. Animals can respond just as well to treatments as humans. Only I'm not sure I have the right bedside manner for animals. I don't like chooks. Cows scare me, and don't even get me started on sheep.'

'Then I guess it's safe to say you better stick to humans for now.'

'Probably for the best,' Rilee agreed.

'How did your meeting with Aaron go?'

'It was promising.' The careers advisor had been interested in her idea, but he had to take it to the principal and then there would be a long way to go to work out how to fund it, and how to get it approved from there. 'It's going to take a long time before it's up and running.'

'You knew that already though, right?'

'Yeah,' Rilee agreed, 'but he has to get the principal on board before he can go any further.'

'And that's bad because?'

'Well, not bad . . . but the principal is apparently an old friend of Ellen's.'

'Oh.' Shae sat back with a twist of her lips. 'You think Ellen would try to sabotage it?'

'I don't know. I hope not. I'm hoping that she's too busy organising this party to be bothered with making any trouble.'

'So what's the latest on the upcoming shindig?'

'Circus more like it,' Rilee groaned. It seemed Dan was right: once his mother got an idea in her head, it was useless to try to stop her. 'It started out as only a few close friends and family, and last I heard the guest list was up to about one hundred and five.'

'Give it time. I'm sure that number will grow over the next few days.'

'I don't know any of these people.'

'It'll be fine. I'm sure most of them will be neighbours and local families, and they're a nice enough bunch. Besides, you'll have Dan there.'

'I guess so. And it's not like I don't want to meet these people, it's just that I feel like I'm on show or something. Like I'm the latest cow they've brought from the saleyards.'

Shae choked on her coffee at that. 'Oh my God, can you imagine? I can just see Dan leading you around the yards on a rope as they all discuss your breeding lines.'

Shae's laughter was contagious and soon Rilee was giggling too. 'Check out the teats on that one,' she said.

They were laughing so much neither of them heard the screen door open until Ellen cleared her voice noisily, bringing an abrupt halt to the hilarity.

'Oh, Ellen, hi, I didn't hear you come in.'

'Apparently,' her mother-in-law said with that annoying eyebrow lift. The woman made Rilee feel as though she were a child being reprimanded. 'I could hear you laughing all the way over at the house.'

So it was official, Rilee thought, her mother-in-law did indeed have supersonic hearing. 'Sorry about that,' Rilee said, carefully avoiding looking at Shae who was pulling an unflattering face, since her back was towards Ellen. 'Would you like a coffee?'

'No, thank you. I came over to go over some arrangements for the engagement party,' she said, before sending a bland look at Shae, 'but I see you have a guest.'

Like that would have been a total surprise. Considering she'd heard the noise from her house. Rilee was more than a little irritated by the woman's assumption she could just invite herself over.

'It's all right, I was leaving anyway,' Shae said, getting to her feet and taking her cup to the sink. 'Thanks for the coffee,' she said. 'Nice to see you, Mrs Kincaid,' she added before disappearing out the door.

Rilee stared at the empty doorway and felt suddenly abandoned. *Traitor*, she thought. Ellen was already busy unloading her notepad onto the table and making herself at home.

Rilee tried to listen as Ellen gave her a rundown of arrangements. Clearly her opinion was not being asked for; everything had already been decided. Rilee continued to fume silently right through the menu plan and on to the decorations.

By the time Dan got home Rilee was ready to explode.

Dan took one look at her face and paused as he reached for the fridge door. 'What's she done now?' he asked wearily.

'She's doing my head in, Dan,' Rilee said, throwing her arms in the air. 'She just walks in the house—never bothers to knock. She basically kicked Shae out so she could discuss the engagement party with me, although I might add she didn't stop to take a damn breath the entire time, and I'm pretty sure I didn't get a word in edgeways.'

'It's just her way,' Dan said, taking out a beer.

'Well, it's rude!'

'Just let her get this party out of her system and things will settle down.'

'Why?'

'What do you mean, why?'

'Why do we have to let her have her way just to keep the peace?'

'Because the alternative is too horrible to think about.'

'She's got like this because no one around here will stand up to her. It's ridiculous.'

'Ri,' he sighed, dropping his head. 'Just trust me on this. Making a big deal about it will only cause drama. We don't want drama, do we?'

'How is standing up for ourselves drama? I just want a little common courtesy. I want her to respect boundaries, Dan. She can't just waltz into our home whenever she damn well feels like it and she can't dismiss my friends as though they're . . . peasants.'

'You have to appreciate that sometimes things are done differently out here.'

'All I'm asking for is a little respect.'

Dan paused, seemingly to gather his thoughts. 'There's a certain order to things around here. You can't just start rearranging things without ruffling everyone's feathers.'

'What are you talking about?'

'Look,' Dan sighed, putting his can of beer down on the table. 'There's a system. You have the hierarchy, which at the moment is Mum and Dad. They run the show. Then there's me, and then there are the workers. The hierarchy doesn't mix with the workers. Anything they need to get across to said workers goes through me. I'm the official channel.'

Rilee stared at him, unimpressed.

'Years ago, my grandparents were the hierarchy and Mum and Dad were where we are. If you start messing with things, then the whole system falls apart.'

'What century are you living in?'

'I know it seems strange, but Mum and Dad are the last of an era. They still hold on to a lot of the social politics that used to be commonplace out here.'

'Well, it doesn't wash with me. I don't care what her views are about *the workers*,' she said pointedly. 'This is my home and Shae is my friend. She has no right to think she can get away with rudeness. I don't care how ruffled her feathers get, if she does it again, I'm telling her how it is.'

'I'll have a word to her,' he promised, tugging at her hand so that she sat down on his knee.

Rilee bit back a frustrated sigh at his words. She knew that Dan having a word to his parents would be about as effective as spitting to put out a bushfire. It wasn't fair that Dan was in the middle and had to be the peacemaker, but she was really beginning to hate the way he always turned to the patronising 'I'll have a word with them' to placate her and end an argument.

'How about we get away for the weekend?'

Her irritation dissolved immediately. 'Really?'

'I want to look at some cattle in Armidale. I was planning on a quick day trip, but we could make it a weekend if you want.'

A few weeks ago she'd have wept with bitter disappointment that he wasn't talking about a trip to the city. Now, though, she didn't care where he wanted to go, as long as she got away from here. 'Sounds great.'

'Righto then. We'll leave Friday night.'

A whole weekend away. Rilee couldn't help the smile that spread across her face at the thought and found herself counting the sleeps until it was time to go.

Sixteen

Two days later Ellen dropped off a large pile of invitations, all addressed and stamped, ready to be posted out. 'Be a dear and run these into town to the post office, will you? I've got far too much on my plate to go myself, and these need to be sent today.'

Rilee forced a smile and made herself think of the king-sized bed and spa that awaited her in Armidale. 'Of course.' It wasn't as though she had anything better to do. She watched Ellen head back to the main house and took a deep breath. She'd just post the damn things and remain calm. She automatically reached for the bottle of Nervine Calm and shook out a few tablets into her hand. It was all very well to tell herself to be calm, but it wouldn't hurt to add a little herbal assistance. It could be worse, she told herself. She could be turning to alcohol.

She flicked through the pile and glanced over the multitude of names she'd never heard of before, then frowned as she reached the end. Sitting at the bench, she went back to the beginning and looked again, her frown turning into a scowl as she slapped the pile of envelopes onto the countertop and headed out the door.

Crossing the yard, she heard a door bang and then the sound of an engine revving before Jacob drove past the house in his big four-wheel drive. *In his usual good mood, I see.* Rilee braced herself as she knocked on the back door and waited until she heard the impatient 'Come in' that followed a long silence.

She pushed the screen door open and went inside, noticing the kitchen was empty. 'Ellen? It's me,' she called.

Rilee looked up as she heard the crisp click-clack of high heels on the tiled hall that pre-empted Ellen's arrival. Rilee caught a glimpse of the older woman's face before she'd managed to hide it by busying herself as she crossed to the kitchen sink. It looked very much as though she'd been crying and it momentarily distracted Rilee from her anger. 'Ellen? Is everything all right?'

'Of course. Why wouldn't it be?' she asked without turning.

'You seem a bit . . . upset.'

'No, just busy,' she said dismissively, before adding, 'organising this *party*,' pointedly.

'Are you sure?' It seemed too coincidental that Jacob's angry departure coincided with an obviously upset Ellen.

'Did you need something, Rilee?' she asked.

There was no mistaking the impatience in the woman's tone, and some of Rilee's previous compassion slipped as she remembered the reason she'd come over. 'Yes, actually, there was something I wanted to talk to you about. It seems Shae and Mark's invitation got lost, and I'm just checking to make sure you've allowed for them in your catering numbers.' Fine, if Ellen wanted to play 'let's pretend no one saw you cry' then she'd cut straight to the chase.

'The invitation didn't get lost. I was only inviting close friends and family.'

'Then I'd like to include them. Shae is a friend of mine.'

'I'm not sure that's entirely appropriate. For starters, they wouldn't feel comfortable, I'm sure.'

'I'm sorry, Ellen, but I don't understand what you're saying.'

'They work for us, Rilee. They are employees. This is a private function.'

'So because they work for you they can't also be friends?'

'It keeps things a lot easier if there are clear divides.'

'Divides,' Rilee repeated dully.

'What happens if Dan is forced to let Mark go one day? When you muddy the employee-employer line, things get messy.'

'I'm sure if something like that were to happen, Mark and Dan would be mature enough to handle the situation.'

'I've found in life that it's always better to avoid unpleasantness in the first place. But, if you want to ignore my advice then by all means invite them along. It's formal, by the way,' she added coldly.

Rilee bit her tongue and forced a polite smile.

*

Rilee was packing an overnight bag when she heard a knock on the back screen door. 'It's just me,' she heard Shae call out.

'Come on in,' Rilee called back, dropping the lacy negligée onto the bed and going to greet her friend. 'Just the woman I wanted to see. I was going to head down to your place later.'

'Whatever it was, I didn't do it,' Shae said, holding up her hands in mock protest.

'Here, this is for you.' Rilee crossed to the kitchen bench and handed Shae a gold-embossed envelope.

'What is it?'

'An invitation to the wedding party.'

'Really?' Shae stared at the envelope warily.

'What's wrong?'

'It's just a bit of a surprise, that's all. We're staff. We don't usually get invited to things like this.'

'Oh my God, not you too,' Rilee sighed. 'I swear if I have to hear one more time about hierarchy and pecking order, I'm going to lose it. You're coming to the party.'

'Rilee, I don't even have anything to wear. It's formal attire.'

Rilee studied her friend across the table thoughtfully. 'Come with me,' she said, standing and heading up the hallway. In the spare room Rilee began moving boxes stacked in a tall pile until she found the one she was looking for. Opening the lid, she searched through the contents, then gave a triumphant smile as she located the garment she had in mind.

'Try this on. I think it will fit.'

Shae took the silky material in her hands and frowned as she examined the dress. 'This says Versace.'

Rilee shrugged. 'It's a cheap knock-off.'

'I know a cheap knock-off when I see one, Rilee, and this is not cheap and it's not a knock-off. It's gorgeous.'

'Just try it on already,' Rilee said, turning back to another box to look for shoes.

Shae stared at Rilee with her mouth gaping as she held out the shoe box. 'Jimmy Choo . . . Oh my God, where did you get all this stuff?' Shae asked, as she slipped on the heels with almost reverent care.

Rilee eyed the dress, tugging at the hem to straighten the fabric. 'What do you think?'

'I think it's amazing. But I'm not sure Mark and I coming is such a great idea.'

'It's supposed to be my party,' Rilee reminded her. 'I want you there.'

'Are you sure it's okay to borrow this? I've never worn a real Versace before. Come to think of it, I've never worn a fake one either,' Shae said, looking at the dress in the mirror.

'I'm positive. In fact, you can keep it. It really suits you.'

'I can't do that,' Shae said, almost giving herself whiplash as she turned to face her friend.

'Yes, you can. I'll never wear it again.'

'I'm pretty sure you'll have more opportunities to wear it than I ever will.'

'My Versace days were brief, and I'm fairly certain they're over,' Rilee said.

'There must be an interesting story behind all this,' Shae said, nodding at the boxes of clothing.

Rilee shook her head. 'They belonged to a very different chapter of my life. I'm not sure why I even bothered to keep them.'

'Ah, hello? Because they're like worth a small fortune! You'd have to be crazy to throw stuff like this away. It's not every day a girl gets the chance to wear fancy designer brands, so I won't knock back your offer.'

Rilee remembered having only ever read about these fashion houses in magazines, their logos instantly recognisable to her in much the same way as car enthusiasts recognise a badge on the front of a car. And then suddenly what she'd only dreamed about was a reality. At first that life was just as perfect as she'd imagined it would be, wearing gorgeous clothes and going to lavish parties, but she'd been too blinded by the illusion to pay attention to the niggle of uncertainty that everything wasn't as perfect as she thought. Eventually she saw it for what it was. Some of the most beautiful people were shallow imitations. Dressing in Versace and draping yourself in priceless diamonds didn't make you beautiful on the inside where it counted. Sometimes she thought about the wide-eyed, innocent kid she'd been and felt sad. But that girl was long gone and in her place was *this* Rilee. She wasn't perfect but she had managed to pick herself up and pull herself together and that had to count for something . . . didn't it?

she'd been and felt sad. But that girl was long gone and in her place was this Rilee. She wasn't perfect but she had managed to pick herself up and pull herself together and that had to count for something ... didn't it?

Seventeen

The view below them was spectacular. A tapestry of colour spread out across the ground with patchworks of browns, yellows and greens as far as the eye could see. Mountain ranges bordered the edges of the horizon, touching the blue sky and melting into an indistinguishable line, seemingly joining the earth and sky together as one.

The property they were visiting was near a small town on the way to Armidale and they were flying there before heading to their accommodation in town. Realistically they could have driven but, as Dan so cheerfully put it, why waste time driving when they could fly?

Rilee had flown with Dan a few times now and knew that he was an extremely capable and experienced pilot, but knowing that and remembering all that separated them from plummeting to their deaths was a very thin sheet of metal and a bunch of engine parts were two very different matters.

The flight itself Rilee found rather enjoyable; it was just the landing and take-off that made her break out in a cold sweat. As they approached their destination—a narrow landing strip in the middle of a wide brown paddock—Rilee felt her stomach lurch and shut her eyes, gripping the seat with her hands. She let out a long slow breath once the wheels touched the ground in a smooth textbook perfect landing and summoned what she hoped was a reassuring smile at Dan when he reached over and placed his hand on her knee.

The McPherson property was not nearly as imposing as Thumb Creek Station, but it was impressive nonetheless. There was no grand residence, no cluster of workers' cottages, but they clearly had a very profitable stud if the quality of fencing and yards was anything to go by.

Bill McPherson drove out in a large four-wheel drive to collect them, helping Dan put chunks of wood in front of the tyres of the plane and securing it before driving them to the homestead.

Rilee liked the silver-haired man instantly. He had a quiet way about him, but his questions and conversation proved him to be shrewd and perceptive. His wife, Marcy, was welcoming when they reached the house and sat them down for a cuppa straight away.

'I understand you were a city girl, Rilee?' Marcy said as she handed over a cup of tea.

Rilee looked up at the woman, unsure if there was going to be a patronising smile to accompany the question. She let out a small sigh of relief when she detected only curiosity instead. 'I'm afraid I still am. I haven't quite got the hang of country life yet.'

'You'll get there,' she said with a small wave of her hand. 'We all do eventually.'

'Oh? You came from the city too?' Rilee asked, gratefully sipping her tea.

'A long time ago now, but yes. Born and raised on the North Shore.'

'Wouldn't know it now though,' Bill chimed in, taking a bite of the homemade date loaf he held in his hand.

Marcy smacked his arm lightly. 'You be quiet. There were many a time I had my bags packed by the front door in the first few years. You're lucky I stuck around.'

'That I am. Luckiest man alive, I reckon,' he said with a soft smile.

She glanced across at Dan and wondered if he was comparing the McPhersons with his parents. She couldn't read his expression, but she wondered if maybe her stoic husband ever wished his family was a little more affectionate.

'Are you interested in the farming business, Rilee?' Marcy asked.

'I find it fascinating, but I think Dan and his family have the business side of things under control,' Rilee said, her smile feeling a little forced. 'I'll just stick to my own profession, I think.'

'Oh? Which is?' Marcy asked, tilting her head slightly.

'I'm a naturopath.'

'Oh, how exciting. My sister swears by her practitioner.'

Rilee felt an instant rush of relief at the woman's words. She had come to expect either contempt or dismissal whenever she discussed her work.

'She had terrible trouble with eczema and allergies for years, and now, not a sign of it,' Marcy said, giving a small shrug of her shoulders. 'So will you be able to continue practising? Or have you given it up for now?'

'Oh no, I couldn't give it up. I plan on opening a clinic in Pallaburra, very soon actually.'

The men stood up, excusing themselves to go look over the cattle Dan was interested in, and Rilee enjoyed finally being able to discuss her work without feeling defensive.

'It's good that you have your own work to keep you busy,' Marcy said as they enjoyed their second cup of tea. 'It's still important to take an interest in your husband's business, though.'

'Between Dan and his parents, there's very little for me to actually do.'

'I know all too well how it feels to come into another woman's domain and try to fit in. Bill was a real mummy's boy too,' she chuckled and Rilee smiled a little at the thought. 'It's hard trying to find your place, especially when you haven't had much experience with farming before. It's certainly a different way of life.'

'I really don't have anything helpful to offer the business,' she said, before adding carefully, 'and I'm fairly sure the Kincaids wouldn't appreciate me trying.'

'You may not have any farming experience, but you can most certainly contribute to the family business in other ways. It's important not to let them shut you out. It may not be intentional, but if you don't establish some kind of interest early on then they'll exclude you in the future. Trust me, I've been there.'

Rilee thought perhaps Marcy was right. Although she didn't want to step in and help run Thumb Creek right now, she should at least have an idea of how it worked. However, she knew exactly what their reaction would be if she tried. Ellen would dismiss her in that condescending, patronising way she so often used, and Jacob would probably just grunt and tell her to stick to being a wife.

Part of her understood how parents might have concerns about a daughter-in-law joining the family business—after all, divorce was common nowadays and she could imagine them being afraid their business would be implicated in settlement proceedings. Nevertheless, Marcy's words hit a nerve. The Kincaids never discussed anything that related to the financial running of the property when she was around. Dan would go to the main house and have meetings or sit in on visits from the bank or accountant, but she was never invited along.

Bill and Dan returned a little while later all smiles and in good humour, which made Rilee wonder if maybe now was as good a time as any to show some interest in Dan's business.

'Thank you for the chat,' Rilee said, giving Marcy a hug of farewell, 'and I'll post that mixture out to you as soon as I get home.'

'That would be lovely, Rilee. Thank you, I can't wait to try it. And remember what I said,' she added in a lower voice.

'They were lovely,' Rilee said once they were back in the air.

'Yeah. He's a top bloke, Bill McPherson. Knows his cattle too.'

'So you were happy with the cattle?'

'Yeah.'

'How many are you buying?'

'None.'

'What? I thought we were coming out here to look at cattle to buy?'

'We were coming out to look over the quality of his stock and check out his bull.'

'I don't understand. You came all this way just to *look* at his cattle?'

'Yep, and make a decision about breeding.'

'So you need to buy a bull?'

'No, not the entire bull,' he grinned across at her. 'Just the semen.'

'Oh.' *Gross.*

Dan looked back at her. 'I want to cross my Black Angus with his Bazadais line.'

'Why a Bazadais?'

'They have better muscle and weight gain.' When he saw that she seemed genuinely interested, he continued a little more eagerly. 'Angus meat has the marbling effect that restaurants and the overseas market are looking for, but if you cross the Black Angus with the Bazadais you retain the marbling effect and increase the size and muscle of the animal, so you get more meat and less waste.'

'And your father doesn't understand this?'

'It's not a matter of him understanding it. Black Angus have been the standard breed on Thumb Creek for generations,' he shrugged. 'I've been trying to convince Dad to introduce the Bazadais for a while now, but he doesn't get why you'd mess around with something that's always been reliable.'

'But you obviously think it's worthwhile?'

'Yeah, I do. I think we could improve the quality of meat, as well as the durability of the animal—make them a lot more drought tolerant, adaptable to different conditions, so we can survive climate fluctuations better.'

'How can he not consider it?'

'Because he's Dad,' Dan said gruffly. 'Because he's always bred Black Angus and he won't consider anything else. He just doesn't want to go through the process of implementing it. It'll take years to build up the stock, and he doesn't see the point of all that stuffin' around, as he calls it.'

'But if he agreed to you coming out to look at Bill's cattle then he must be coming around?' Rilee gave a small lopsided grin at her husband's guilty look. 'Oh. I see. He doesn't know you came out here to look at the cattle.'

'I'm going to do it on my own.'

Rilee frowned. 'You can do that?'

'I can, if I use my own money and resources.'

Rilee frowned. 'When were you planning on filling me in on these plans?'

'Filling you in?' He sounded confused.

Marcy was right. Maybe she should have taken a more active interest in the business side of things. Wasn't it normal that married couples would discuss things like venturing out on their own? Then again, Dan had shown little interest in her business plans. 'Well, if you're thinking about starting up your own business, shouldn't I be part of that discussion?'

'It's not really my own business, it's more a sideline—something I want to do to prove to Dad that what I'm saying can pay off.' He glanced at her, his expression cautious. 'It wasn't a big secret, I brought you along.'

'Well, yeah.' Okay, so that was true.

'What's going on?'

'Nothing, forget it,' she said with a quick smile and wave of her hand before looking out the window.

'I didn't know you were interested in any of this.'

'Well, I wasn't . . . but that was before I realised you were planning on doing this without your parents. If this is your project then I want to learn more about it. I'd like to be part of it.'

'Really?'

'Of course. You're supposed to be my husband. Married couples usually take an interest in each other's business—'

'There's no *supposed* to be about it. I *am* your husband,' he said in a low, deliberate tone, and Rilee swallowed a little nervously at the steady look he gave her.

'Would you keep your eyes on the . . . out there!'

163

With a small chuckle he returned his gaze to the front window and Rilee let out a slow breath. The man was far too potent for his own good: with just a look he could send her heartbeat into overdrive.

❀

Their Armidale accommodation took Rilee completely by surprise. She'd been expecting an impersonal motel room, but instead Dan drove their rental car through town and turned off down a dirt road that seemed to go for miles without giving any hint of where it headed. Dan slowed as they approached a sign, which read *Wood Smoke Cabin*, and then turned down a long gravel driveway bordered by a manicured hedge. At the end of the drive was a clearing where a little cabin sat on the edge of a ridge overlooking the bushland and valley below.

Rilee gaped at the scene before her as Dan retrieved their overnight bag and led the way up the three steps to the verandah.

'This is where we're staying?'

'Do you like it?' Dan asked as he dropped the bag on the verandah and linked his arms around her waist.

Rilee turned and held him tight. 'It's beautiful. How did you find it?'

'I remembered a mate telling me about it once. He stayed here for his honeymoon a few years back.'

'It's perfect,' she sighed, laying her head against his chest and breathing in the heady mix of mountain air and man.

'Wait till you see inside,' he promised, opening the front door.

Rilee gasped as she walked into the cabin and looked around. A huge fireplace dominated the living area and scented candles flickered gently all around the room. A giant wrought-iron bed sat facing a large window which provided stunning views of the mountains, and on the other side of the room a decadent-looking spa bath sat surrounded by a recess of glass, facing a wall of natural rock. 'This is amazing,' she breathed and Dan's smile widened at her delight.

'You're amazing,' he corrected, brushing the side of her cheek tenderly. 'I know I've thrown you in the deep end back at Thumb Creek. I'm sorry things have been so hectic.'

'It's not as though you didn't warn me,' she shrugged.

'Yeah, but I just wish it could have been different.'

'I get to spend every night with you beside me,' she smiled, slipping her arms around his hips.

'You don't regret saying yes?'

'Of course not,' Rilee pulled back to look her husband in the face and caught a glimpse of doubt shadowing his expression. 'Are you serious?'

'I've never had anyone to worry about before, Ri. I don't want to stuff this up.'

'I love you, Dan. There's nowhere else I'd rather be than with you.'

They spent almost the entire weekend locked inside their little cabin, only venturing outside to explore the bushland and tracks before hurrying back inside where it was warm, once more.

Eighteen

The sound of a plane droning grew louder and Rilee felt the leap of butterflies inside her stomach. *Just be yourself*, she recited. Dan gave her hand a squeeze and she looked up to find him watching her with a crooked smile.

They stood side by side at the airstrip, watching the small plane grow bigger as it circled for landing. Jacob had flown down to Sydney to bring the girls home on the final leg of connecting flights. Ellen hadn't come with them to the airstrip; she was waiting up at the house instead, putting the finishing touches to the party arrangements.

'Stop stressing. They're going to love you,' Dan said.

She managed what she hoped was a confident smile in return, but it did nothing to pacify her nerves. She was pretty sure he'd said the same thing about his parents.

The plane taxied to a stop outside the hangar and Dan tugged her along behind him as they made their way towards the aircraft.

The door opened and steps dropped down moments before a face, similar in features to her husband's, popped through the doorway wearing a wide grin.

'Danny boy!' The excited squeal was followed by a human catapult that launched at Dan in a blur of blonde hair and long denim-clad legs.

Dan barely had time to drop Rilee's hand before he caught his sister and swung her around in a huge bear hug. 'Hey, squirt,' he chuckled as he set her down on her feet. 'How was the flight?'

'Long! How come you didn't come and pick us up?' Natalie demanded.

'Someone has to work around here,' he shrugged.

A second woman emerged from the plane, a stark contrast to the first. Rilee knew what to expect from the photos around the house of the two women, but seeing these two opposite personalities in the flesh was unexpectedly surprising. Megan was tall and slender and dressed impeccably in a skirt, jacket and heels.

She was almost as tall as Dan as she leaned in and kissed his cheek before pulling back and looking at Rilee. 'This must be our brand-new sister-in-law,' she said in a low-pitched, almost sultry tone.

'Nat, Megan, this is Rilee. My wife,' he added, slipping his arm around Rilee's waist and pulling her close to his side.

Natalie grinned, pushing her brother aside and giving Rilee a friendly hug. 'I always wanted a younger sister, and now I have one.'

'Trust me, they're more trouble than they're worth,' Megan drawled, aiming the playful insult at her sister without moving to hug Rilee.

Jacob called out to Dan to give him a hand with the luggage and suddenly Rilee was alone with the two women.

'I'm so glad you were both able to come home for the party. Your mother's been looking forward to you arriving.'

'We wouldn't have been game not to come. In case you haven't figured it out yet, you don't say no to my mother,' Natalie told her dryly. 'Besides, there was no way I was going to miss out on meeting my baby brother's new bride.'

'I know it was a bit of a surprise,' Rilee started.

'You think?' Megan said with a smile that didn't reach her eyes as she headed towards the vehicle.

Rilee stared after her with a sinking sensation in her stomach.

'Don't worry about her,' Natalie said, nudging her shoulder. 'She'll come around. She just seems like a cold-hearted bitch until you get to know her.' Rilee started to protest, but Natalie laughed and shook her head. 'Trust me, she's worked hard at perfecting that image. In her line of work it comes in very handy. She just forgets to leave it at the office sometimes.'

Rilee soon forgot about Megan as Natalie distracted her with questions about naturopathy. As they chatted they found more than a few common interests which kept them deep in conversation until the men had loaded the luggage into the four-wheel drive and they all headed back to the main house.

It was interesting to watch the dynamics of the Kincaid family in action, Rilee thought as they gathered in the lounge room a little later, sipping port and eating a light supper of cheese and fruit.

Ellen seemed to relax—well, as much as Ellen could relax. The woman never seemed to sit still for more than a few minutes. She was always doing something. Rilee put it down to her dominating nature: if ever there was a control freak it was Ellen Kincaid. However, tonight she did at least seem to enjoy catching up with her daughters.

Megan was very much like her mother, and yet probably had a great deal of her father in her as well. Jacob seemed different around his daughters too. With Dan he was always so blunt and demanding. As she watched him with his daughters, she saw him listening, nodding and even smiling. She glanced sideways at Dan now and again to gauge his reaction to his parents' changed demeanours, but he didn't seem perturbed by it. It was clear that the siblings, although divided by quite a large age gap, were close.

'When do your parents arrive, Rilee?' Ellen asked as she passed around a platter of cheese and biscuits.

'The day after tomorrow,' she answered, and hoped she didn't look as nervous as she felt about her parents' visit.

'We look forward to finally meeting them,' she said in a polite tone.

'So tell us the story of how you two met. I haven't really gotten to the bottom of this yet,' Natalie said with a teasing glint in her eye. Rilee shifted her gaze to Dan uncomfortably. Was this what siblings did? Tried their best to make each other squirm?

'Yes, go on, Dan, we could use a little entertainment,' Megan added, reclining in her chair.

'We met at a bucks party,' Dan supplied unhelpfully.

'A bucks party?' Megan grinned at Rilee. 'What on earth were you doing at a bucks party?'

No doubt she was already imagining there was jumping out of a large cake involved. 'I was waitressing.'

'So you saw each other from across a crowded room?' Natalie prodded.

'Not quite,' Rilee hedged.

'I came to her rescue,' Dan corrected.

'Like a knight in shining armour,' Natalie sighed.

'Are you sure you're a high-finance wiz?' Dan asked drolly.

'Hey, a girl can be brainy and still like a bit of romance, you know,' she informed him.

'He *thought* I needed help,' Rilee amended lightly, 'but then he came back the next weekend and asked me out.'

'And a few months later you were married,' Megan finished, although it sounded more like an accusation than a happy ending. 'I didn't know people actually did that, you know, other than in the movies—waking up in Vegas and discovering you got married to a complete stranger.'

'We got to know each other a bit better than that before we decided to get married,' Dan said.

Even though he still looked relaxed, Rilee detected the slight shift in his mood and sensed a tension between him and his eldest sister that hadn't been there moments before. 'When you know it's right, why waste time waiting?'

'Why not,' Megan shrugged. 'A few months is ample time to get to know the person you're about to spend the rest of your life with.'

'I guess we could have lived together for a couple of years first, but then that's not always a guarantee that you will actually know someone, is it?' Dan said and Rilee saw Megan's expression change, the sarcasm of moments before melting into cold disdain.

'Is there any more food, Mum? I'm actually starving. Airline food still leaves a lot to be desired,' Natalie said, jumping to her feet.

Rilee wasn't entirely sure what had just happened, and judging from the bemused glance his parents had exchanged, she wasn't the only one, but the moment passed and Ellen left the room to organise food, Natalie in tow.

'I'm heading to bed,' Megan said, standing gracefully and stopping by her father's chair to kiss his forehead. 'Goodnight.'

She didn't kiss Dan, or say goodnight to him.

∞

Later, in bed, Rilee turned on her side and tucked her arm under her head as she watched Dan take off his watch and place it on the bedside table before getting in beside her.

'I think I made an impression on Megan,' she said dryly.

Dan grunted. 'She's all right once you get to know her.'

'Why does everyone keep saying that when what you should be saying is, "Yeah, she acts like a jerk, but you'll get used to it."'

He turned his head at that and she caught a slight smile in the moonlight. 'She's not always *this* much of a jerk.'

'Well, that's comforting,' she muttered. 'So what was all that about anyway?'

'What?'

'You know what. You obviously said something to her that hit the mark.'

When he didn't answer straight away, Rilee thought maybe he was going to shut her out of what was clearly something between the three siblings. 'I shouldn't have said it, I guess, but you're right, she was acting like a jerk towards you and it just came out.'

'What was it about?'

'A few months ago Megan broke up with a boyfriend she'd been with for about two years.' He paused. 'After she discovered he was actually married and had a family.'

'What?' Rilee gasped. 'I don't understand. How do you have a boyfriend for two years and not know he's married?'

'My point exactly. Who the hell is she to sit there and say we rushed into something when she had two years with a bloke and didn't know something like that.'

Rilee pushed up on her elbow and looked down at her husband. 'So how *didn't* she know something like that?'

'He worked away a lot,' he said. 'Apparently he was a pretty convincing liar.'

'How did she find out?'

'His wife got suspicious and hired a private investigator to follow him, and then turned up on Megan's doorstep.'

'Oh my God.' Rilee could only imagine how that scene would have played out. 'And Megan had no idea at all that this guy was married?'

'Nope. He had it all nicely worked out. His wife and kids lived in Sydney and he commuted to the Melbourne office for three weeks at a time. He told Megan he had to work one week a month in the Sydney office and would fly out and spend that week playing happy families.'

'And he managed to keep this up for two years?'

'Apparently.'

Rilee couldn't get her head around it. Poor Megan. She could only imagine how devastating it must have been to discover the man you loved had a whole other life he'd kept secret from you. How could someone even do that? Then something else occurred to her. 'Your parents—I take it they don't know about it?'

'No. They just know Megan broke up with him, they have no idea why. The only reason I know is because Natalie called and asked me to come down to be there when Julian turned up to move his stuff out. He was giving Megan a hard time.'

Rilee placed a hand on his bicep and smiled. 'You're a great brother to go all that way and help.'

'That's what family do,' he said simply.

'I know, but the way you three stuck together was special, which makes me feel bad about you and Megan and what happened tonight.'

She saw Dan's face tighten a little. 'She's still torn up about Julian. I get that and for the most part I can give her a break, but not when she takes it out on you and me. There's no excuse for that.'

Rilee snuggled into her husband's side and closed her eyes. It explained Megan's attitude, so maybe she shouldn't take it personally, and yet, for some reason she had a feeling there was more to it. She smothered a wide yawn. It had been a long day. Maybe things would be better after they'd all had a good sleep.

Nineteen

Rilee walked around the back of the chook pen and into the shed and let out a small squeak of surprise to find Megan inside.

'Sorry, you gave me a start,' Rilee said.

Megan's hand was resting on a saddle which sat on a small stand with bridles hanging on the wall above.

'Were those yours? Did you have horses?' Rilee asked. She'd wondered about the riding gear stored inside the old shed. It hadn't been used in a long time judging by the dirt and mould on the leather. There were no horses on Thumb Creek; everything was done on motorbikes, quads or motor vehicles. She'd been disappointed to discover this: it didn't fit her romantic image of stockmen on horseback riding into the sunset.

'A long time ago,' Megan said and Rilee caught the slightest of hitches in her tone before she cleared her throat and dusted off her hands.

Rilee put back the shovel she'd been using to clean out the chook pen. 'How long since you were last home?' she asked.

'A while. Work keeps me fairly busy.'

'Well, I'm glad you could make it back for the party. It means a lot to Dan, and to me as well.'

Megan's eyes narrowed and her head tilted slightly, reminding Rilee of the chooks as they sized up the scraps she threw to them. 'I hope you married my brother for the right reasons and you know what you're getting yourself into.'

'Sorry?' Rilee frowned.

'It's a big gamble to marry someone you hardly know. If down the track you decide you made a mistake and you divorce my brother, you should be aware that there won't be a hefty settlement.' She gave a tight smile before adding, 'One of the benefits of having a solicitor in the family is making sure the Kincaid assets are protected.'

Rilee was too shocked to speak, but Megan didn't wait around for a reply.

'Don't take it personally.'

For the second time that morning, Rilee jumped as Natalie stepped into the shed. What was it with these people and all the sneaking up on a person! 'It's a little hard not to.'

Natalie walked across to the saddle and ran her hands over the smooth seat. 'Megan used to compete,' she said with a wistful smile. 'She loved showjumping. She was good too—did the show circuit and won loads of competitions.'

'What about you? Did you ride?'

'Yeah, but my heart was never in it the way Megan's was. She and Clancy were a team.'

Rilee thought back to all the photos hanging on the walls or sitting on side tables throughout the huge homestead, but she couldn't recall a single one that had a horse in them.

'They were inseparable, until the accident.'

'What happened?'

'Clancy stumbled on a jump and fell and they had to put him down. Megan almost didn't make it either. She was in hospital for over a month.'

'Oh wow.'

'She was different after that. She wouldn't talk about it and she never looked at another horse again.'

'How sad.'

'Yeah, it was. She threw herself into uni over the next few years, and then law school and work,' Natalie shrugged. 'I think she got so used to keeping busy to forget about Clancy that it just became a habit. Work has been her whole life.'

'Is that why there are no photos?' Natalie gave a surprised look, and Rilee added hurriedly, 'It's just that your mother seems to have photos of *every* other occasion or event in your life, but I haven't seen a single one of either of you with a horse.'

'Mum and her photos,' Natalie sighed. 'There used to be. In fact, it was rare to find a photo of Megan *without* Clancy,' she said sadly. 'After she came home from hospital, I think Mum thought seeing pictures of Clancy everywhere would slow down her healing process—she was so withdrawn and miserable.' Natalie ran her fingertips across the bridles on the wall. 'I guess there was never a good time to put them back up.'

Rilee shook her head; it must have been a traumatic experience and one that seemed to have shaped the woman Megan was now. Maybe she'd never allowed herself to grieve the way she'd needed to. Or maybe, she conceded, hearing Dan's voice in her head, she should just mind her own business and stop diagnosing.

'Come on, let's get out of here, this is far too depressing.'

The two women walked up to the main house. Natalie poured two glasses of iced tea from the fridge and led the way back outside to an elegant wrought-iron setting under a large shady tree.

Across the manicured lawn, tables were being set up and a team of people Ellen had hired were busy hanging lights. Ellen herself had gone into town earlier, which had given everyone at home a few hours' breathing space. At the pool, Rilee spotted Megan lying on a sunlounge, reading the paper, and she smiled at her, but Megan simply lifted the paper higher to block her from view. Natalie gave a twist of her lips as she exchanged a look with Rilee.

'I just wish she didn't see me as some kind of threat. She really doesn't like me very much,' Rilee said, taking a sip of the cold beverage. She had to admit it was pretty refreshing on a hot day.

'Megan has always had trust issues. It takes her a long time to open up to people, even more so lately.'

'Dan told me about her break-up. But don't worry,' Rilee added quickly, 'I wasn't planning on mentioning it to her. I figured I'd be the last person she'd want knowing something that private.'

'Probably a good idea not to say anything,' Natalie agreed.

'So how come *you* don't think I'm the devil incarnate?'

Natalie threw her a grin. 'You're the woman my bonehead brother chose over every other woman who was dangled under his nose. I trust his judgement.'

'I'm glad *someone* does.'

'Look, Megan's attitude sucks, but if there is one thing about her that's never changed it's that she's loyal to a fault.'

'I don't understand.'

'Her best friend is Priscilla's older sister, and the whole Montgomery clan still have a bit of a bee in their bonnet over Dan slipping through their fingers.'

'Oh great,' Rilee groaned.

Natalie chuckled. 'I know, it's all very Romeo and Juliet. Megan'll get over it, I promise. She's just feeling obliged to act all high and mighty, but she'll come around.'

'I could seriously wring Dan's neck sometimes. If I had any idea this marriage would have caused so much friction, I'd have thought twice about it.'

'No, you wouldn't,' Natalie said, shaking her head. 'Any fool can see you're crazy about my brother. Nothing would have stopped you two getting together.'

'I would have fought harder to make him do it properly, then,' she conceded.

'Probably wouldn't have made any difference,' Natalie said and then gave a grimace. 'Sorry, but you're an outsider. That's just the way it is out here. Wouldn't matter what you did.'

'Well, that's comforting.'

'But who cares, right?' she lifted her glass and tapped it against Rilee's. 'You make my brother happy and that's all I care about. So ignore the rest,' she said, getting to her feet. 'I better finish the list of jobs Mum left before she gets back.'

Rilee grinned and shook her head. She wasn't sure she would ever understand this place, but at least she had one ally in the Kincaid camp, which was one more than yesterday!

Twenty

Rilee heard her parents' arrival long before she saw them. The unmistakable drone of a VW Kombi was hard to miss, especially out here. Rilee braced herself; even though there was a bubble of excitement at seeing them, she was worried her parents would be completely out of their element at Thumb Creek Station.

All worries disappeared as soon as she caught sight of the pale blue van and the woman with wild hair hanging out the passenger window and waving like a crazy person. A smile broke out over Rilee's face as she waved back, opening the cottage gate and hurrying towards them.

Within moments she was engulfed in a warm hug and lemongrass, rosemary and sandalwood filled her senses. 'Hi, Mum,' she said, pulling away and blinking back happy tears. Her mum's baggy, brightly coloured batik-style pants and loose-fitting tie-dyed top was an eruption of colour that somehow just seemed to work.

Her dad made his way around the van and lifted her into a bear hug, dressed in his usual mismatched faded shirt, board shorts and grey hair pulled back in a short ponytail.

'There's my favourite daughter,' he said, grinning.

'I'm your only daughter,' she added.

'That I know of,' he replied. It was their usual banter and it brought home just how much she'd missed these two crazy people. After hugging her dad, she looped her arms around their waists and led them towards the house.

'It's just like you described, darling,' her mother said as she ran her hands along the backs of the scrubbed timber table setting in the kitchen.

'Where's this husband of yours?' her father asked after she'd handed him a cup of fragrant tea she'd prepared in their honour.

'He'll be home soon. He just had to go and check on a few things.' No sooner had she spoken than she heard the ute pulling up outside.

Rilee wasn't sure why she was feeling so nervous about this meeting—she'd been preparing Dan for this for months, and truth be told, Dan was the least of her worries. She couldn't bring herself to think about the meeting with his parents. She'd deal with that when the time came.

Dan took his hat off as he came through the back door, hanging it up before heading across the room to greet her parents. Rilee didn't miss the surprise on her husband's face as he extended his hand to her father only to be dragged into an embrace and slapped heartily on the back. To his credit, Dan recovered quickly and he was obviously more prepared for her mother's hug when it came.

They moved out onto the verandah with their tea and conversation for the most part stayed on relatively safe subjects. When something came up about pesticides, her heart swelled with love that her husband seemed genuinely interested in her father's opinions and allowed him to put forward his case for permaculture's approach to farming.

The afternoon went by way too fast and before long it was time to prepare for dinner over at the main house.

'Darling, would you please just calm down,' her mother said as she watched Rilee fuss about the kitchen while they waited for Dan to finish his shower.

Her parents had taken time to freshen up after their trip, her mother in a long peacock blue kaftan dress and sandals, while her father had swapped his board shorts for a pair of cargo shorts and a clean shirt for the occasion.

'I'm sorry, Mum. It's just that . . . I don't think you understand what they're like,' she said, lowering her voice.

'I'm pretty sure your father and I can handle the situation.'

'Although the way she's pacing around like a caged lion, I'm thinking it might not hurt to have a quick puff—' her father started before Rilee cut him off.

'Dad, don't you dare!' Rilee gaped at her parents as they chuckled. That's exactly what she needed right now: her parents meeting her in-laws for the first time reeking of pot.

'Fine, we'll do this your way. Stiff upper lip and all that.'

'No, I'm sorry. This shouldn't be such a huge deal. I know you guys will be fine. Just be yourselves.'

'Only way we know how to be, kiddo,' her father said, standing up and kissing her temple.

The walk up to the house seemed longer tonight and the sound of gravel beneath their feet was loud in the quiet evening air. The sun was sinking and a splash of orange, pink and yellow stained the sky beyond the open paddocks that stretched out before them.

'What a beautiful place,' her mother sighed. It was beautiful. There was a wildness about it—a rugged, dangerous kind of beauty that Rilee loved.

Dan squeezed her hand as they headed up the steps to where his parents were standing by the grand entrance like statues.

'Mum, Dad,' Rilee started, wishing her voice wasn't coming out like a timid mouse, 'this is Ellen and Jacob. My parents, Shelly and David,' she finished, holding her breath as the two sets of parents smiled and the Kincaids extended their hands. *Don't hug them, please don't hug*, Rilee repeated silently as she watched her mother glance at Ellen's outstretched hand before stepping closer and wrapping her arms around the stiff older woman. *Oh God.* It was like watching a train crash and being helpless to do anything to stop it. Her father pulled Jacob in for a hearty man hug. Beside her, she felt Dan chuckle silently and she glared at him in reproach. Yes, she had told them to be themselves, but couldn't they have shaken hands like normal people?

To their credit, Ellen and Jacob recovered their composure quickly, hastily ushering their guests inside to meet the rest of the family.

'Stop worrying,' Dan said when she shot him a helpless look. 'Your parents are awesome. It'll do Mum and Dad good to be kept on their toes.'

It turned out Dan was right, her parents were the life of the party. Megan seemed to thaw a little as her mum recounted some of the wilder days on the commune. She even seemed to have won over Dan's mother.

'Your gardens are just gorgeous, Ellen. I saw them as we walked up.'

'Thank you,' Ellen said, venturing a small smile across at Shelly as she daintily sliced her meal. 'I do love gardening.'

'It's a real credit to you.'

Rilee had to look twice at her mother-in-law—was that a blush?

'Thank you, Shelly. From what Rilee's been telling us, I believe you have a bit of a green thumb as well?' Ellen asked hesitantly.

'I do, but for some reason I can never grow roses. Maybe you can give me some pointers. I'd love to have a tour of your garden before we leave.'

'Yes, well, I think we can arrange that,' Ellen replied with a decisive nod.

Rilee smiled and shook her head; they had everyone eating out of their palms of their hands. It was touch and go for a moment over dinner when conversation turned to farming and a heated debate broke out between her father and Jacob, but it defused quickly enough when Dan cut in.

'I took David out to show him the back paddock where the worst of the mother-of-millions outbreak is.'

'Mother of what?' Rilee asked, sending her husband a doubtful glance. It sounded like something from *Game of Thrones*.

'Mother-of-millions. It's an extremely aggressive weed,' Dan explained, before turning back to his father. 'David reckons we can clear up the remainder by introducing some African thrip.'

'Thrip?' Ellen said with a lift of her eyebrow.

'Some kind of imported bug,' Jacob muttered. 'Heard something about it a while back. Waste of time when you can just spray or burn it.'

'Jacob's correct, it's a type of insect,' her father explained. 'Barely visible to the naked eye, but they work a charm on cleaning up the mother-of-millions infestation and they have less impact on the environment than chemicals or fire.'

Jacob gave a contemptuous snort at that, but Dan ignored him. 'Apparently, they're having huge success with them up in Queensland. And they'd be a cheaper alternative to pumping a crapload of insecticide onto them like we have been.'

'If it ain't broke,' Jacob said, sitting back in his chair and crossing his arms.

Rilee could see her husband's frustration, but she could also see the fire in his eyes and knew that he wasn't giving up on the idea either. Clearly he knew when to choose his battles and she was relieved he didn't push the subject tonight.

'Oh my God, your parents are the coolest,' Natalie grinned as she helped Rilee dish up dessert.

'They're pretty amazing,' Rilee agreed.

'I can see where you get your love of natural medicine. I was just talking to your mum and I had no idea there were so many natural alternatives for treating everyday problems.'

Pride filled Rilee as she looked across at her parents. It felt good having them here with her. She felt less of an outsider. How had they managed that? She'd been trying for months to break through the wall the family had put up and her parents had managed to smash it within five minutes. *Just enjoy it,* she told herself firmly. Who knew how long it would last.

Twenty-one

The homestead was done up like something out of a *Home Beautiful* magazine shoot. The gardens had been pruned and manicured, and the new seedlings, planted only a week before the party date, had amazingly all blossomed, right on cue. A small army of workers had miraculously appeared and set up a huge marquee on the lawns and catering staff and waiters were bustling everywhere.

'I'm so glad your mother didn't go over the top with this party,' Rilee murmured as they walked across to prepare for greeting guests.

'Trust me, she didn't. This is understated,' Dan told her dryly. 'You look stunning by the way, Mrs Kincaid.'

It had been a long time since she'd worn this particular dress. She hadn't imagined she'd wear it again, or any of the others she had packed away, but she hadn't been able bring herself to throw away such beautiful garments, and she was glad of that now. This had been her favourite with its v-neckline and silver sequined bodice. The low-cut back was a bit daring, as was the slinky black skirt with the slit on the side, but it made her feel confident and sexy, and she needed that given there would be more than a few guests ready to judge the new wife of Dan Kincaid.

Rilee smiled, allowing her gaze to roam the length of her husband's body, clad in black trousers and jacket, over a deep blue shirt and black tie. 'You don't scrub up too badly yourself, Mr Kincaid.'

'If I didn't think my mother would come and drag us out the door, I'd turn you around right now and take you back to bed.'

Rilee gave a rather unladylike snort at the thought. She had no doubts whatsoever that Ellen Kincaid would do exactly that. 'Let's get this thing over and done with then, shall we?' she sighed.

'A woman after my own heart.' He took her hand and tucked it under his arm, Rilee wasn't sure if it was for support or as insurance that she couldn't run away. Whatever the reason, she was grateful to have him beside her. She had a feeling this party Ellen was throwing was less of an introduction to the community and more of a throwing her to the wolves.

Ellen came towards them as they walked under the elegant archway of white roses. She frowned as they stopped in front of her. 'Darling, why didn't you come up to the house and ask for a tie? Your father has plenty to choose from.'

'This one's fine,' Dan said, brushing his mother's hands away as she fussed with the knot.

'Well, there's no time now, it'll have to do. Come on, we've got guests waiting.'

Dan exchanged a brief look with Rilee and slid his hand around her waist, pulling her close to his side. 'I'll make it up to you later tonight, I promise,' he whispered close to her ear, sending a shiver of anticipation down her spine.

'You better believe it,' she murmured. If she survived the party, that was.

Rilee smiled and nodded as she was introduced to a sea of new faces. Some were nearby graziers, long-time residents of the area, but there were also quite a few people who had flown in from the city and different parts of the country. Rilee knew that this was what their wedding would have been like and she was grateful they'd eloped. As she looked around at all the glitz and glamour, she caught a glimpse of her parents chatting to a small group of couples across the lawn. She'd thought they would stick out like a sore thumb in this crowd, but her mother looked stunning in a simple silver and black sarong and high heels. Her father had scrubbed up pretty well too and was wearing a suit, albeit with a bright lime and orange Hawaiian shirt under the jacket. She grinned despite herself. They were making an effort, and yet they somehow managed to remain true to themselves. Rilee's heart filled with pride.

No, she was glad they hadn't had a traditional wedding; here when everyone mingled, it was fine, but seated in a church? The Kincaids' side would have been overflowing and hers would be practically empty. Her father had no parents or siblings, and her mother's side of the family had disowned her when she'd fallen pregnant with Rilee at a very young age. She'd never even met them, and while she'd occasionally thought about trying to track them down, she realised that if her grandparents had wanted to get to know her, they could have just as easily tried to make contact with her. She wasn't sure she really needed people in her life who were capable of turning away their daughter because of one mistake. She was grateful her parents were nothing like that or she would have found herself with no one, seeing as she'd made more than her fair share of mistakes over the years.

Rilee felt Dan's arm tighten a little around her waist and glanced up, noting the sudden tightening of his features. Before she could ask what was wrong, a silky voice said, 'Well, aren't you the sly one, Dan Kincaid.'

'Priscilla,' Dan said politely. 'I think you've already met my wife.' He pulled Rilee closer to his side.

'Hello, Kylie,' she said, dismissing Rilee after a brief once-over.

Rilee didn't bother correcting her. Either the woman had serious short-term memory problems or she was doing it deliberately to get under her skin, in which case she wouldn't give her the satisfaction of seeing that it bothered her.

'I didn't know you were coming.' Dan's tone suggested he was not happy about the fact.

The woman shrugged delicately. 'I was out here this weekend visiting Mum and Dad. It was too good an opportunity to miss.'

A silence fell over their small circle, although Priscilla didn't seem at all fazed by the awkwardness of the situation. No doubt this was her intention, to make Dan squirm in front of everyone as payback for Priscilla's humiliation at being rejected for a stranger.

'We're very happy that you could make it,' Rilee said, plastering on a bright smile. 'It's always nice to meet Dan's old friends. Enjoy the party, we need to go and mingle.'

'Nice move,' Shae said a few moments later when Dan left Rilee to get another drink. 'But it's a good thing looks can't really kill.'

Rilee discreetly followed her friend's small toss of her head and caught Priscilla watching her from across the garden.

'What did she hope to achieve by coming here?' Shae mused.

'I feel kind of bad for her. I mean, if she didn't come, people would probably be thinking she was bitter about it all, so maybe she figured she'd come and show everyone she's moved on,' Rilee suggested.

'Oh yeah,' Shae scoffed. 'She seems to have moved on really well.'

Rilee had to agree, looking at her glaring across at them now. She was doing very little to hide her resentment. It was irritating. It wasn't as though she'd deliberately stolen

Dan out from under her nose; until coming out here, she hadn't even been aware the woman existed.

'If it's any consolation, it is completely obvious to anyone with eyes that Dan is head over heels in love with you. And from the comments I'm overhearing you've made a big impression too.'

'Maybe I should have been handing out business cards after all,' Rilee murmured as she took a sip of wine. 'And you look gorgeous, by the way,' she added, admiring her old dress. 'It never looked that good on me.' The nude pink colour looked stunning against Shae's complexion, and clung to her hourglass shape, showing it off to perfection.

'Ellen almost smiled welcomingly at me before she realised I wasn't one of her hoity-toity guests,' she said dryly. 'I wish I'd had a camera to take a photo of her face.'

'There weren't very many locals on the invitation list, were there?' Rilee commented as they surveyed the crowd.

'It's a rather elite circle the Kincaids mix in. These are most of the big property owners from all over the region. Cattle breeders and the like. The rest are all the self-important mob from the charity boards Ellen's on. They don't throw a shindig like this just for the locals.'

Rilee wondered again at the complex world her mother-in-law had woven together, and she silently mourned the simple life she'd once imagined the Kincaids would lead on Thumb Creek.

Rilee touched her fingertips to her throbbing temple. She'd been doing her best to ignore the headache for the last hour or so but without success. It was too far to dash home for her remedies, so she'd decided to raid the guest bathroom at the main house instead. Rilee swallowed two of the small white pills and sighed as she looked at herself in the mirror. The last time she'd worn this dress had been at a casino on the French Riviera. A ghost of a smile touched her lips at the memory. The shimmery silver fabric sparkled under the bathroom lights. She might be wearing something from her past, but the woman who stared back at her in the mirror was completely different to the carefree, naive young woman she'd been back then.

Rilee left the bathroom and braced herself to head back out to the party. As she approached the end of the hallway, she heard the low murmur of voices and paused, unwilling to intrude on a private conversation.

'I just don't understand what he could possibly see in her,' said one of the voices, and Rilee recognised it instantly.

'Priscilla, I know this is difficult for you, dear,' Ellen soothed in a gentle tone she'd never used with Rilee. 'But we must accept Daniel's decision on this and make the best of it.'

'But she has no right to be here.'

'She is Daniel's wife, and whether we like that or not, there is nothing we can do about it.'

Heat sprang to Rilee's cheeks at the curt remark as fury and hurt battled for control inside her. Clearly these two women despised her, but it still stung to hear it so openly, especially from the woman who was supposed to be family now.

'I wouldn't be so sure about that, Ellen.' The angry clack of heels on the hard tile floor echoed through the quiet house.

Priscilla's parting threat didn't worry Rilee in the least. She knew that her relationship with Dan was secure. The bond they shared had only grown stronger since their hurried wedding. It was no mere infatuation but something deep and enduring. Priscilla might be no threat, but Ellen's lack of support hurt more than she cared to admit. She'd truly hoped her mother-in-law could get past her disapproval and they could become friends. It seemed unlikely that would be happening anytime soon after what she'd just overheard.

Rilee returned to the party and forced a bright smile to her face, determined not to let Priscilla and Ellen ruin what was left of the evening. Maybe she couldn't make her mother-in-law like her but she'd do her best to win over all the woman's neighbours and friends. She'd be the happiest, most endearing daughter-in-law she could possibly be, at least for tonight.

Twenty-two

It had been three days since the party and life was only just beginning to return to normal. She'd stood at the gate long after her parents' departure, fighting a lingering sense of abandonment. Everything had seemed so different when they'd been here—more attainable. Now that they'd gone, Rilee was feeling more than a little lost and very much alone.

While Natalie and Megan had been home, family dinners and conversation had been almost enjoyable. There was no business talk, and no arguments between Jacob and Dan—clearly the girls brought some kind of civility to the place that wasn't usually there. After they'd left, it seemed oddly quiet. While Megan hadn't exactly shed a tear over saying goodbye to Rilee, she had given her a brief, somewhat stiff hug farewell, so Rilee was taking that as a small win.

Maybe there was hope after all. She did miss Natalie's smiling face, though; the two women had become close in the short visit and Rilee wished fervently that she didn't live so far away.

Rilee knocked on the back door of the main house and waited until she heard footsteps approaching.

'For heaven's sake, Rilee, you don't need to knock, just come in.'

'Sorry, old habit,' Rilee muttered. How was she supposed to enforce boundaries in her own home if she was expected to just walk into her in-laws' house whenever she felt like it? 'I'm just wondering what time you need me to be ready tomorrow.'

'Tomorrow?' Ellen looked at Rilee in confusion.

'Isn't that when the church group meeting is? I have a few ideas I thought the group might like to hear about.'

When Ellen continued to stare at her, Rilee fought hard to keep a lid on her irritation. 'At the last meeting you said to bring along some ideas and we'd discuss them.'

'Oh, that,' she said, giving a small flutter of her hands. 'Heavens, I've had so much else on my mind since then, I'd forgotten all about it. I didn't think the ladies' church group was really your thing.'

'I never said that. I just think it could take on a few more local projects.'

'I was under the impression that you'd found it all a bit backward.'

Rilee shook her head. 'Of course not.'

'Well, I'm not so sure you're a good fit for the group. Maybe once you've settled into the community a little more, got used to the way things are done, perhaps then you could come along and see if you'd like to join.'

Was she really being told thanks but no thanks? 'You were the one who invited me.'

'I realise now that it was probably a little premature to get you involved so soon after arriving. Never mind, I'm sure you'll be so busy with your little business you won't have time for much of anything.' She clasped her hands together in front of her and Rilee got the message the visit was over. Well, she wasn't about to go down without a fight.

'I'd like to put my ideas forward, Ellen. I feel very strongly about them and I think the group would be a great vehicle to get things done.'

The phone chose that moment to ring and Rilee wondered if Ellen had some secret hand signal to alert it to do so when she needed an out. 'Excuse me, dear, I best get that. We can discuss this later.' She was already heading up the hallway towards the ringing phone.

'I'll wait out the front tomorrow morning,' Rilee called after her and Ellen waved a hand over her head distractedly in acknowledgement.

As she walked back home, she mentally went over her preparations for the following day. She was going to be heading into battle and she needed to be ready.

∽

198

The air smelled clean and crisp as she stepped out onto the verandah early the next morning. She'd spent the night before tossing and turning as she thought about the meeting today.

Dan had shaken his head at her as she'd made him sit through her proposal yet again. 'Ri, you're going to be fine. Stop stressing, would you?'

It was easy for him, he wasn't the one who had to stand up in front of his mother and her friends. Truth was, neither did she; there was nothing stopping her from simply not going to the meeting. Ellen had made it perfectly obvious yesterday that she didn't want her there. She hadn't even wanted to go to the first one, but every time she recalled the irritated rebuke she'd received last time, her resolve strengthened. Not only was it a question of pride but it was a cause that *mattered*. Were they all going to stand by and watch as more young girls lost their chance to live their own lives, thanks to a lack of education or simple boredom? No. This was important.

She was just finishing with her makeup when she heard the sound of a car engine. She quickly finished applying her eyeliner before dashing down the hall and into the kitchen, grabbing her handbag off the back of a chair and shoving her feet into the shoes she'd put out earlier. As she pushed open the screen door she saw a trail of dust disappearing down the driveway and found herself staring after it in shock. Ellen had left without her.

Muttering an expletive, Rilee headed back inside and called Dan.

'Your mother's left without me,' she said without a greeting.

'Are you sure?' Dan sounded weary and distracted.

'She drove off, just then.'

'Maybe she assumed you were getting there on your own.'

'Well, how am I going to do that now? You have the ute.'

'Has Dad left yet?'

'Yes, he went earlier.'

She heard Dan swear and silently repeated a few choice words of her own. 'I can't bring the ute back. We're stuck out here for a while yet. Hang on,' he said and the phone went silent for a while before he was back. 'Mark said to call Shae. She wanted to head into town today.'

'Okay. Thanks.'

'And Ri?'

'Yes?' she said, failing to keep the frustration from her voice.

'You'll be great.'

She'd almost decided not to bother going, but Dan's confidence gave her the boost she needed. 'Thank you. See you tonight,' she said, pulling her shoulders back and placing her hands on her hips. 'You can't get rid of me that easily,' she said with newfound resolve.

Twenty-three

'Rilee,' Ellen said, raising an eyebrow slightly as Rilee approached her moments before the meeting was due to start.

'We must have got our wires crossed about this morning,' Rilee said, holding the woman's gaze innocently. 'Luckily Shae was heading into town.'

'I was sure you'd decided against coming along to the meeting.'

'Oh no. In fact, I've been busy coming up with some great ideas I think everyone will approve of.' Two could play this game of social niceties.

'Yes, well, we'll see if there's time at the end of the meeting,' she said, clapping her hands briskly to get the attention of the women chatting in the seats nearby. 'All right, we have a lot to get through today, ladies. Let's get started, shall we?'

Rilee sat quietly, biding her time as the meeting seemed to drag on endlessly. Finally, Ellen stood and took the microphone from the last of the speakers and began to wrap the meeting up as food was brought out to the side tables and cups and saucers rattled in the kitchenette.

'Actually, Ellen, if I can quickly have a word?'

'I think we're almost ready for morning tea, Rilee, dear.'

'It won't take long, I promise,' she said, surprising herself as she stood up and walked towards the small stage. She'd come too far now to shut up and sit down quietly. 'At the last meeting I commented about the projects this group is sponsoring. I realise I may have come across as a little critical, but I can assure you that was not my intention. I've been thinking long and hard about this, and maybe it's because I'm new to town, but I see so much potential for this group to make a difference locally. You do such an amazing job with your overseas projects, but if you took on something to make a difference right here in town as well, you'd be helping *our* kids.'

'As I said before, Rilee, we're committed to more than our fair share of projects at the moment. It's not practical to take on any more.'

'I wouldn't mind hearing about her ideas.'

All eyes turned on the voice from the back row, and Rilee recognised the woman with bright red lipstick immediately. Edna. Bless her heart.

'The fact is, due to the lack of a medical practitioner and, from what I can gather, a slightly outdated pharmaceutical practice, the wellbeing of teens in this town has become a serious issue. If kids can't get access to appropriate contraception then pregnancy and STDs soon become a major concern. It has a massive impact on the whole community.'

'What's this got to do with the church group?' one of the women asked.

'I'm suggesting that the group implements specific strategies to curb the problem.'

There was an undercurrent of conversation humming throughout the room.

'And just how do you propose we do that?' another woman asked.

'We need better access to health care, counselling and support,' Rilee said, looking around the room. 'Look, most of these kids can't drive, so they can't get to Narrabri or Gunnedah to see a practitioner. They're wary of going into the chemist here because they're worried about word getting back to their parents, not to mention they feel they're being judged. So what's their alternative? They opt for crossing their fingers and *hoping* they don't get pregnant or contract a sexually transmissible disease.'

'Perhaps if they practised crossing their legs instead they wouldn't have to worry about it.' The snide remark from the middle row sent a trill of sniggering around the room.

'And I'm sure no one in this room ever had sex when they were a teenager,' Rilee snapped and noticed a few women of varying ages drop their gazes as she looked about the room.

203

'Teenage pregnancy should be a community issue. In most cases, the young women who end up pregnant drop out of high school and then depend on social security because they don't have the education to access further studies, not to mention there are very few local jobs available in town to start with.'

'So what are you proposing?' asked a woman from the front row.

'Ideally we need to get something into place so kids have access to contraception, but the bigger issue is educating kids earlier, to show them they can do more with their lives than remain in Pallaburra.'

There was another murmur of unease and Rilee hurried on. 'The church group could fund excursions aimed at kids most at risk of falling into the welfare cycle. These excursions take at-risk kids to Sydney university campuses and regional TAFE colleges. They explore the city, show them how to catch trains and buses and basically give them a taste of city life—what's out there. They show them a life they could have if they choose to study and go on to university. A lot of disadvantaged kids rarely ever leave town. They become trapped here and need help to break the cycle.'

'I don't actually see how an all-expenses paid trip to the city is going to stop teenage girls having sex.'

'It won't stop them having sex,' Rilee said, forcing a calmness into her tone she was far from feeling. 'But combined with some kind of education and showing them there's a whole different future they could aim for might just encourage more of them to stay in school and go to university. Or at the very least, realise they can choose more than Pallaburra.'

A low hum like a hive of angry bees ran through the room and Rilee immediately realised her mistake.

'There is *nothing* wrong with growing up and living in Pallaburra,' a woman at the front of the room spoke up. 'I was born here and raised my family, and both my girls are still in town and raising their own children. I might add, *neither of them* got themselves pregnant while in school,' she added with a sharp nod.

A few other women muttered indignantly as they glared at Rilee.

'I'm not implying that there is anything *wrong* with living in Pallaburra or that every teenage girl is out there having sex and falling pregnant. But for every household that has a supportive home life and parents who care, there are at least a dozen more out there with no positive role models. Those kids are basically bringing themselves up due to broken homes and parents with addictions. You don't have to look very far to realise this town has more than its fair share of these kids. They're the ones we need to help. They should be a community concern.'

The undercurrent in the room was still hostile and Ellen glided to the front of the stage, bringing an automatic hush to the room and leaving Rilee to wonder how on earth the woman did that.

'Thank you, Rilee, for your *suggestion*. You may take a seat now and we'll close the meeting.'

As Rilee sat down she felt the weight of the other women's stares on her back. It seemed one wasn't supposed to point out the less attractive parts of one's town. *Great job, Rilee,* she chastised herself silently. *You really should write a book on how to offend a whole town in three easy steps.*

After suffering through a frosty morning tea, she had to endure the ride home with Ellen.

'That went well,' Rilee said, half-heartedly attempting to lighten the mood.

'What did you expect, dear? You marched in there and practically told everyone that their children ought to move as far away from Pallaburra as they could. Perhaps you could have handled it with a little more tact.'

Rilee bit her tongue, focusing on the landscape flashing by outside the window.

'This isn't the city,' Ellen continued.

'I'm fully aware of that fact.' God, she was sick of hearing this.

'There's no need to be petulant. I'm trying to help.'

'I could have used your help earlier, instead of being sent back to my chair like a recalcitrant child,' Rilee said.

'I'm the president of ladies' church committee, Rilee. I can hardly be seen to be showing favouritism to a family member, can I?' She gave a short sigh. 'I guess I'm partly to blame. I invited you along thinking it might help you meet people, but I realise now that the group is not a good fit for you.'

A few days earlier and Rilee would have been jumping for joy over the fact she no longer had to attend the meetings.

Now she felt insulted and indignant. How dare Ellen sit there and tell her she didn't belong? What had started out as a challenge to find a worthwhile local cause had now become a mission. The more she'd researched, the more she'd realised this was an important issue.

'I understand that hearing the facts from an outsider was probably a little . . . confronting,' Rilee said finally, 'but you have to admit this is something that needs to be addressed.'

'It's not something that the church committee would normally take part in.'

'Why not?'

Ellen made an irritated sound before waving a hand in the air. 'It just isn't.'

'Isn't the church part of the community? Shouldn't it be trying to help kids? This is an important issue.'

'There are plenty of important issues, Rilee. And we have our hands full raising money for the ones we are already supporting.'

'This is a local social issue where the group could make a real difference. If you could turn just one girl's future around, wouldn't that be worth the effort?'

'I think you may be reading far more into this than you should. Where is the evidence that the kinds of things you're suggesting would make any difference? Besides,' she added, taking her eyes off the road briefly to pin Rilee with a look, 'there would be an enormous amount of organising. You'd have to get the high school on board, which would involve the department of education and all kinds of red tape. We wouldn't even get something like this up and running before the end of the year. It just isn't practical.'

Rilee shook her head sadly as she looked back out the window. She'd been so sure this would be something the women in town would embrace.

Later that afternoon she was venting over coffee at Shae's house. 'You know what sucks the most about all this?'

Shae shook her head patiently.

'If Priscilla had been the one who'd brought up this idea, Ellen would be falling over herself to make it happen.'

'I wouldn't be too sure. I think it's more that underage sex is a taboo subject for a church committee.'

'Taboo?'

'There's no way people around here are going to feel comfortable providing access to contraception for high school kids. Besides, most of the women in that group send their kids away to boarding school. They don't really see what happens to the disadvantaged kids in town. I'm not sure they care whether or not they make poor choices that affect their lives.'

Rilee gaped at her friend in shock. 'Well, that's just stupid.'

Shae shrugged and emptied her cup in the sink. 'There's a lot of outdated thinking around here. You'll get used to it.'

'No,' she said, clearly louder than she'd intended judging by the way Shae swung around and looked at her. 'No, I'm not going to let them win. If they won't help me do this then I'll find a way to make it happen without them.'

'How are you going to do that? You need to raise a lot of money, and Ellen's right, there'd be more than a little bit of red tape to wade through before you could get something like this off the ground.'

'I don't know how I'll do it . . . yet. But I'm not giving up before I've even tried.'

'I think you're seriously taking on too much. You've got a business to start.'

'It's important, Shae. Have you looked around in town lately? Have you seen some of these kids? There has to be more to life than popping out babies and walking down to the shops to buy cigarettes.'

'Yeah, it's hard not to see what's happening, but you can't singlehandedly step in and change the world.'

'I don't want to change the world,' Rilee said simply. 'But if I can offer an alternative to just one girl, doesn't that make it worthwhile?'

Shae smiled. 'Well, I guess no one can argue with that logic.'

'Good, so you'll help me then?'

'What?' Shae's smile soon disappeared. 'Hey, wait a minute, I don't recall volunteering for anything.'

'You didn't. I nominated you. Thanks for the coffee . . . partner,' Rilee said, hurrying to the door. 'I'll be in touch!'

As she walked up the dirt track towards her cottage, Rilee felt a renewed surge of optimism washing through her. She was not going to stand by quietly and let them sweep her concerns under the mat; out of sight, out of mind. It was time Pallaburra had a bit of a shake-up.

Twenty-four

The next day Rilee met with the local real estate agent for another look through the two office spaces she was considering for her business. It was sad that there were so many empty storefronts to choose from in the main street, testament to the struggles which seemed to plague so many rural towns.

After looking through both premises, she finally decided upon the little cottage at the end of the main street, which had once been a corner store. She loved that it was its own building, complete with front awning and large window overlooking the main street. With a bit of remodelling, she could already imagine her little practice here. There was enough space to make two treatment rooms, with a small kitchen and bathroom in the rear of the building, and a large airy waiting room.

Rilee smiled as she turned in a slow circle and surveyed the premises. 'It's perfect,' she whispered.

'So . . . you'll take it?' the real estate agent asked eagerly.

'I'll take it,' she beamed across at him. All of a sudden, her dream was within reach. It might not be the bustling inner-city practice she'd been picturing, but it was hers. She straightened her shoulders. From here on in, she could start a fresh chapter of her life. It was time to get to work.

∞

Life suddenly became a whirlwind of activity. Rilee spent the next few days travelling into town and overseeing the set-up of her office. When she was at home she was busy sorting through a million different lists of things to do and trying to get some kind of system in place for her business.

She knew Dan was feeling a little put out by the end of the week; he'd been going to bed before her and she'd noticed that he'd stayed on his side of the bed, without throwing an arm across her and pulling her tightly against the front of his body as was their usual routine when they fell asleep at night. It had been weighing heavily on her mind. Tonight she'd decided she was not going to look at paperwork or go online to order supplies. She'd make sure she went home early so she could spend some time with her husband.

She looked up as the front door of her clinic opened and the man himself stepped inside. 'Hey there, stranger,' she said, smiling as she stepped into his embrace. 'What are you doing in town?'

'Had to come in and grab a part for the tractor. Figured this might be the only chance I get to see you today.'

Rilee pulled back slightly to look up into his face. 'Tell me you are not pouting, Dan Kincaid,' she said.

Dan rolled his eyes before giving her a sheepish grin. 'Can't a fella miss his wife?'

'Absolutely,' she said, kissing his chin. 'I'm sorry I've been so busy. I promise, today I'll finish up early.'

'I know you're excited,' he said with a sigh, 'I guess I have been acting like a—'

'Spoilt brat?'

'Jealous husband,' he finished with a cringe.

'Jealous?'

Dan took her hands in his and looked down at them. 'I have to admit something and I don't want you to get angry,' he warned. 'I've liked that you had nothing else to keep you busy since we moved home. I love walking in the house at night and you're there. I like that we spend so much time together. I didn't realise how much I took you being there for granted. I've really missed you this week.'

She couldn't be annoyed when the man looked so dejected. He really did look cute when he pouted, not that she'd ever admit that out loud. 'I love that we've spent so much time together too, but it's time I found my own thing to do. I need this, Dan. This is where I know what I'm doing. This is where I don't feel like a complete idiot all the time.'

'You're no idiot. You're smarter than just about all of us put together,' he said with a rueful half-smile, 'but I get what you're saying. I'm just going to miss the way it's been, I guess.'

'It'll be different,' she agreed, 'but not every couple get to spend the amount of time together that we have. Sooner or later the honeymoon had to end. We'll just *both* go to work now,' she said gently. 'But the best thing about having my own practice is that I can choose the hours.'

'So now you know you've turned me into a sook and I'm completely under the thumb, is there anything you need doing around here?' he asked, looking around at the bare walls.

'Well, you could come and take a look at this back room,' she said, locking the front door and leading the way to the rear of the building.

'What's wrong with it?' he asked, looking around the room.

'It needs a little something.'

'Like what? Furniture?' He looked confused as she walked across and slid up onto the desk, crossing her legs and leaning forward to wave him closer with her finger.

'I'm pretty sure we can work with what we've got,' she said, uncrossing her legs and slowly pulling her skirt higher up her thighs.

His confusion was quickly replaced by a very different expression, not unlike a wolf about to devour its prey. 'I think I can help you out.'

He nudged her legs apart and moved between them, pushing her back until she was resting her weight against her elbows.

Rilee watched him with undisguised longing. She could never get enough of this man. She loved everything about him: his large, callused hands, and the gentle way they could stroke a newborn calf or send goosebumps along her flesh when he trailed his fingers across her skin as he was doing now. She loved his eyes, the way long hours out in the sun had given him laugh lines that crinkled when he smiled. He had the kindest eyes she'd ever seen, even when they were alight with fiery need like they were at the moment. And she loved his voice, that deep rumble which sent shivers of longing through her when he whispered things against her ear that made her face burn and her body ache. She loved . . . *him*.

He didn't waste time with clothing, his lazy seduction quickly melting into carnal lust as he pushed her skirt up around her waist. He let out a whispered curse that somehow managed to sound like a prayer before he moved back just enough to unbuckle his jeans. This was no slow, gentle Sunday morning loving; they were making up for lost time.

Rilee gasped as he pushed into her, and Dan stilled, his face a mask of restraint as he hovered above her. 'Don't stop,' Rilee moaned and instantly she saw relief flood his features. This was a new experience for them. Usually their lovemaking was gentle and slow, but this was different.

There was an urgency to it which set something free inside Rilee she hadn't even realised had been trapped.

She saw the surprise briefly light up Dan's eyes when she told him rather explicitly what she wanted him to do, but he wasted no time following her instructions. The table beneath them banged against the back wall, and the echo of their mutual groans and sighs filled the room.

Dan collapsed against her, breathing heavily, and slowly the world around them came back into focus.

'I think I'll drop in here more often through the day,' Dan said, easing his weight off her.

'I can't guarantee you'll get that kind of reception every time.'

'Then I better make an appointment.'

'What kind of establishment do you think I'm running here?' she asked haughtily.

'A very exclusive one, I hope,' he said, leaning over to kiss her tenderly.

'Your mother would have me burnt at the stake. I'm pretty sure she thinks I'm the witch who stole her son.'

'She'll come around eventually,' he said, slowly getting to his feet and doing up his jeans.

'I have a shower out the back. You wanna test it out?' she asked, wiggling her eyebrows.

'It's tempting,' he said, kissing her, 'but Dad's probably already sent out a search party. He'll be waiting for the tractor part I was supposed to be bringing back.'

'Spoilsport.'

'You can help me out in the shower tonight, at home.'

'Fine,' she pouted, but kissed him goodbye as he left the office. After the unexpected visit, the rest of the day went by in a satisfied daze. Late afternoon she locked up the clinic and headed for the grocery store on her way home.

❧

Rilee pushed the shopping trolley along the aisles, dropping in the items she needed for tonight's dinner. As she picked up a packet of pasta from the shelf she heard two women talking in the next aisle.

'I heard she reads those tarot cards. Maybe I should get one done.'

The other woman let out a dismissive grunt. 'Load of rubbish if you ask me.'

'Well, I don't know, she's married into the Kincaids, so she must have something going for her.'

'Way I heard it she was a big surprise to Ellen and Jacob. Dan just walked in and announced they were married. All a bit hurried, if you get what I mean.'

Rilee's mouth gaped as she listened to the two women gossip about her.

'You think she's knocked up?'

'I don't know, but apparently it was all very unexpected. Besides, why else would he suddenly turn up with a wife when he had one already picked out for him?'

'Getting some girl pregnant isn't that big a deal these days.' The other woman sounded doubtful and Rilee felt marginally better that not everyone was small-minded enough to jump to that conclusion. 'Then again, we are talking about Kincaids. They're hardly likely to allow a grandkid of theirs go without their name, are they?'

'What? A Kincaid with human feelings like the rest of us?' the woman said sarcastically, and Rilee listened as the two women chuckled.

She wasn't sure if she should be insulted on behalf of her husband's family or relieved that she wasn't the only one who thought Ellen could be a pretentious pain in the neck. But tarot cards? Really?

She finished her shopping and paid for her purchases. Her earlier buoyant mood had dimmed by the time she arrived home, but she forced the overheard conversation from her mind as she carried the shopping inside and began preparing a special meal for her husband. She had a lot to be grateful for, but that old familiar loneliness hovered in the background. All she wanted was to fit in here and yet the divide between her and the town seemed to be wider than ever.

Twenty-five

Rilee looked up at the knock on the front door and waved as Shae poked her head inside. She mouthed a hello as she listened to the customer service operator on the other end of the line.

'This is the third time I've called about this order,' Rilee said. 'I finally received the delivery yesterday, but there are items missing. No, I don't want to hold—' Rilee groaned in frustration and Shae held up a mug to ask if she wanted coffee.

'Yes, please,' she said wearily.

'Not going well?'

'Nothing is going right with this order. I open tomorrow and I still don't have most of the stock I've ordered.'

'Just relax. I'm sure you can manage for a few days before you need the stuff that hasn't turned up.'

'That's what Dan said this morning. But it's not the point. It doesn't look very professional if I'm a naturopath who can't prescribe anything.'

'Maybe you should prescribe yourself something to chill out,' she said, grinning as she worked the coffee machine.

'I'm already taking the maximum dose.'

'I won't come to you for stress relief then.'

Rilee let out a long breath and realised her friend was right. She was supposed to be the damn professional here and she was allowing the situation to get on top of her.

The operator came back on the line and Rilee switched her attention back to the conversation, listing the items she hadn't received before being reassured they were coming in a separate package and should be there by tomorrow.

'See? It's all going to work out. Just breathe.'

'Yes, doctor,' she said, accepting the fragrant cup of coffee with a moan of gratitude.

'Aren't you supposed to drink green tea or something healthy?'

'Probably. But I prefer this. And if you ever tell anyone, I'll have to kill you.'

'Your secret is safe with me,' Shae vowed.

'Shae, have you been hearing any gossip about me lately?'

Shae lifted an eyebrow. 'What do you mean?'

Rilee toyed with a pen on her desk, avoiding her friend's eyes. 'I overheard two women in the supermarket and they were speculating about why Dan married me.'

'The general consensus is that he's knocked you up.'

Rilee sent her friend a wry glance. 'So I heard.'

Shae shrugged. 'If it's any comfort, the pregnancy rumours are old news. The fact you think living in Pallaburra is the pits, and you think kids should leave town as soon as possible so they don't get stuck here like their parents,' Shae said, 'that seems to be getting far more mileage at the moment.'

Rilee groaned and hung her head. The bloody ladies' church committee meeting. She knew there would be some kind of fallout from it.

'It'll blow over,' Shae told her calmly.

'But it probably hasn't done my business any favours, has it?' Rilee said, slumping back in her chair.

Shae didn't answer straight away and Rilee felt what little hope remained plummet.

'Look, your being a naturopath was always going to be hard enough for this place to get used to,' Shae started. 'Being a newcomer is another roadblock . . . but managing to offend half the town is probably not the best way to generate new clients.'

'I didn't mean to insult them. God, Shae! It wasn't even like that,' she said, tipping her head back to stare at the ceiling. 'I just wanted to make a difference to some of these kids' lives.'

'It *will* blow over,' Shae said, leaning across and gently placing her hand on top of Rilee's.

Rilee managed a weak smile at her friend's support. She hoped Shae was right. This business was a dream she'd been fostering for a long time now. Had she managed to destroy her chance before she'd even started?

⁓

Rilee unlocked the front door the next morning and let out a long, slow breath. Today was the official opening of her very own clinic. A bubble containing equal measures of pride and anxiety floated inside her chest. She took a photo of the front door. The rustic timber of the original door softened the sparkling glass behind which she'd paced the sign: Rilee Kincaid MHSc (Herbal Med), BEd, ND, AdvDipHom.

There were a lot of initials after that name, and her shoulders straightened a little more as she thought of the years of studying and hard work she'd put in to achieve them. 'You can do this,' she whispered.

Rilee spent the first hour sitting behind the front counter, trying to keep occupied as she waited for a potential client, but so far not one person had come by. Even the phone had remained stubbornly silent. She'd called the number from her mobile to double check it was working and it rang through.

Dan had messaged her to ask how it was going and when she'd told him it was quiet, he'd suggested he come in and see if she had any jobs for him to do. She'd declined his offer, but now, more than two hours later, she was almost wishing she hadn't. At least that would have meant she'd done something productive all day—even if it had only been cavorting with her husband.

The phone finally rang and Rilee almost fell off her seat in her eagerness to answer. 'Natural Healing Centre, this is Rilee.'

'Hello, darling. Just calling you to say happy first day of business. How's it going?'

'Oh. Mum. Hi.' She strove to hide her disappointment. 'Yeah, it's going really well.'

'You've been busy? That's fantastic.'

Rilee didn't have the heart to correct her, then felt even worse as her mother continued. 'I am so proud of you, sweetheart. You've worked so hard. Your father and I are just the proudest parents you could ever imagine. We love you, Apple Blossom.'

Rilee silently groaned her dismay, both over the use of the blessing name her parents had given her in lieu of a traditional christening and at the slight quiver of emotion she detected in her mother's voice. She knew she'd given them many disappointments over the years. Through it all, they'd never once wavered in their love or support, even when she'd turned her back on them. When she'd come home with her tail between her legs, her life in tatters, her parents had been there with opened arms and nothing but love to help her heal.

She could not disappoint them again. She wouldn't. This business was going to be a success. Besides, it was only the first day. Surely tomorrow things would pick up.

∽

They didn't. Rilee spent another long day hovering by the phone. She did have people through her door . . . two to be exact. The first woman she suspected was the one she'd overheard gossiping in the supermarket, because she asked for a tarot reading and left more than a little disappointed when Rilee told her she didn't read cards. The second was a man . . . a delivery man, who was asking for directions.

It was getting harder to remain positive, despite reminding herself that new businesses were always slow to start out. But deep down she knew this was because she had stood up and told a few home truths about the town at that stupid meeting, and now she was paying the price. Why hadn't she just let Ellen have her way? Because she'd stupidly thought she could make a difference. *And look where that got you.*

She was out the back refolding the towels for the fifth time that day when she heard the front door open. Bowing her head, she whispered a fervent prayer that may or may not have involved the selling of her soul, then plastered a professional smile on her face before walking out to greet the arrival.

Shae stood at the front counter and Rilee felt her face begin to fall. She really wasn't sure she could keep this up for much longer.

'Hello, I heard you're a naturopath?'

Rilee sighed. 'You wouldn't have heard it from around here. No one apparently knows what a naturopath is, exactly.'

Shae sent her a sympathetic smile. 'Then maybe you need to do something about that. We need to get some information out there.'

'I've been thinking about that. I started working on a flyer, listing the most common ailments and how I can help treat them . . . Can you take a look and see what you think?' She opened a file on her computer and turned the screen around so Shae could read it.

'That's great. You've already worked out your demographic. You need to be to the point. Too scientific and you risk losing their trust.'

'Usually the more scientific the more trustworthy.'

'Maybe in other places, but around here we're limited in the number of different therapies available. Change still comes slowly. But I think you're on the right track. You just need to win over a few of the toughest critics and you'll be set.'

'What do you suggest I do—force them to come to a consultation?'

'Not force. But maybe offer a free mini consultation first.'

Rilee considered her friend's advice and nodded slowly. 'I think you're right.' Enthusiasm bubbled back up inside her once more at the new plan.

'But that's not why I came here,' Shae said, making Rilee glance up again. 'I'm actually here as a patient.'

'Shae, you don't have to do this. Seriously.'

'I am serious. I'm not here to help you out. I've actually been working up the courage to ask you for help ever since we met.'

The note of uncertainty was something Rilee hadn't heard from her friend before. 'Why would you be nervous?'

'Because . . .' Shae started then swallowed, lowering her gaze to the floor. 'I'm afraid.'

Rilee came around the desk and touched her arm. 'Why?'

She looked up and the hopelessness Rilee saw there made her catch her breath. 'Because if you can't help me, I'll be forced to give up the one thing I've always wanted.'

'What's that?'

'A baby, Rilee. I want a baby.'

She'd figured from their conversations that she and Mark had been trying for a baby, but she hadn't suspected there were any problems.

'We've been trying to have a baby for the last two years. It took forever to conceive, but I miscarried after only a few weeks, and since then we've kept trying but we've had no luck.'

'How far along were you?'

'About twelve weeks.'

Rilee gave Shae's hand a sympathetic squeeze. The loss of a baby, no matter how far into a pregnancy, was always devastating.

Rilee reached down behind the counter and took out a clipboard, then turned back to Shae. 'Come with me into the consulting room,' she said with a gentle smile. 'Let's see what we can do.'

An hour later Shae sat back in her chair. 'Wow, that was really intensive.'

'Sorry about all the questions, but I need to know everything before I can work out a treatment protocol for you.'

'So what do you think?'

'Well, Mark's low fertility would explain the length of time it took before you were able to conceive, but then if your oestrogen and progesterone levels are out, it would make falling pregnant in the first place difficult and it would be almost impossible to hold the embryo once you did conceive.'

'So what do we do now?'

'First thing we need to do is chart your cycle so I can get a clearer picture of what we're dealing with, and then we'll do a blood test and check your oestrogen and progesterone levels. I'm fairly confident it's low progesterone that's the problem.' She jotted down some notes on the file quickly before looking up to give Shae a confident smile. 'In the meantime, I can give you something that might help Mark and I'd also like to work on your nervous system. Stress can play havoc with hormones and we need to get that under control first.'

'And you think after all that . . . I'll be able to have a baby?'

Rilee saw the guarded look in her friend's eyes. She didn't want to give false hope, that would be too cruel, but she truly believed there was a good chance she could help. 'I wish I could give you a guarantee, but I can't.' She saw a look of reluctant acceptance cross Shae's face and hurried to add, 'It's not to say I don't believe you will. I've seen it help people before, but you know as well as I do that sometimes life doesn't always go according to plan. But if you'll trust me, I promise I won't give up until we've exhausted every possible treatment.'

Shae gave a shaky sigh that was filled with relief. 'Okay.'

Long after Shae had left the surgery, Rilee was buried in research as she worked on the treatment protocol and she hardly noticed that no one else came into the office for the rest of the day. It didn't matter so much when she had at least one patient in need of her help. This was the reward she'd been working towards. Her first patient in her very own practice. Someone she could help—really help. This was what all those long years of study had been for. This was what she was born to do. Her confidence levels lifted higher than they'd been in a very long time and it felt good.

Finally, things were back on track.

Twenty-six

The sound of the door opening alerted Rilee to a visitor and she crossed her fingers that it was a customer. As she walked out to the front of the clinic she stopped short. 'Oh. Hi,' she said, trying not to sound as stunned as she felt.

Talissa dug her hands into the front pockets of her jeans and pulled out two crumpled ten-dollar notes before taking a step closer and thrusting them out at Rilee. 'I haven't forgotten about payin' you back. This is all I got so far. I'll get the rest later this week.'

'Oh.' Rilee shook herself mentally before reaching for the money. 'Are you sure? I don't mind if you want to keep this and use it for more important things.' *Like food for your child,* she added silently, sending a glance at the baby kicking in the pram.

'We're good.'

'Well, okay then,' said Rilee, realising it was obviously important to Talissa's pride that she pay back her debt.

'I forgot to ask before, what's bub's name?'

There was a definite hesitation this time and a frown. 'Khaleesi.'

Rilee couldn't help the flicker of surprise and the girl instantly hunched her shoulders. 'So you're a *Game of Thrones* fan then?'

Talissa tilted her head slightly and some of the tension left her body. 'Yeah.'

'Me too. I have the books if you ever want to read them,' Rilee said casually.

'Why would you want to read books when you can watch it on DVD?'

'I love the DVDs too, but the books are so much better.' At the girl's doubtful look Rilee chuckled. 'Honest. When you read the books you get more of the story and you get to know the characters and what they're thinking.'

'I never liked reading much . . . at school.'

'It's not too late to try it and see if you like it now.'

'I don't get much time to read. Not with a baby to look after,' she said, checking on the child quickly.

'I noticed you bottle-feed her. You didn't like breast-feeding?' Rilee couldn't help thinking how much healthier and cheaper it would have been for her to have breastfed instead of buying all that expensive formula.

'Nah. It was too hard.'

'You didn't get any help at the hospital?'

Talissa shrugged and turned away to look around the room curiously. 'I wasn't there long.'

'Does the baby nurse clinic come here?'

'Nah. You gotta go to Narrabri for that. I went the first time, but I haven't been back.'

This news made Rilee uneasy. Why wouldn't they have a nurse come out to the women here in Pallaburra? It was bad enough that any new mum had to drive all that way with a newborn for weekly check-ups, but for these kids too young to drive? How were they supposed to get regular baby checks? Not to mention the normal antenatal care that was important to help with breastfeeding education and the mother's health.

'I hate going to that place anyway. All the other older women sit there and look down their noses at me and Khaleesi, just cause I'm younger than them.'

She'd seen it around town, the subtle change in expression as a young mother walked past a group of older women, the knowing glances they'd silently swap.

'I don't give a toss what other people think of me, but I just wish it was fair, you know? No one looks at teenage dads like that, cause they're hardly ever around anyway.'

'What about Khaleesi's dad? Is he around?'

Talissa turned away with a brief shrug of one shoulder. 'Nah. He dumped me when I told him I was pregnant. He told me to get rid of it. But that's when I knew I was gonna keep it,' she said, looking up at Rilee with a determined glint. 'I know what it feels like not to be wanted by anyone. I wasn't going to do that to my baby.'

Rilee felt her throat thicken with emotion at the quiet yet strong words the young girl spoke. 'I heard the cashier mention your mum the other day. Does she help you out?'

'Sometimes,' she said, crossing to the desk and picking up the small brown bottles of premixed remedies Rilee had on display.

'How old are you, Talissa?'

'Fifteen,' she said calmly.

'Do you have any plans to go back to school?'

'No. What's the point?'

'You don't want to study and get a good job?'

'Study what? In case you haven't noticed, there's not that many *good* jobs in Pallaburra.'

'You wouldn't have to get a job here. You could get a job somewhere else. As for studying, there's a whole range of things you could study if you finished school.'

Talissa put the bottle she'd been holding down and gave Rilee an odd look. 'How would I do that with a baby?'

'It wouldn't be easy,' Rilee conceded, 'but I'm sure there would be a way to do it.'

'Maybe for someone like you.'

'That's not true. If you want something bad enough there's always a way to make it happen.'

'If you have money.'

'Not everyone starts out with money, Talissa. I put myself through my naturopathy degree by working in a bar.'

'Yeah, but you didn't have a kid.'

True. And therein lay the problem. 'Would your mum help you out with taking care of the baby?'

'Maybe. But I wouldn't ask. Khaleesi is my responsibility. Look, thanks for the other day, but none of this is any of your business.'

'I'm sorry. I ask too many questions,' Rilee said with a slight wince. 'Force of habit. That's how I get to the bottom of people's health problems, but sometimes I forget that I do it.'

'Yeah. I'll get the rest of the money to you when I can.' She pushed the pram towards the door and Rilee crossed the room to hold it open for her.

'It was good to see you, Talissa.'

The young girl looked at her briefly, but didn't comment.

Rilee sighed as she turned away from the door, feeling a mixture of frustration and helplessness. As a healer she had a natural desire to fix people, but in this case it wasn't a matter of treating them with a remedy, it was knowing that in order to 'fix' them she'd have to change their whole environment. She wasn't naive enough to believe she could wave a magic wand and change things for Talissa, but putting a face to the problem in this town certainly made it far more personal. Changes had to happen or there would be more Talissas left to believe Pallaburra and fatherless children were the only future they could hope for.

Twenty-seven

Rilee pushed open the café door and prepared to summon a smile for the two women working behind the counter. It was slow progress but she was slowing chipping away at Pru and Shaz's stand-offish ways.

At first she'd brushed off the idea that the prejudice she sensed from some locals had anything to do with her new surname. It had seemed silly to her that in this day and age there could still be a class division in a town, but the matter of the party invitations had been disturbing proof that this division was firmly in place in Pallaburra. Anyone with links to the Kincaids was friendly enough towards her; it was the people who didn't run in the same circles that she was finding hard to win over.

'Morning, Pru,' she said as she reached the counter and the middle-aged woman looked up.

'Havin' your usual today, pet?' she asked as she finished wrapping a sandwich she'd been making and placed it in the front of the glass counter.

'Yes, please.' Surely it had to be a good sign that they knew her usual, she thought. While she had a perfectly acceptable coffee machine in her office, she had to give the café credit—they made coffee so much better than she did. But aside from that, she couldn't ignore the tiny part of her that refused to give up on trying to win over these women. She'd never felt this need to have people like her before. Maybe it was pride, maybe it was just pure stubbornness, she wasn't sure, all she knew was she was determined to win Pru and Shaz over . . . even if that meant buying coffee here every day until it happened.

The door to the kitchen swung open and Shaz came out carrying a divine-smelling parcel of hot chips. Her chubby face would be pretty if only she'd smile a little more often, Rilee thought, not for the first time. Gloom seemed to hang about the young woman like a rain cloud, making her a difficult person to warm to, but Rilee wasn't giving up.

'Heard you're chummy with Talissa Barnett,' Shaz said after she'd deposited the chips into the heated food warmer awaiting collection.

Rilee wasn't sure what direction this conversation was headed, but it never ceased to amaze her how eyes were everywhere, watching everything. 'As chummy as you can get with anyone around here.'

'Those Barnetts are bad news,' Shaz continued, seemingly oblivious to Rilee's light sarcasm.

'Old Lyle Barnett was a nasty piece of work,' Pru added with a shake of her head.

'Is that Talissa's father?'

'Grandfather. He's dead now. Died a few years back,' Pru said with a dismissive wave of her hand. 'But he made old Dotty and Cheryl's life a misery.' At Rilee's confused look, she clarified patiently, 'Talissa's grandmother and mother.'

'Oh.'

'No surprise about how Talissa turned out. Poor kid had no chance being born into that family.'

'Well, it's not the end of the world just because she had a baby. She can still make something of her life.'

'Yeah, right,' Shaz scoffed.

'She can. In fact, I'm looking into some study options to show her next time I see her.'

'Waste of time,' Pru said, shaking her head.

'Not if she wants it. Not if she has enough people around her to give encouragement.'

'I heard you were on a bit of a campaign to save the town,' Pru said, eyeing her curiously.

'I'm not trying to save anything. I just think there needs to be more incentives for kids around here to do something with their future.'

'Too late once you're knocked up,' Shaz shrugged.

'Which is why we need to work on getting better access to things like contraception to stop it happening. I was thinking about a public forum, inviting local community leaders together to get some kind of action happening.'

'You won't get any help from anyone around here. They're all too busy being high and mighty to bother working out how to teach kids about safe sex.'

Rilee frowned. 'What do you mean?'

'Your so-called community leaders are people like old Errol Stetton and they're all tied up in the church. You won't get much cooperation out of that lot.'

'But Errol Stetton is a pharmacist. It's part of his *job* to provide health care to his community.'

'As long as it doesn't interfere with his own personal beliefs. Which kids having sex does.'

'He's always been a judgemental old bastard,' Shaz interrupted. 'I had a friend who went in to ask for that morning-after pill you can get now, and he yelled at her in front of other customers, completely humiliated her. Her parents found out she was pregnant before she'd even got home that afternoon.'

Rilee stared at Shaz in open-mouthed disbelief. 'That's so . . .' There were no words for how outrageously inappropriate that was. Not to mention the concern that this girl was under the misconception that the morning-after pill would have worked if she'd already been pregnant. One of the first rules of any health profession was to respect a patient's privacy. How dare Errol Stetton publicly humiliate someone asking for his help?

Shaz gave an offhand shrug. 'That's the way it is.

Everyone knows not to go to Stetton's. So they either have the baby or take matters into their own hands.'

'You're not saying girls are aborting their babies . . . without a doctor?'

'Some of them get desperate enough to try stupid things they hear about. There was a young girl a while back who heard of kids taking these hormone drugs used to abort pregnancies in livestock. She got hold of something similar and almost killed herself in the process.'

Rilee stared at the women, feeling sick to the stomach. 'Is this true?' she demanded, turning to Pru for confirmation.

'From what I've heard,' she agreed, placing her coffee on the top of the counter.

Rilee couldn't believe what she was hearing. She knew that Errol Stetton's pharmacy presented a barrier to young kids seeking help, but for a pharmacist to abuse a young girl who approached him for a legitimate medication was beyond comprehension. It was a woman's right to obtain the morning-after pill if she had concerns that there was a risk of ineffective or no contraception used and did not want to risk an unwanted pregnancy. Originally it had only been obtainable through a doctor's prescription, but once it had become obvious that those most at risk—namely young teenage girls—weren't accessing the medication, it had been made available without prescription through a pharmacy.

How dare this man deny a woman's right to have access to something that could prevent so many unwanted pregnancies. This wasn't the nineteen fifties for goodness sake!

'Three-fifty, love,' Pru said, eyeing her curiously, and Rilee realised she was still in a state of shocked disbelief.

'Sorry.' She dug through her purse and handed over the correct change. 'Thank you.'

Rilee turned away and headed outside, filled with a whirl of emotions. Anger was the most vocal, followed swiftly by a desire for retribution and a strong urge to do some kind of physical harm, but she managed to get that under control as she opened the door to the pharmacy.

'Why, hello, dear, how can I—' Betty started but Rilee cut her off sharply.

'I'd like to speak with Errol, please.'

'I'm afraid he's busy at the moment, perhaps—'

'I'd like to speak to him right *now*,' Rilee insisted, holding the woman's nervous gaze.

'I'll just . . .' Her hand fluttered to her throat as she glanced over her shoulder at the rear of the store. 'See if he . . .' She let the sentence fall away when Rilee lifted an eyebrow at her in silent challenge.

As a rule, Rilee wasn't a confrontational person, but at the moment she was too outraged by what she'd just learned to settle for tiptoeing around.

She heard the murmur of voices from the back in the preparation area, one low and faint, the other loud and abrupt, before Betty reappeared, stepping behind the counter and busily rearranging pamphlets on the counter.

Moments later Errol strode through the doorway, his owlish eyes, magnified behind his thick glasses, fixed upon her in a stern manner. 'Mrs Kincaid. What can I do for you?'

'I'd like to clarify something with you. The morning-after pill,' she said, getting straight to the point, 'do you supply it to your customers?'

Rilee watched as his eyebrows dipped low towards the bridge of his nose and his thin lips tightened. 'No, I do not,' he stated emphatically, and from the corner of her eye Rilee noticed Betty had ceased her rearranging and was staring across at them with her mouth gaping.

'And why not?'

Errol drew back his head and straightened his bony frame to peer down at her. 'Because I find it immoral and offensive.'

'You're responsible for this community's wellbeing,' Rilee told him, her voice rising despite her best intentions to remain calm. 'You're supposed to use medication to *help* them.'

'And I do so. But I am completely justified in refusing to prescribe anything that goes against my moral judgement.'

'Withholding any kind of medication that can treat a patient is not only unprofessional, it's negligent,' Rilee said, struggling to regain control of her temper.

'Unprofessional? Negligent?' he spluttered, his usually pale face turning bright red. 'How dare you!'

'How dare *you*!' Rilee snapped back. 'Because of your so-called morals, you've condemned God only knows how many young women to unwanted pregnancies, ruining any hopes they may have had for their future.'

'They made the choice to partake in unprotected sex, therefore they must take responsibility for their actions. I can hardly be blamed for the choices they made.'

'This is unbelievable,' Rilee said.

'And you're wasting my time,' he snapped, turning his back on her as he stormed back to his work area.

'I think you should go now,' Betty said from behind the counter, twin red spots marking each of her plump cheeks as she glared at Rilee. 'And don't think I won't be mentioning this to Ellen.'

Rilee suppressed the urge to stick her tongue out at the annoying woman and walked out of the shop. Her hands shook as she unlocked the door of her clinic and put the coffee cup down on her desk.

If kids couldn't or wouldn't use contraception, for whatever reason, and the only other avenue for protecting themselves from pregnancy was denied them, no wonder the rate of teenage pregnancy in this place was so high. Everything was stacked against them. The remoteness of the town, and the fact it had no medical practitioner of its own, reduced access to appropriate contraception and sexual health education, and now this. Moral objections? That was this idiot's reason for denying medication, Rilee fumed. How dare he!

She'd been thwarted by Ellen's influence on this last time, after the principal had politely but firmly ended any hope of a school-based program, but not this time. She'd bypass local organisations and look further afield for help. She wasn't sure where yet, but the time had come to take action.

Twenty-eight

Rilee spent the rest of the day on the phone and online, desperate to find someone who could help her. During her research she came across a program located in Tamworth. It was a service designed to provide assistance to young people and their families in relation to mental and physical health, work and study support, and alcohol and other drug use. Rilee reached for the phone and called the number on their web page, eager to speak to someone who might be able to give her some advice.

An hour later she hung up the phone and looked at the notes she'd been taking while she spoke to Teal, a case-worker at the centre, ideas flying about in her head at the possibilities available for Pallaburra.

The service had had Pallaburra in its sights for a while, as well as several other outlying towns with similar issues, and Rilee was encouraged that while it felt to her as though no one really cared about the youth out here, this service was at least aware of their situation. While the ball was not exactly rolling, she certainly had quite a few avenues to explore to initiate something and she was beyond excited by the prospect.

Rilee called Shae and told her about the encounter with Errol—she was rather surprised the news hadn't reach Thumb Creek yet—and the resulting call to the Tamworth youth program.

'Basically they're looking at setting up some kind of outreach community centre where a counsellor and doctor would be available once a fortnight for appointments. Kids would also have access to computers for online consultations and help. Shae, this is exactly what Pallaburra needs.'

'How come I've never heard of them before?' Shae said, sounding blown away by the news.

'They've only been set up in Tamworth for a few months.'

'So what's the next step? What are they planning to do?'

'At this stage not a great deal. Teal's taking it up with his area manager and having a meeting to see what resources they can offer us, but he did warn that it might take a while. There's a huge demand for their services.'

'I guess we're at the bottom of a long list of towns with the same problems,' Shae sighed. 'Still, at least this is something positive. Hey, while I've got you here,' Shae said, 'you're not the only one who's been busy. You are now on social media,' she announced proudly. 'I'm going to email through the links and give you the passwords so you can manage the pages.'

'Social media?' Rilee sighed. 'Really?'

'Yes, Miss Anti-Social Media. Now you're a business owner, you *need* to be out there on Facebook and Twitter. Trust me on this.'

'Why don't you keep the passwords and tweep or cheep or whatever for me?'

'That would be tweet, and actually that might not be such a bad idea for now,' Shae said dryly. 'But don't think you're getting out of it. Set aside a day next week so we can go through it together.'

'I can't wait,' Rilee replied and Shae scoffed at her distinct lack of sincerity.

The door opened a little while later and Rilee looked up and smiled as a somewhat frazzled-looking woman came into the surgery. Her frizzy red hair sprang from her head, clearly defying any efforts by brush or comb. She was dressed in a faded flannelette shirt and pair of old jeans that were tucked into large black gumboots.

Rilee greeted the woman, who stood on the other side of the counter eyeing her strangely. 'Is there something wrong?' Rilee asked, feeling suddenly self-conscious.

'It's just that you look so . . . normal.'

Rilee was too surprised to laugh, but after a moment managed to gather her composure and smile. 'What were you expecting?' Maybe it wasn't such a good idea to ask.

'I don't know . . . maybe a few warts and hairy armpits.'

Rilee did laugh then, although she wasn't altogether sure the woman was joking. 'Well, I'm sorry to disappoint.'

'Nah, it's a relief actually.'

'I'm Rilee. How can I help you today?'

'It's not actually me,' the woman hedged. 'It's Harry. He doesn't have much longer, you see.'

Rilee heard the woman's voice quiver slightly and nodded encouragingly for her to continue.

'It's just that . . . he's in so much pain. I know I should have helped him . . . you know . . . end it, everyone keeps telling me to, but I just can't bring myself to do it.'

Rilee stared at the woman and tried to keep the alarm from her face. Was she trying to ask for something that would help end a man's life?

'Then I heard about you and I thought, maybe as a last resort . . . maybe you had something that might help?'

Rilee brushed aside the *last resort* comment. She was used to people consulting her profession only after exhausting conventional medical avenues. It didn't really bother her; after all, natural medicine and modern western medicine were supposed to work hand in hand. It just frustrated her that sometimes people wasted so much time before they tried naturopathy. 'It would help if I knew what was wrong with Harry.'

'It's his lungs. He can't breathe.'

'I'd have to give Harry an examination before I could see if there's anything I can do. Do you think he'd come in?'

'Oh, I expect he'll be okay with you. He usually doesn't much like strangers, but he's that weak now, I'm sure he wouldn't bite.'

Rilee raised her eyebrows at that; maybe Harry was suffering from dementia and had bouts of violence. 'When do you think you could bring him in?'

'I'll go get him. He's just outside in the car,' the woman said, heading for the door.

Rilee would have preferred to get a bit more background information from his carer before she examined Harry if he was that near the end of his life; however, seeing as he was here now, she was just going to have to make the best of it.

'I'll give you a hand,' Rilee said, following quickly, unsure how the woman would handle a man that weak on her own. Rilee's mind was racing with possible scenarios as they headed towards an old Holden parked outside.

'I think I'll be able to carry him, I'll just need to swing him around from this side,' the woman was saying as she opened the rear of the station wagon.

Carry him? The woman looked as though she could handle a hard day on the farm, but carry a man?

'Maybe we should see if we can get a lend of a wheelchair first?' Rilee said and the woman gave her a doubtful look over her shoulder.

'I heard you lot were a bit out there but I really don't think that'll be necessary.'

'I don't think . . .' Rilee's words tapered off as the woman leaned into the back of the vehicle and then straightened, a large lump of fur in her arms.

'That's a dog,' Rilee gaped.

'Of course it's a flaming dog.'

'Harry's a dog,' Rilee groaned.

'And he's not getting any lighter. You want to show me where to put him?' the woman said briskly, jolting Rilee into action.

'In here,' she said, somewhat disconcerted, but the woman was about to drop the animal if she didn't put him down soon, so she led the way into the first consultation room and pointed to the examination table.

The great lump of fur blinked up at her through heavy, pain-ridden eyes and Rilee felt only a moment of hesitation before she gingerly approached the table. She could hear the raspy, heavy breathing of the animal and saw the struggle it took to pull in each breath.

'The vet said I should put him down . . . but I just can't do it. Not until I know I tried everything possible. Is there anything you can do?'

Rilee placed her stethoscope against the dog's chest and listened, hearing the crackle and rasp inside his lungs. This was one very sick old dog. She looked over and saw the woman's weathered hand stroking the animal's soft caramel fur. Her heart tugged at the look they shared— the dog's resigned but adoring, while the woman's was pained, desperate to help her beloved pet find comfort. While theoretically she could use her herbs on animals as well as humans, other than Red the rooster, she'd never actually done it before—and certainly never for anything this serious. She couldn't cure this dog, but she could maybe make him a little more comfortable for the time that he had left.

'Let me see what I can do.'

Twenty-nine

Rilee turned her face to accept a kiss from Dan as he walked into the kitchen. 'How was your day?'

'Flat out. How was yours?'

'Oh you know . . . the usual,' she said, shaking her head. 'Two cats, a dog and an enquiry about treating anxiety in a goldfish.'

Dan laughed but stopped when he caught her unamused glare. 'Oh come on, Ri. Animals need help too.'

'I know,' she groaned, 'and I know I should be happy that word seems to be spreading about the practice, but I'd like to treat *people* occasionally as well.'

'They'll come.'

She wasn't so sure. She'd had to explain that while she could treat certain ailments in pets, she was not a replacement for a veterinarian—the closest being over an hour and a half away. It had opened her mind, though, to the possibility of including animals in her practice in the future and she'd made enquiries into undertaking accreditation.

Dan sank down onto the lounge with a long sigh and Rilee crossed the room to stand behind him, placing her hands on his shoulders and gently kneading. Over the last few evenings they'd been working together preparing a business plan for his cattle venture. Rilee was impressed by the thought Dan had been giving the whole idea. This wasn't something he'd just thrown together in his head. He knew where he wanted to go and he knew how to get there. Rilee found the experience almost as exciting as he did. She loved that they were both bringing something to the table—while Dan had the knowledge and knew how to set up the day-to-day handling of the project, he was more than happy to hand the business planning over to Rilee. Despite the fact she was also running her own business, she was filled with optimism at the prospect of their joint venture.

She smiled as Dan let out a long, deep moan of approval and forced herself to ignore her immediate reaction to the sound. How long until this newlywed thing wore off? she wondered. She hoped it never did but was realistic enough to expect that eventually life and other distractions would get in the way of their, up to now, insatiable and spontaneous sex life.

'God that feels good,' Dan groaned, his eyes closed in a state of painful bliss.

'What have you been doing? Why are you so tight?' As her hands warmed up his tense muscles, she began to work deeper, trying to loosen some of the tension.

'I had to cover for Mark and ended up shovelling the whole load of fertiliser myself.'

'Why were you covering for Mark?'

'I dunno, he got called home for something urgent.'

Rilee stopped massaging and frowned. 'Is something wrong with Shae?'

Dan shook his head. 'He said everything was fine once he got back, but he's been going home for lunch a lot the last few days.'

Rilee slowly smiled and relaxed a little. 'Oh.'

Dan opened one eye and turned his head to glance at her. 'Oh?'

'Nothing,' she dismissed, returning to kneading his strong shoulder muscles once more.

'I know that nothing,' he said. 'What's going on?'

'I have no idea.' Well, none that she was at liberty to share with anyone other than Shae, given she was her practitioner. But she could take an educated guess that the horny goat weed supplement she'd sent home for Mark was doing the trick.

'Ri? Is there something going on I should know about?' Dan asked, turning to look at her.

Rilee required a distraction. 'I need you to get naked.' And that would do it, if the look on her husband's face was any indication. 'Those muscles need working and I can't do it out here. Spare room. Now,' she instructed.

'Only if you get naked too,' he said with a slow smile.

'I'm a trained professional. I'm not supposed to get naked.'

'You're not on the clock now,' he reminded her.

'Well, I guess that's true,' she said, pulling her T-shirt over her head and tossing it on the back of the lounge chair, before reaching behind her and unhooking her bra.

Oh well, there was always more than one way to relax tense muscles, she thought as Dan swooped her into his arms and carried her into their bedroom.

The phone rang as they lay together a little while later. 'Just let it ring, pretend we're not home,' Rilee said when Dan moved to get out of bed.

'Can't, it might be important,' he said with a grin as he disentangled Rilee's fingers from the sheet that covered them.

Rilee pouted as he stood up, but consoled herself by enjoying the view of her naked husband strolling through the house on his way out to answer the phone. Her smile soon melted when she heard him mutter a low curse.

'What?' she asked, disappointed when he didn't return to bed but started getting dressed instead.

'I forgot all about dinner tonight.'

'No,' Rilee said, glaring up at the ceiling.

'Come on, Ri. It's my fault. Mum sent me a message when I was on the way home but I got distracted when my wife lured me with the promise of a massage and forgot all about the fact we were supposed to be getting ready for dinner.'

'I'm tired, Dan. Why do you always say yes? Can't you just for once say no thanks when she invites us to dinner? Or at the very least ask me first before you accept?'

'I thought I was doing you a favour.'

'How do you figure that?'

'Well, since you've been busy all week with work and stuff, you'd leap at the chance not to have to cook dinner.'

'She's just . . . such hard work,' Rilee sighed.

'I know. But they're my parents, Ri. It's what we do.'

She knew she sounded petty and mean when she protested about accepting dinner invitations, but that was just it—a normal dinner invite was one thing, Ellen's invites were summonses. To anyone else, turning down dinner wouldn't be an issue. To Ellen it would be a personal insult, and it drove Rilee up the wall.

Rilee knew the moment they walked into the dining room that they were in the poop. Ellen and Jacob sat at the dining table, where they'd been waiting on Rilee and Dan, and one glance at Jacob's empty Scotch glass and Ellen's tight smile was enough to alert her that they were in for an even cooler evening than usual.

'Sorry we're late,' Rilee began.

'Yes, well . . . it's lucky it's a cold chicken salad then, isn't it,' Ellen answered curtly as she picked up her cloth napkin and gave it a crisp flick before placing it on her lap.

Jacob reached for the decanter and poured himself another Scotch.

Rilee raked her mind for something to break the tension in the room but she had a feeling, in Ellen's current mood, anything she said would only cause more irritation, and so she followed her mother-in-law's lead and busied herself with placing the napkin on her lap and making sure she had all the creases out of it.

Mrs Pike wheeled the little trolley in with their plates, and Rilee marvelled at how the older woman could go about her duties without a blink of an eye at the thick silence which hung in the room.

It was a relief to have the meal to focus on, and Rilee dug into her chicken salad with enthusiasm, anything to avoid the uncomfortable disapproval radiating from the woman across the table.

'I received a phone call earlier today from Betty Stetton,' Ellen threw in casually as she sliced through a portion of chicken on her plate. 'I believe you paid a visit to their store a few days ago, Rilee.'

The tender chicken, which had moments earlier almost melted in her mouth, instantly became dry and tasteless as she tried to swallow it quickly. 'Yes, I did.'

Beside her Dan looked up warily.

'Would you care to explain?'

Rilee set down her cutlery and rested her folded hands on the table, striving for calm. 'What exactly do I need to explain, Ellen?'

The older woman's eyes narrowed and her tone was sharp. 'The reason you felt a need to verbally abuse Errol Stetton in his store would be a good start.'

'I did not abuse him, I simply stated that he was being unprofessional.'

'You cannot go walking around town dishing out whatever opinions you think you're somehow entitled to.'

'I'm not entitled to an opinion? That's funny, everyone else around here seems to think they are.'

'These people are upstanding members of our community. They're also personal friends and fellow parishioners in our church. Do you have any idea how embarrassed I was to have to apologise to Betty today?'

'There was no need for you to apologise. It had nothing to do with you, Ellen. If she wanted to make such an issue out of it then she should have called *me*.'

'It has everything to do with me. Everything you do reflects upon this family. I've put up with the natural medicine thing, and all the whispers around town regarding that. I've embraced you as a member of our family.' She waved a hand blithely, 'I even threw you a party to acknowledge you as our daughter-in-law, and then you go and do something like this without even a shred of remorse.'

'Mum,' Dan tried to intervene but Rilee cut in.

'Are you serious? You think I should feel bad for calling out a supposed health professional for refusing care to vulnerable members of this community? I can't believe no one had the guts or sense to it before now.'

'Errol Stetton and his family have been pharmacists in this district for generations,' Ellen snapped.

'And unfortunately Errol Stetton seems to believe he's still living in a bygone era, and this town has been suffering because of it.'

Ellen wiped at the corner of her mouth delicately with her napkin. 'I've never had an issue with Stetton's pharmacy,' she said dismissively.

'And you're never likely to, as long as you and Errol continue to believe in the same things.'

'He's a chemist, not a doctor—I don't see what the big deal is,' Jacob put in from across the table, topping up his glass yet again.

'He's the only access to health care this town's got. He's deliberately withholding treatment based on his own personal beliefs.'

'Which he's entitled to do,' Ellen added.

'Except that he's playing God with young people's lives and taking none of the responsibility for his actions.'

'This is all because of that dreadful abortion pill.'

'It's not an abortion pill,' Rilee said patiently. 'It's taken to induce—'

'I don't wish to discuss all the details at the table, thank you very much. However, the fact still remains, these girls think they can just take care of any oversight on their behalf by taking a pill the next day. They're treating the whole creation of life and the sanctity that goes with that as though it's nothing more than a common cold or a headache—just take a pill and get rid of it.'

'I'm not going to argue the virtues of marriage and sex, but I am going to defend any woman's right to have access to contraception. Sex is not always consensual, Ellen. Does Errol Stetton even bother to think about this when he's humiliating young women who come to him for help? I doubt it, because clearly if she's had sex, then she needs to be punished for it! If you'll excuse me, I've lost my appetite.' Rilee pushed the chair away from the table and left the room.

She was just pulling on her pyjama top when she heard the screen door open and Dan's footsteps echoing up the hallway. Rilee looked over to find him leaning against the doorjamb watching her silently.

'I'm not apologising, Dan.'

'I didn't ask you to,' he said, shaking his head but still not moving.

'She enjoys playing these power games, you know,' Rilee said as she dragged the brush through her hair in quick, rough strokes.

'Rilee,' he sighed.

'Don't say it, Dan,' she said, turning on him swiftly. 'I swear to God, if you say it's just the way she is One. More. Time. I'm going to lose it.'

She watched as Dan pushed away from the door and came to a stop before her. 'I wasn't going to say that.'

'What were you going to say? Because I noticed you didn't really *say* anything back there.'

'Like I could have gotten in a word edgeways if I wanted to.'

'I'm sick and tired of being spoken to like I'm a child.'

'Then stop acting like one,' Dan said, raising his voice, surprising Rilee into silence. 'You reckon you're sick and tired? How do you think I feel when I'm stuck in the middle of you two? I have Mum calling me while I'm trying to work, and you when I get home, both complaining about what the other one did. I've just about had a gutful, Ri.'

Dan had never raised his voice to her before and it took a moment to get her head around the surprise. 'Well, I wasn't the one who set up an ambush disguised as a dinner invitation,' she said bluntly, before walking into the bathroom and slamming the door behind her.

Rilee glared at the mirror, too furious to do more than replay the evening's dinner over in her mind. How. Dare. She. Rilee noticed the twin spots of colour in her cheeks and turned on the cold water with a vicious twist, splashing her face and trying to wash away the humiliation of being lectured like a disobedient child at the dinner table.

Thirty

Rilee was too restless to sleep, but she knew Dan needed as much shut-eye as he could get and carefully eased out of bed, pulling on a T-shirt and a pair of tracksuit pants.

She hated going to bed angry. Not that she was angry at Dan, exactly. More that his mother had ruined what had started out as a perfect evening. She was a little miffed that Dan couldn't see that by not standing up to Ellen he was enabling her to continue with her demanding tirades.

She stood at the kitchen sink and filled the kettle. As she did so, she looked out the window and her attention was caught by a light on up at the main house. She turned off the tap and hesitated for a moment before replacing the kettle and heading out the back for a pair of shoes.

The dogs over in the kennels paced up and down in their enclosures, excited by movement, but didn't bark. She ignored them, moving through the garden gate and around the side of the house towards the dim light in the window, shining out from the office. No one worked at this hour of the night. What if something was wrong?

She was glad she wasn't any shorter; as it was, she was only just able to catch a glimpse in the window. Jacob sat leaning forward in his chair, arms braced along his thighs as he stared at a photo frame he held in his hands.

It was rare to catch this man looking so vulnerable and Rilee felt a surge of unexpected protectiveness swell up inside her. He was a cranky old coot, but Rilee suspected it was a form of self-protection.

She let herself in the back door, which was never locked, and made her way to the office. Rilee didn't bother knocking—she didn't want to wake anyone else and eased the door open a fraction to slip inside. Jacob was so lost in his thoughts he didn't even glance up.

She walked softly and the movement caught his eye, making him gasp and then let out a low string of expletives.

Rilee pretended not to hear them, her gaze focused on the frame in his hands. It was a photo of Ellen and himself on their wedding day.

'What the hell are you doing in here?' he demanded harshly, slipping the photo frame back into the drawer of the desk.

'I saw the light on,' she shrugged. 'Is everything all right?'

'Course it is. Can't a man have a moment's peace without you buttin' in all the damn time?'

'Do you really want to live like this?' she asked quietly when he glared at her.

'Like what?'

'Like this,' she waved a hand at him. 'You're miserable. Ellen's miserable. I know you love her, I can tell, and yet you've let pride and embarrassment push between you.'

'You don't know anything,' he said, although some of the fight seemed to have gone out of him. He sounded sad and defeated.

'I know two unhappy people when I see them. I know that Ellen is just as lonely as you.'

'I should never have married her.' The admission came out of the silence which followed, and surprised Rilee.

'Why would you say that?'

'She didn't belong out here. She never wanted to leave the city.'

'She wouldn't have stayed all these years if she didn't want to.'

'She's got a bigger stubborn streak than even I have, in case you haven't noticed,' he scoffed. 'She couldn't leave and admit to her family she was wrong and they were right. They never liked me—thought their precious daughter deserved more than a farmer. Didn't matter to them how hard I worked, or how far back the Kincaid family name went out here. Theirs went further.'

'She must have loved you very much to go against her family's wishes in the first place,' Rilee ventured gently.

❦

Things had been crazy busy, between running the clinic and implementing the first stage of Operation Bazadais. True to her word, Rilee had involved herself in every step of the process and was, to her surprise, finding it fascinating. Most of their spare time was filled doing research and making phone calls, tracking down the perfect cattle. There was so much to research. The cattle had to be a certain build for ease of calving, while still having good yields and growth rates.

Dan took her for a drive early one morning and proudly showed her an expanse of land at the edge of their holding. Rilee hadn't ventured this far before and it still boggled her mind to realise just how much land her husband's family owned.

'This is where the magic's going to happen,' Dan said as they drove slowly over the rugged ground.

'It looks a bit . . . sparse,' she said uncertainly.

'Yeah, well, the old man wouldn't give me the good stuff, would he,' Dan said with a lopsided grin. 'The paddocks further over have some good feed in them. We'll work on these others—plant them for later feed.'

He pulled the ute to a stop and they got out. Rilee walked across to a nearby fence line and bent to take a closer look at a rather pretty plant growing there before Dan yelled out for her not to touch it.

'Why?'

'It's mother-of-millions,' he said, walking across to her with a frown on his face. 'It's toxic to livestock and humans.'

She looked down at the reddish-orange cluster of flowers and wondered not for the first time how even the prettiest of nature's creations could be deadly.

'Bloody nuisance. The paddock over there was thick with it a few years ago before we burnt and sprayed it, but thanks to your dad we might finally be getting on top of it.'

For a moment Rilee was confused, until she recalled the dinner conversation when her parents had visited. 'The bugs?'

'Your dad sent me a few plants with thrip on them, and already they've started to work.

'Does your father know about this?'

Dan gave her a brief grin and she couldn't help but chuckle. 'He's not going to be happy that his son is using hippie mumbo jumbo to fix a problem,' she said, imitating her father-in-law's impatient growl as she snaked her arms around his waist.

'He gave me this area because he knew it was hard work. If I fix the problem and restore it back to viable grazing land, there's not a hell of a lot he can complain about, is there?'

She loved that he was such a quiet achiever. His father hadn't been encouraging about the new cross-breed project, and he hadn't made it easy for his son. If Dan wasn't so determined, he probably would have given up on the idea a long time ago. Instead he'd found ways to overcome the problems and make the best of the less than ideal tools he had to work with. His vision and hard work filled Rilee with pride.

'It's so vast out here,' she said, looking out over the seemingly endless land surrounding them.

'Yep, there's a lot of country.'

'I'm really proud of you, Dan. All your hard work is paying off.'

He gave her a squeeze and looked down, making her breath catch. '*Our* hard work,' he corrected. 'This is going to be our future, Ri.'

She was touched that he was so accepting of them working together, but a tiny part of her felt like a failure at her own business. Her dreams had once been big like this. She'd only envisaged the success. The reality was turning out to be a lot different to what she'd imagined.

Thirty-one

Rilee picked up the plastic shopping basket as she walked into the supermarket. While perusing the shelves in search of inspiration for dinner, she heard her name being called and turned to find Edna making a beeline towards her.

'Have you heard, dear?'

'Ah, heard what?' Clearly it had to be pretty big news if it replaced even a hello.

'Errol Stetton died.'

'What? When?' Rilee gaped.

'At lunchtime. He went home for his usual lunch break, told Betty he was going to have a lie-down for a few minutes and never woke up.'

'That's terrible.' She couldn't say she had any fondness for the man, but it was still a terrible shock to hear that he'd died so suddenly. 'Poor Betty.'

Edna shook her head slowly. 'Yes. It would have been horrible.'

'Does she have any family in town?'

'In-laws and such,' Edna nodded, 'but Lisa, their daughter, will be here tonight apparently. Which is nice, considering the whole falling-out business between Lisa and her father.'

'Well, I'm glad she won't be alone.' She chose to ignore the piece of gossip Edna was dangling in front of her. Or maybe she wasn't dangling it, Rilee couldn't be sure, since everyone around here seemed to know everything about everybody. Maybe Edna just assumed Rilee knew what she was talking about. Edna took her leave and Rilee finished her shopping in record time, eager to avoid any further discussion about the Stettons' sad news.

She looked up from making a salad when the back door opened and Dan walked into the kitchen, hanging up his hat and taking off his boots.

'How was your day?' he asked, snagging a slice of carrot as he leaned down to kiss her hello.

'Fine. Although I heard some sad news about Errol Stetton.'

'Yeah. Bummer, huh.'

'Wait, what? How did you know?'

'Mum. Passed her when she was on her way into town with a casserole.'

It was seriously scary the speed at which news travelled in this town. 'Oh, that was nice of her.'

Dan shrugged as he chewed on the carrot stick. 'The church women usually cook enough food to sink a ship in times of crisis.'

'I think it's nice,' Rilee said as she carried the food to the table. 'I wonder what will happen with the pharmacy now.'

'What do you mean?'

'To operate, there needs to be a pharmacist working there. Without a qualified dispenser, the chemist will have to close, which means we'll no longer have even *that* limited access to medical treatment.'

'They'll figure something out. Lisa will help sort it, I'm sure.'

'That's the daughter? I heard she was on her way back. What's she like?'

Dan forked a piece of steak from the serving plate. 'Dunno, I haven't seen or heard of her for years. I always remember her being a bit . . . different.'

'Different how?'

'She was pretty quiet, always had her head in a book. I didn't really pay much attention, to tell you the truth.'

With a bit of luck maybe Lisa would be able to find a pharmacist to take over her father's business. Without a functioning chemist, the town was going to suffer terribly. A lot of people depended on it for regular medications. Losing it would be a massive headache. And yet another service they'd have to add to the growing number of resources that were being lost from the town.

When Rilee got home from the clinic earlier than usual, Dan was just finishing a phone call and looking across at her with excitement. Her spirits lifted, the worry she was feeling about the lack of clients momentarily forgotten.

'You're in a good mood,' she said after Dan had swept her into his arms and kissed her soundly.

'I just got some great news. Mick Honeywell has found a mob of cows going for an absolute steal at a dispersal sale. They've got calves at foot and are already in calf again.'

'What does this mean?' she asked slowly.

'It means this is the equivalent of winning the cattle lottery. We'll be two seasons ahead of what we were planning. And I spoke to Bill McPherson earlier and made him an offer on that bull we were looking at online.'

'But he was worth *thirty thousand dollars*,' Rilee gasped.

'Yeah, but seeing as we'll be so much further ahead when we get these cows, it suddenly makes it viable.'

'But we weren't going to go in this big this fast. I'm not sure how we can work that much outlay into our business plan.'

'Look, Ri, this is an opportunity we need to grab. They don't come along very often. This speeds up our time frame, the game's changed.'

'But that's why we made a business plan, so we had something to stick to and so our expenses didn't get out of control.'

'Rilee, you have to trust me on this. I know on paper your plan looks great, but I'm talking as a farmer here—you can't always plan for things like this.'

'Well, why do we need the bull now? If they're already in calf, can't we just wait a while before we decide what to do? You said artificial insemination was the way to go. Why are we changing our minds now?'

'Because they're in calf we need to make a decision about remating now. We'll only have a few weeks after they've delivered to implement the decision. Besides, this bull is too good to pass up. Not only can we breed from him, but we can sell his semen as well—double the investment.'

Rilee chewed the inside of her lip as she mulled over his arguments, but her gut was telling her outlaying this much money in the early stages of their business was not a smart move. And yet this was an industry she knew next to nothing about and Dan was asking her to trust him. 'Can we think on it a few days before we make our decision?'

She hated seeing the light go out of Dan's eyes; she knew she'd ruined his excited mood by being the voice of reason, but she just couldn't shake the feeling that this was a bad idea.

'There's really nothing to think about, Ri,' he said, taking his hat from the hook and putting it on. 'I've got some stuff to do out in the shed. I'll be back in a little while.'

Rilee let out a long, tired breath as she closed her eyes and tipped her head from side to side to ease the tightness that had been building all day.

She opened the fridge and took out the ingredients for dinner and started preparing the meal. When Dan came in and they were seated at the table, Rilee broached the subject once more.

'I've already told McPherson we'll take the bull,' he said without looking up from his plate.

Rilee blinked, uncertain that she'd heard him correctly. 'I thought we were thinking it over?'

'Like I said before, there's nothing to think about.'

'But I thought we were partners in this.'

'We are. You handle the books and I handle the farming.'

'I can't very well handle the books when you spend money we don't have.'

'Damn it, Rilee,' he said, looking up and holding her gaze angrily. 'I get this shit from my old man. I wanted to start my own business so I didn't have to deal with someone second-guessing me all the damn time.'

She could see his frustration and she immediately felt bad for doubting him. Maybe he was right. Maybe she just needed to shut up and let him do what he thought best. 'All right. If you think it's a risk worth taking, then okay.'

He visibly relaxed, his mouth losing the tightness of moments before. 'It's worth it,' he said softly.

She managed a smile. She needed to ignore the whisper of unease she felt; after all, what would she know about running a business? All she had at the moment was a shopfront and no customers. At the rate she was going, this cattle venture might be the only thing she was involved in that was a success.

Thirty-two

The kitchen door opened and Ellen swirled in like a mini cyclone, ending the peaceful early morning cuppa Rilee and Dan had been enjoying.

'I just popped over to remind you that the funeral is at ten, but I need you to help set up for the wake and deliver those tables for me.'

'Yeah, I remembered, don't worry,' Dan told his mother.

Rilee cradled her mug. 'I'm not sure I should be going.'

'You have to,' Ellen said, turning to face her.

'I don't *have* to,' Rilee disagreed calmly. 'It's not like I knew him very well.'

'Then you go to support the family.'

'It feels strange going to a funeral of someone I didn't really know.'

'It's how we do things here.'

'We'll be there, Mum,' Dan cut in smoothly.

Rilee glanced over at her husband but didn't bother protesting. She wasn't about to give Ellen a front-row seat to a disagreement.

'I know you didn't get on with Errol, but Mum's right. It's for the family. You show up at these things to support them,' he said after ushering Ellen towards the door and waving goodbye.

'Fine,' Rilee said, putting her hands up in front of her. 'I just feel like a hypocrite, that's all.'

Dan snagged her hand and tugged her closer to him, drawing a reluctant smile from her. 'I don't know,' he said, lazily running his hands up and down her sides, 'you feel pretty good to me.'

'I'm serious, Dan,' she laughed, slapping at his hands. 'I yelled at the man. I feel really bad.'

'Has your opinion of him changed?'

'No,' she said slowly. 'Which makes me feel even worse. The guy's dead, but I still think he was arrogant and self-righteous.'

'Well, then, you're not a hypocrite, are you?' he surmised.

'No, I'm just a horrible person.'

'You're not a horrible person. You have a right to your opinion. It doesn't mean just because you didn't get on with him that you can't show up as part of the community and give his family your support. Imagine if everyone he pissed off in his time decided not to show up at his funeral? It'd be half the town,' he grinned. 'But imagine how Betty and Lisa would feel if no one showed up.'

Put like that . . . Rilee gave a short huff. 'Fine. I see your point. Okay, I'll go to the funeral.'

'That's my girl,' Dan grinned. 'You know, you're kinda cute when you're annoyed.'

'Oh really?'

'Yep,' he said, nuzzling her neck. The phone interrupted and Dan groaned when he pulled out his mobile and looked down at the screen. 'Yes, Mum?' he answered, sending a regretful look down at Rilee. 'Okay, I'll grab the extra seats as well. Yes, as soon as I finish my cuppa. Bye.'

Rilee pulled away from his embrace and went back to clearing the breakfast dishes. 'You better drink fast. I have a feeling that won't be your last reminder call this morning.'

∞

The church service went on for what seemed an incredibly long time, and Rilee was surprised by the number of people in attendance. It was crowded and people were squeezed into the pews like sardines. Rilee concentrated on the stained-glass windows around the little church to take her mind off how hot and stuffy it was inside. She loved the way the light streamed in through the beautifully coloured glass, casting rays of reds, greens and yellows across the congregation seated inside.

When the last hymn had been sung, Rilee stood with everyone else as the family rose from their seats and left the church. Betty was supported on either side by her brother and a younger woman Rilee assumed was her daughter. Her heart clenched at the sight of Betty dabbing her eyes with a scrunched-up tissue, her pain and sadness palpable. No matter her personal feelings towards Errol, Rilee felt the woman's grief and she quickly wiped at a stray tear she felt falling.

It was a welcome relief to move outside into the fresh air. People mingled in groups, and smiles and conversations replaced the sombreness of inside the church. Rilee stood beside Dan as he chatted with various people and as always the conversations centred around the usual farming topics: weather, crops, livestock and the market.

From the corner of her eye Rilee saw Betty's daughter disappear around the side of the church and quickly made the decision to follow her.

She wasn't sure what she expected Errol and Betty's daughter to look like—a woman in her fifties maybe; after all, Betty and Errol were no spring chickens—but this woman looked to be in her late thirties. She clearly took after her mother, being somewhat short and plump, with curly black hair, and was currently digging through her handbag.

'Hi,' Rilee said as she approached, and pulled out a clean tissue. 'Here,' she said, holding it out.

A flash of confusion crossed the woman's face as she looked down at Rilee's outstretched hand before she shook her head. 'I don't suppose you have a lighter?'

'Umm, no. Sorry. I just assumed you were looking for a tissue.' *Being that you're at your father's funeral and all,* she added silently, somewhat taken back by the dry-eyed woman who seemed remarkably calm.

The woman gave a soft grunt. 'I need a cigarette a lot more.' She zipped up her bag with a defeated sigh before looking back at Rilee. 'I picked a great time to quit smoking.'

Rilee shoved the tissue back in her bag and held out her hand. 'I'm Rilee Kincaid.'

'Lisa,' the woman said, hesitating only briefly before shaking Rilee's hand and leaning forward slightly to add with a conspiratorial whisper, 'the wayward daughter.'

Rilee couldn't help a brief smile. 'I'm sorry about your dad.'

Lisa brushed at her silky black top, lowering her gaze. 'Thanks, but we weren't close. I'm here for Mum.'

'I'm sure she's really glad to have you home. How long are you in town for?'

'A few days. I can't stay away from work too long.'

'What is it you do?'

'I'm a pharmacist.'

'Oh.' Rilee wasn't sure what she'd been expecting, but it certainly hadn't been that.

'What can I say,' Lisa shrugged. 'It's in the blood.'

Rilee found herself biting the inside of her cheek as she pondered her next question. 'Do you think you might . . . I mean, is there a *possibility* that you might take over your father's pharmacy?'

Lisa lifted an eyebrow at the question. 'Leave Melbourne to move back to Pallaburra . . . to *live*?'

Okay, clearly *not* a possibility then.

'No, I don't think so.'

Rilee tried not to let her disappointment show. Betty wouldn't be able to operate the business without a pharmacist in store. She'd have to advertise the position, but if they couldn't get a doctor to open a practice out here, chances were they wouldn't be able to entice a pharmacist either.

Lisa was right. Who in their right mind would swap the lights of a big city for Pallaburra? 'That's a shame. The pharmacy has been in your family for a long time, I heard. The locals will be sad to see it close.'

'That's life. Things change . . . although not so much in Pallaburra.'

Rilee exchanged a rather dry grimace of agreement. 'Well, I better go and find my husband.'

'Hold on . . . did you say Kincaid?'

Rilee studied the woman cautiously. 'Yes.'

'I know you . . . the new witch doctor. My father's words, not mine,' she added and grinned at Rilee's dismayed expression. 'Oh, don't worry, I heard all about *the incident*,' she said, lowering her voice.

'I'm really sorry, I didn't mean to upset him that day. I was just so . . . angry,' she said apologetically. She was *so* going to hell for speaking ill of the dead. Errol was probably going to haunt her.

'Seriously, it's okay. Trust me, I had my fair share of stand-up arguments with the stubborn old bugger over the years. You're preachin' to the choir, girlfriend,' she smiled sadly. 'Anyway, thanks for coming today.'

Rilee gave a sympathetic smile before waving goodbye and crossing back to Dan as he was saying his farewells.

A few minutes later she spotted Lisa walking with her mother towards a navy SUV in the church parking lot. With Errol's passing, lots of things had changed, not just for the town but for Betty and Lisa too.

Thirty-three

The bell above her door tinkled while Rilee was out the back making up a list of things to order.

'Lisa, hello. It's lovely to see you again,' Rilee said once she saw who it was.

'I just thought I'd drop by and take a look,' Lisa smiled, turning to take in the shelving that housed a pretty display of natural creams and soaps. 'Do you make all this yourself?' she asked over her shoulder.

'No, not the beauty range. They're actually made by my mother. She has her own line of natural products. I have samples if you'd like some,' Rilee said, getting them from behind the counter and handing them over.

Lisa thanked her, tucking the little sachets into her small handbag. 'Actually, I was hoping we could have a bit of a chat, if you're not too busy? I could shout you a coffee.'

'I'm run off my feet, as you can see,' she said dryly, waving a hand around the empty waiting room. 'I have a coffee machine out the back.'

While Rilee prepared the coffee, Lisa surveyed the room. 'I love what you've done with the place. This used to be a corner store when I was a kid. I remember buying bags of mixed lollies from a big glass display case,' she said wistfully. 'It never looked this classy though.'

'It's been a labour of love so far. It's taking a while to build up the clientele.'

Lisa gave a snort as she pulled out a chair and sat down. 'I'm surprised you've done as well as you have. They're a tough mob to crack.'

Rilee detected an undercurrent of bitterness in the woman's voice. 'How long since you've been back here?' she asked, placing the cup in front of Lisa.

'Be close to twenty years, I suppose.'

'That long?' Rilee hadn't meant to sound so surprised but it seemed a terribly long time without coming back to see her parents.

Lisa's lips twisted as she lowered her gaze to her cup. 'My father and I had a difference of opinion. He told me not to come home until I changed my ways.'

'Your ways?'

'Until I decided I wasn't gay any longer.'

'Oh.'

Lisa raised an eyebrow. 'I thought you must have heard by now. Wow, the gossip mill's certainly slowed down on this one.'

Rilee chuckled and shook her head. 'No, I had no idea.'

'Being a single woman in her forties wasn't a giveaway?' Lisa joked. 'That's the usual cliché, isn't it?'

'Maybe, although I'm pretty sure that's not a scientifically proven method of determination. I can see how that would have been difficult with your parents.' She couldn't imagine Errol being supportive of something like that if his views on birth control were anything to go by.

'Nope. Apparently it was too much for a God-fearing Christian to accept. I guess he and I were a little too alike when it came to being stubborn. It didn't matter, I couldn't wait to leave this place back then,' she said, tracing her fingernail around the top of her cup thoughtfully. 'It wasn't the kind of town where you could be different and be accepted . . . if you know what I mean.'

'What about your mum?'

'She's okay with it now,' Lisa said, 'and when I say okay, I mean as long as we don't mention it.' She gave a half-smile. 'She chooses to believe I'm a spinster. But at least she didn't cut me out of her life the way Dad did.'

'So you left and never came back?'

'I came back once. I don't know why I thought he'd have changed his mind. I tried for Mum's sake . . . Anyway, no huge loss. I haven't missed this town at all. Mum would come down to the city to visit occasionally. She'd tell him it was a shopping trip. He knew what she was doing, but I guess he chose to ignore it to keep the peace. Big of him, huh?'

'I think it's sad,' Rilee said softly. 'He wasted all those years just because he wouldn't accept that you were gay.' How did a parent even do that?

Lisa gave a half-hearted shrug. Somehow Rilee suspected she wasn't as unaffected as she'd like people to believe. 'Anyway, I've been thinking about what you said at the funeral . . . about taking over the pharmacy. Mum wants me to, and with Dad gone, I don't know, I feel as though she might need me around for a bit. I guess it can't hurt to keep it open for a while and see how things go.'

'Really?' Rilee felt herself gaping at the other woman, unsure she'd heard her correctly.

'Yep.'

'Lisa, that's fantastic news,' she said, slightly floored by the sudden announcement.

'I know about Dad's stance on contraception and the morning-after pill,' she said, looking up at Rilee. 'I wanted to let you know that I'm not of the same beliefs, in case you had any concerns.'

'You have no idea how much of a relief it is to hear that.' Rilee hesitated briefly. 'Actually, I'm wondering if you'd like to be involved in a new initiative I'm trying to get up and running. I'm working with a youth program to bring health services and counsellors to town, and I think with your experience, you'd be a huge asset.'

Rilee spent the next hour showing Lisa her plans and filling her in on everything she hoped to achieve, and by the end she could see there was a distinct gleam of interest in the other woman's eyes.

'I wish there'd been something like this out here when I was a kid,' she said solemnly. 'I think this is a brilliant idea. I'd be happy to help where I can.'

The two women clinked coffee cups in celebration and Rilee sat back in her chair with a satisfied smile. With Lisa on board, the plan seemed that much closer to becoming a reality. Finally, she thought, things were beginning to look up.

∽

A week later Rilee sat down at her desk to check her emails when her gaze latched onto the name of the Kincaid family doctor. They'd struck up a good working partnership, especially seeing as Jacob was a difficult man to pin down—even more so when he was avoiding the doctor's calls. Rilee had been working as the middle man and the arrangement was surprisingly successful. His GP had already run one blood test and examination and found that there was something to be concerned about and was following up with a second blood test. Rilee's fingers hovered apprehensively over the keyboard before she hit enter and waited for the email to open.

After a quick scan of the letter, she opened the attached pathology reports and read over them carefully. She'd been hoping the results would indicate something simple since there were many treatable ailments in men of his age caused by declining testosterone and other hormone levels. Deep down, though, she'd known it was something more serious.

She picked up the phone and waited for it to be answered on the other end.

'Kincaid.'

'Jacob, it's Rilee.'

There was silence, and then a sigh of resignation. 'You got the results back, I take it.'

'Can you come into the clinic sometime today or would you rather I saw you at home?'

'Just tell me now.'

Normally she'd prefer to discuss things like this face to face, but Jacob wasn't a normal client. 'Your doctor is requesting a biopsy. But,' she added quickly, 'this is good. There's still a chance that a biopsy will reveal the growth is benign, but even if it's not, it's early stages, which is good news.'

Jacob snorted. 'I'd hate to hear what you think is bad news then, girl.'

'I know cancer is a scary word, but out of all the cancers you could have, prostate is one of the very few we have successful treatments for, and we've caught it in the early stages, which means it can be treated and managed.'

'What's involved?'

'Well, your doctor will be calling you soon to explain this all to you, so answer the damn phone, okay? He'll be referring you to an oncologist who will organise a treatment protocol for you. He's happy to liaise with me if you still want that. I can provide a variety of supplements to complement the drug protocol from your specialist.'

'So I'll have to take another trip to the city then?'

'You'll probably be taking regular trips for a while,' she said gently. 'You'll have to tell Ellen and Dan. You're going to need their support with this.'

'No. Not yet.'

'Jacob, how are you going to explain taking so many trips to Sydney? It's not going to be practical to do this alone.'

'I'm not doing it alone. You're supposed to be helping me.'

'I am helping you. But you still have to be treated by an oncologist. I don't see how you will be able to hide that, or why you'd want to, for that matter.'

'Because Ellen will only nag. I can fly down and do what I have to do and fly home without causing all the drama and stress.'

'They're your family, Jacob. They'll want to know what's going on. Besides, you may not be able to fly yourself home after a treatment. You're going to need Dan at least for that.'

'I'll manage.'

The man was so damn stubborn. 'Okay,' she sighed. 'We'll wait until you've spoken with the doctor, then we'll be in a better position to work out the details. In the meantime, I can start you on some supplements to boost your testosterone and help with some of those symptoms of yours.'

'Just remember the deal. This is between you and me.'

Rilee opened her mouth to warn him it wasn't a good idea, but heard the beeping of a disconnected call and bit back a sharp curse as she hung up the phone.

'Small victories,' she muttered quietly. With Jacob Kincaid, that was all she could hope for.

Thirty-four

Rilee let out a short, impatient huff as she stared at the schedule book and her nonexistent appointments. She couldn't understand it. She'd tried everything: the free samples, the mini consultation, the flyers, and still there was no show of clients. She knew damn well this town was full of potential ailments she could treat, but no one was giving her the chance. Last night she'd made a serious decision: she was giving herself a deadline of six more weeks. After that she couldn't justify flushing her hard-earned money down the drain in wasted rent when she wasn't generating enough business to pay for it.

Rilee looked up when the screen door opened and her mother-in-law stormed into the kitchen. Clearly this was not going to be a social visit.

'I want to know what's going on, and don't deny it. I've been watching you two. What have you been giving him?'

'First of all, you could actually try knocking before you come in. This is my home. And, secondly, I can't and won't answer any of your questions about client matters. If you want answers, you'll have to ask your husband.'

'You think I haven't?' The tightness of the older woman's expression would have been cold if it weren't for the slight shimmer of tears in her eyes. Rilee felt her irritation slip a notch.

'I'm sorry, Ellen.'

'You're not sorry!' she snapped. 'You're practising this naturopathy stuff on him and I demand to know why.'

'There's nothing I can say.'

'I am his wife,' she declared, clearly outraged that Rilee refused to discuss the matter.

Rilee crossed to the door and held it open. 'Then go and act like one. Talk to your husband.' At any other time, the stunned look on her mother-in-law's face would have been priceless.

Rilee closed the door behind Ellen and realised that her hands were shaking. Oh God, what had she done? Ellen wasn't a woman you kicked out of your house without there being some kind of fallout.

∽

The next day, as Rilee headed down the driveway on her way to work, she found Jacob leaning against the side of his four-wheel drive and she slowed down to a stop beside him.

'Everything okay?' she asked, watching his stern face staring into the distance behind her.

'Ellen wants to know what's going on. Tell her,' he said before getting back behind the wheel.

Rilee watched as he drove off. 'Thanks, Rilee. If you wouldn't mind, Rilee,' she muttered. *Would it hurt to say please?* She had to admit, though, that she was relieved she wouldn't have to stonewall Ellen again. Despite being annoyed by his blunt demand, a bud of optimism began to unfurl inside her chest. This might be the new beginning for her in-laws she'd been hoping for. It was a baby step, but a step nonetheless. She cranked up the radio and sang along to the music as she headed into the clinic.

Later as she sat at her computer writing up notes, she glanced up as the door opened and found Ellen paused on the threshold.

'Ellen,' Rilee greeted.

'Jacob said you would fill me in,' she said without preamble.

'Yes, he mentioned that this morning. Come on through, we'll go out to my office.'

When they were settled at the desk, Rilee had a sudden attack of nerves until she took a deep breath and reminded herself she was a professional. She linked her hands together in front of her on the desk before deciding that looked a little pompous and picking up a pen instead.

'I've been concerned about Jacob's frequent urination through the night, as well as a few other things, all of which are symptoms for a variety of different conditions. I urged him to go and see his doctor, which thankfully he eventually did. Over the last few months he's been undergoing different tests and recently a biopsy. His doctor has been sending me the results, and they've come back indicating that Jacob has what they refer to as a moderately aggressive prostate cancer. It seems to be localised, which means it's contained within the prostate.'

'Cancer?' Ellen repeated stiffly.

Rilee nodded. 'It's been caught reasonably early and it can be managed.'

'Why isn't he undergoing treatment in a hospital?'

'His doctors are in the process of figuring out what method of treatment is going to be the most suitable. In the meantime, I've started him on a variety of herbs and vitamins that will work to support his treatment.'

'When will he start this treatment?'

'Maybe you and Jacob should make an appointment together to see the doctor,' Rilee suggested, and saw Ellen nod after a moment of consideration.

'These herbs you've been giving him . . . what can they do?'

'They can help manage the symptoms and give him a better quality of life.'

'Is there anything I can do?'

Rilee heard the stiffness in the woman's voice, but also detected a hint of vulnerability. 'He needs to cut back on work. I tried to tell him, but he won't listen to me. He needs to get away somewhere and just relax.'

Ellen gave a bitter laugh. 'I've been telling him that for years. I don't expect he'll listen now.'

'Maybe this time he will. Perhaps all he needs is for you to ask him.'

'You haven't been married to him all these years. You don't know him.'

Rilee shook her head. 'No, I don't, but you do. If anyone can get through to him, it will be you. He loves you very much.'

Ellen stared at her, her expression wide-eyed and shocked. Not for the first time, Rilee wondered how these people had become so emotionally cold. Ellen got to her feet and straightened her skirt, avoiding Rilee's gaze. 'He won't listen to me. He'll do as he pleases, just as he always has.'

'I hope for his sake that this time he listens. Reducing his stress levels will make a huge difference to his overall prognosis. Oh, and before I forget, here,' Rilee stood and reached for a small brown paper bag she'd prepared this morning. 'I was going to drop it in to you this afternoon when I got home.'

'What is it?' Ellen reached hesitantly for the bag.

'That tea I mentioned to you a while back. To help you sleep. I wrote the instructions on the back.'

'Oh. Well, thank you,' she said somewhat stiltedly. For a moment Rilee thought she caught a softening of her expression, then it was gone, replaced by her usual brisk manner once more. 'Maybe I'll give it a try. It's not like anything else seems to be working.'

Rilee felt a smile tug at the corners of her mouth as she watched Ellen walk to her car outside. If she could just hold on a little longer and continue to chip away at their reserve, eventually they would relent and let her in, surely. This family wasn't for the faint of heart, but if she could help this pair, she knew she could help anyone.

∽

The door closed as Dan came inside and she looked up from the notes she was writing. 'You're home early.' Her smile faltered as she caught the serious expression he wore.

'I've just been talking to Mum.'

Rilee stood from the table slowly.

'When were you going to tell me about Dad?'

'When, or *if*, he told me I could. It wasn't my place.'

'He's my father, Ri.'

'Yes. And he's my patient. I can't reveal personal inform-ation, no matter who it is.'

'You could have warned me.'

'You knew he had a problem. Why do you think I've been trying to help him all this time?'

'You could have told me he'd been to see you. A little warning would have been nice.'

'How was your mother?'

'Upset. They're heading down to the city tomorrow to see the doctor apparently.'

'That's good.'

'I thought you were treating him.'

'I am, in conjunction with his doctor and oncologist.'

'So it's definite? It's cancer?'

'That's what all the tests have confirmed, yes. But there are treatments available. It's not as aggressive as it could be. Now that he's getting treatment, it can be managed, but he's going to have to give up the labour side of work and avoid stress.'

'I can't see him giving up too much around here. It's not in him to sit back and watch. You know how he is.'

Rilee shrugged. 'Hopefully he'll learn.'

Dan gave a doubtful snort at that.

'On the bright side, you'll finally have a chance to prove to him that you can handle things. Once he sees that you're more than capable of running this place, he'll be able to relax.'

'This isn't how I wanted to prove it to him.'

'I know,' she said, moving closer to wrap her arms around him. 'But maybe being forced to slow down is exactly what he needs.'

'I'm not so sure he'd agree with you there, Ri.'

'It'll be a big adjustment for everyone, and it's going to take time, but maybe it'll bring you all closer.'

'Guess we'll have to wait and see, won't we?'

They stood in the middle of the kitchen and held each other silently for a long time. Change was never easy, and Dan was probably feeling more than a little anxious about how his parents were going to handle such a dramatic shift in their lives. All she could do was be there for him and help out where she could.

Dan's spirits lifted significantly over the few days with the delivery of his cattle, followed a few weeks later by his bull. Dunvegan Sir Walter was an impressive animal, although Rilee wasn't sure whether his name was inspired by a type of grass or taken from a medieval name generator. They dubbed him Walter and even a novice like Rilee could tell he came from a very well-bred line.

He was to be kept separate from his little harem until after they'd delivered their calves, which hopefully would be within a matter of weeks, and then he'd be turned loose to do his thing.

It was nice to have a happy husband back, and Rilee was glad that the cattle took his mind off his father for a while.

Thirty-five

Early the next week, Rilee looked up as Lisa walked into the
pub and waved. With everything going on at home, it was
nice to get away and talk about the community centre again.

'Okay, fill me in,' Lisa said as she sat down.

'Teal called this morning and he's organising a school visit.'

'What does that involve?'

'They come out and talk to the high school kids about
what the service offers and hand out info packs. He was
very interested in the discussion we had the other day about
doing a talk to the kids about sexual health and the kinds
of services that are available. I thought it would be a good
opportunity to promote the privacy area you've set up in
the pharmacy.'

Lisa had allocated a small room in the pharmacy for one-on-one consultations. No longer did anyone have to discuss private matters out where everyone else in the store could hear. The other notable addition was the availability of the morning-after pill. However, Rilee and Lisa both agreed there needed to be a great deal of education around what it could and couldn't be used for.

Lisa nodded slowly. 'Only, I'm not so sure I'm the best option for public speaking—it's not something I'm exactly fond of . . . and in front of a whole school. I don't know, Rilee.'

'The whole school that has about two hundred kids in total,' Rilee pointed out dryly. 'You'd only be talking to a certain age group, maybe year nine to year twelve? So that cuts down the audience size significantly.'

'I guess that's not so bad . . .'

'You're great with kids. You talk to them on their level and they really respond to it. Just be yourself.' Rilee had heard Lisa speaking with kids a few times in store and had been impressed by her easy banter and approachability.

'I almost changed my degree from pharmacy to psychiatry,' she said as they read over the pub menu.

'What changed your mind?'

'Dad. Well, kind of. I never told him I was considering it, I just knew he'd flip his lid,' she said with a wry twist of her lips. 'Actually, I guess I was thinking that if I studied psychiatry I could diagnose my own screwed-up life. Turned out I just needed to get out of this town and away from judgemental eyes. Once I was in the city I realised I wasn't as messed up as I thought. I wasn't crazy, I was just gay. Who knew?' she added, attempting to ease the painful memories with humour.

'I'm sorry,' Rilee said, lightly touching her arm. 'That must have been really hard.' *And so completely unnecessary,* she thought angrily. No matter how hard she tried, she couldn't understand how a parent could turn their back on their own child because of their sexuality. It was barbaric.

∽

Rilee was unlocking the front door when she heard her name being called. It was Shae and she was looking worried. 'What's wrong?' Her immediate fears were there'd been a complication medically. So far there'd been no pregnancy, but it was still early days.

'You're going to need to see this,' she said, moving around Rilee to cross to the desk, then sliding into the chair behind the computer. Rilee watched as her friend pulled up the clinic's Facebook page. She was still learning about social media and so far Shae had been happy to run it for her. She saw the familiar logo at the top of the page and was momentarily distracted by how great it looked. Shae was very good at what she did, but right now as she pointed with a grim face to a section on the screen, Rilee had a very bad feeling that what she was about to find out wouldn't be good news.

'I think I've discovered why you're not getting any business.' An area marked 'reviews' had quite a few comments, which should have alerted her to trouble since she was pretty sure she hadn't treated that many clients yet. There was a rating scale of stars and as she scanned through the list she discovered that all of them were one star. The comments ranged from 'terrible customer service' to 'unsanitary and a waste of money'.

'There has to be some kind of mistake,' Rilee said, confused by the sheer number of comments. 'I haven't even had this many customers.'

'Unfortunately there's no mistake. They've been deliberately posted under fake accounts.'

'What? Why? Who would do that?'

'Someone who wants to sabotage your business would be my guess.'

Rilee didn't have to think too hard. 'Priscilla?'

'She's had it in for you,' Shae confirmed.

'But . . . surely this is going too far, even for her?'

'It's effective.'

Rilee slumped onto the corner of the desk and dropped her head in defeat. 'Well, that's it then. It's over. I can't keep this place open if she's turned everyone against me.'

'So you're just going to give up and let her win?'

'What can I do, Shae?' Rilee asked, throwing an arm out towards the computer screen. 'She's completely destroyed my reputation.'

'All you need is one person to sing your praises. Not everyone is on Facebook—Priscilla can't get to them all. You need to fight this with your skills as a practitioner. Cure one person and you'll have them lining up out the door,' she said, leaning back in her chair.

Was that all? It was a bit hard when she couldn't even get anyone to step through the damn door in the first place. How on earth was she supposed to come back from this?

ॐ

As Rilee got out of the car she heard raised voices. She walked around the side of the house and spotted Dan, Mark and his father, as well as a few of the other stockmen, gathered near the cattle yards.

Rilee hesitated before heading over.

'I told you before—if you do this, you do it on your own time.'

'It was an emergency, Dad.'

'I don't give a damn what it was. You had these men off doing stuff for you for three flamin' hours.'

'Fine, I'll pay their three hours, happy?'

'Damn right you will. We're not running a charity here in case you hadn't noticed.'

She watched as Jacob stalked off back to the main house, leaving Dan and the other men behind.

Rilee frowned as she noticed the animal in the yards. The big bull stood docilely and, if the worried looks on the men's faces were anything to go by, this was not a good sign.

Dan climbed over the rails into the yards, looking over Walter with a tight-lipped expression.

'What's going on?' Rilee asked.

'Bull got into the back paddock and got stuck into the mother-of-millions.'

'But isn't that stuff toxic?'

Dan's slanted look told her exactly how serious this situation was. 'I don't think he ate much or he'd be in worse shape than this. It was just lucky we found him when we did. The vet's on his way.'

Rilee stepped out of the way, finding a seat on the open back of the ute to wait for the vet. She didn't know a lot, but she did know that if this bull died they'd just have lost a substantial amount of money. Even a vet bill and treatment was not an expense they needed right now either. Today was going from bad to worse.

When the vet finally arrived, he looked as grim as Dan as they stood together and discussed treatment options.

'We've got to do everything we can,' Dan was saying as Rilee climbed the fence and stood beside him.

'It's not going to be cheap,' the vet warned. 'And I can't guarantee it's going to work.'

'How much are we talking?' she asked, somewhat alarmed.

'It doesn't matter, Ri. We can't afford to lose this bull. Just do whatever needs to be done, Rob,' Dan said, walking towards the rail and climbing back over.

Rilee glanced at the vet, who gave her an apologetic smile, and Rilee felt the sharp sting of embarrassment at her husband's abrupt dismissal of her question. She turned on her heel and followed him across to the ute.

'What was that all about?' she demanded.

'Rilee, I don't have time right now.'

'You made me look like a complete idiot just then.'

'Babe, I've had a shit of a day, and it's going to be a long night. Can we please not do this right now?'

He didn't wait for her reply, taking out the radio and calling for Mark.

❧

Rilee tossed and turned, having finally gone to bed after midnight without any sign of Dan joining her. He'd been droving the cattle to a safer area, not taking any chances that they'd somehow get out and find the mother-of-millions as well. Cattle raised in the area knew not to eat it, but cattle brought in from an area that didn't have the toxic weed weren't aware of the danger and were at risk of eating it and dying.

She sat up in bed and turned on the bedside lamp when she heard the back door open and held her breath as he entered their bedroom.

'Any news on Walter?'

'He's pulled through. Rob said we're over the worst of it.'

Oh thank God. The sick sensation that had settled in her stomach eased as relief rushed through her. Dan stood just inside the doorway, still dressed in his work clothes, covered in a combination of dust, oil, sweat and goodness only knew what else. His eyes were bloodshot from the late night and the dust and wind while he'd been out moving the cattle. He looked exhausted and Rilee climbed out of bed and crossed to his side, wrapping her arms around him, not caring about his filthy clothing.

'I'm sorry about earlier, Ri.'

She wanted to say it was okay, but it wasn't. Not really. And yet, at this late hour, it wasn't the time to sit down and have a deep and meaningful. Tomorrow she had the high school presentation and Dan would be up again in only a few short hours. He kissed the top of her head and moved away to take a shower and Rilee climbed back into bed. As she listened to Dan's soft breathing beside her, Rilee couldn't shake the feeling that while one crisis may have narrowly been averted, there were more hanging around like vultures, just waiting for their opportunity to swoop.

Thirty-six

Rilee felt unusually nervous as she watched the school hall fill up with high school students. She'd been keeping going on strong coffee after her sleepless night. She was really only here for moral support. Lisa was the one giving the presentation, along with Teal who would be talking about the centre and the services they were offering, so Rilee wasn't exactly sure why she was feeling so nervous.

The school's vice-principal, who had taken over while the principal was on long service leave and who had become a strong advocate for the program, took the stage to make introductions and then handed over to Teal. Rilee was impressed with the amount of information the young man was able to give the kids. Dressed in jeans and a faded T-shirt, with shaggy hair and dirty old sneakers, he didn't inspire a great deal of confidence at first glance. However, as soon as he started talking about the program, his eyes lit up and his face became animated in a way only true passion could create. After listening to him talk, Rilee was positive that the community centre and its services would be critical in helping young people in town reach their full potential. There were plenty of resources available; the only obstacle was access. They needed to get the community centre up and running sooner rather than later.

And then it was Lisa's turn. Rilee was in awe of the way she spoke to the teenagers. She began telling them how difficult it had been for her growing up gay in a small town and how isolated she'd felt. She told them about the pharmacy's private consulting room and then launched into a sexual health talk. Typically there were nervous giggles and a few unsavoury comments that had teachers frowning silent warnings to the instigators, but Lisa took it all in her stride.

'The morning-after pill,' Lisa said, bringing up the next slide. 'You've probably heard of it, and until now it's not been readily available in Pallaburra. I wanted to talk to you all about what it is and what it *isn't*.'

Rilee noticed a few of the older girls in the hall seemed interested, even if a lot of the others, particularly the boys, weren't.

'It's a form of emergency contraception that can be taken up to seventy-two hours after unprotected sex to prevent pregnancy. The sooner it is taken the more effective it is. It's used after unprotected sex, or when the condom has broken or fallen off during sex, or a girl has missed taking the pill.' Lisa pressed the keyboard to show the next slide.

'The morning-after pill is basically a very high dose of hormones. It is *not* an abortion pill. The hormones help prevent the girl's egg being fertilised by delaying ovulation or preventing a fertilised egg from implanting in the womb. The morning-after pill can be given by a doctor or a pharmacist. Here in Pallaburra, because we have no doctor in town at present, you'll need to come in and see me. I'll take you into the consulting room and ask you some questions about your general health and tell you how to use the pill. I'll let you know about any side effects and what to do next. It will be all completely private, so anything that you tell me will stay between you and I.'

Rilee felt her throat tighten a little at Lisa's words. She thought about Shaz's friend and how she was humiliated when she asked for help. She wasn't sure if Lisa understood the extent of what she was offering here today. For these young girls to know they had someone who cared running a place in town that they could go to in times of need was an enormous support.

'While the morning-after pill is a relatively safe backup for an emergency, it should never be used as the only way of preventing pregnancy. It's designed for short-term use only. So let's talk about what other kinds of contraception are available.'

Rilee gave Lisa a thumbs-up after she finished her talk and for the rest of the day couldn't wipe the smile from her face.

The next morning as she walked towards the clinic, Rilee glanced up and stopped in her tracks. A large spiderweb of cracked glass covered the lower section of her office window. She looked around and spotted a rock a few metres away on the footpath, her heart thudding painfully against her ribs as she tried to process the damage.

'You got yourself a broken window.' The slow drawl came from behind her and Rilee spun around to find an older man leaning out of his car window.

'Yes, looks like it,' she said despondently.

'Young kids up to no good, if you ask me,' the man put in. 'You need to give the coppers a call, I reckon.'

'Yes, well, I better go inside and find someone to fix it,' she said, politely trying to escape. She was shaken by the unexpected vandalism and needed a moment or two to process it all.

Her fingers fumbled with the key as she unlocked the door, but eventually she got it open and hurried inside, closing it firmly behind her. Before she had time to think, the phone began to ring and she moved across the room to answer it. She was too shaken to give the usual greeting, barely managing a breathless, 'Hello.'

'Good morning, Rilee. It's Priscilla Montgomery.'

'Priscilla,' there was no way she could hide the surprise in her voice, and she didn't bother trying.

'You haven't wasted any time stirring up trouble, I hear.'

'I'm not sure what you're talking about.'

'I think you should brace yourself for some backlash over your little sex ed campaign. I wanted to let you know that I'm taking a personal interest and intend to assist disgruntled parents in taking it up with the school.'

'I don't see what it has to do with you—you don't have children there.' She knew she sounded blunt, but this woman's sugary tone grated on her nerves.

'My family are long-standing members of the community and anything that affects the town affects me.'

'Really? So *now* you and your family are interested in helping out the local community? I seem to remember you weren't overly keen on the idea when I brought it up with the ladies' church committee.'

'I'm born and bred in this community. You'll always be an outsider. I think you should remember that.'

'And I think you should stop wasting my time. I have work to do.'

'I was just trying to give you a heads-up, but if that's the way you feel . . .' She let her voice trail off and Rilee could only imagine the sly smile on her face as she hung up.

Rilee glanced down, noticing the messages light flashing on her phone.

'How dare you talk to our kids without our permission? Parents should have been informed about this,' a woman said briskly before the phone call disconnected.

Rilee hung up but pressed the message recall button, a feeling of dread pooling in her stomach.

'Who gave you the right to tell our kids about contraception?' was the next message, and the following three were in the same vein. Her mobile began to ring and she reluctantly dug through her handbag to locate it, breathing a small sigh of relief when Lisa's name came up on the screen.

'You won't believe what's been happening all morning,' she started.

'Abusive phone calls?' Rilee asked.

'How'd you . . . Are you getting them too?'

'Yes, I just walked into the clinic and I've got about half a dozen voicemail messages and a broken window. I'm pretty sure I know who's behind it too.'

'A broken window? Have you called the police?'

'Not yet. I'm not sure there's anything they can do about it.'

'You have to report it, Rilee. This is serious.'

'We can't be sure it's even connected to the phone calls,' although she found that a little hard to believe.

'It might not be worth opening today,' Lisa said with a weary sigh.

'I can't afford *not* to open. I'll just mute the phone and hope they get tired of leaving messages. I'm sure it'll all blow over.'

Lisa hadn't sounded very confident, but they hung up and Rilee felt her shoulders slump as her gaze drifted to the smashed front window. While she didn't think Priscilla would actually stoop to vandalism, she was sure that it was a consequence of the woman inciting outrage amongst high school parents. Insurance would take care of her broken window, but bringing the police into the situation and throwing around accusations was probably only going to make things worse. She couldn't afford to become any more alienated from the community than she already was.

The day dragged by, the phone ominously silent. No bookings, no enquiries, nothing. By the time she locked up for the day and drove home, Rilee's energy levels were flagging badly. The last thing she felt like doing was having a discussion with Ellen, but it seemed she had little choice as she parked her car and saw the woman heading across the yard towards her. There was no need to wonder what it was about. Rilee gave a small groan at the furious expression on her mother-in-law's face and braced herself. 'Let me guess, you had a call from Priscilla?'

'And just about everyone else from the church committee. What on earth were you thinking?'

'Oh, I don't know . . . maybe that with a bit of education we can stop a few kids becoming teenage parents?'

'You being part of all this nonsense is reflecting upon us all. How dare you decide to do something like this without consulting us first?'

'Consulting you?' Rilee stared at the woman. 'I beg your pardon?'

A ute pulled up behind them and Rilee absently noted Dan's arrival, but she was too furious to bother with a greeting.

'Daniel, were you aware of what your wife has been up to lately? Have you heard about the uproar she's caused?'

'Mum, why don't we come over later after everyone's had time to calm down—'

'We are *not* going to go over there,' Rilee snapped, turning to face her husband. 'This is none of your business, Ellen.'

'Are you going to stand there and let her speak to me like that, Daniel?'

'Oh for goodness sake!' Rilee threw her hands in the air and walked towards her house. She needed to get away before she said something she would regret forever.

The door banged a few moments later as Dan came inside and slammed his hat on the hook. 'What the hell is going on?'

'Apparently I'm corrupting the innocent children of Pallaburra.'

'Mum said she's been getting phone calls from people all day about you attending some meeting and telling kids where to get abortions.'

'Oh for the love of God,' Rilee said shaking her head. 'Do you honestly think I'd do something like that? Seriously, Dan, sometimes I think you're just as bad as she is.'

'What's that supposed to mean?'

'Did it ever occur to you to *ask* me what she was talking about instead of coming in here and accusing me of something so ridiculous? I'm your wife, surely I deserve the benefit of the doubt?'

'I did ask you!'

'You accused me. There's a difference.'

Dan pinched the bridge of his nose and hung his head. 'Can you please just tell me what is going on?'

'I attended an information session at the school yesterday,

which I told you about but you were obviously too preoccupied to bother listening to.'

'What kind of information session?'

'To tell the kids about the Tamworth youth service, and the fact they've decided to go ahead and rent a room from me once a fortnight for appointments, until we get a community centre up and running.'

'Then where did all the abortion talk come in?'

'Lisa talked to them about accessing the morning-after pill and contraception. There was nothing about abortions.'

She saw Dan flinch and his hands clench. 'And you didn't think that some parents might have concerns about their kids being given that kind of information?'

'It's only what they're supposed to be learning in health education anyway.'

'This is *not* the city, Rilee.'

'When are you going to stop using that stupid argument, Dan? No, it's not the city and, yes, things are different out here, but we're all living in the same times and, like it or not, Pallaburra needs to get its head out of the sand and wake up to reality.'

'You're stirring up trouble. You just can't go rushing at it like a bull at the gate. You're only going to get everyone off side.'

'Well, it's going to take more than a few abusive messages and a broken window to stop me.'

'Wait. What? Broken window? What are you talking about?' He frowned at her.

'I don't know, it was probably some kids mucking around or something.'

He stared at her open-mouthed for a moment, setting both his hands on his hips. 'Why the hell didn't you call me?'

'Because I fixed it.'

'Someone smashed a window. They were sending you a message, Rilee. This is serious. What did the coppers say?'

'I didn't call them.' She saw his look of disbelief and didn't give him a chance to protest. 'There was no point, Dan. It was easier just to get the damn thing fixed. It's over and done with.'

'Easier?' he said with an incredulous laugh. 'It would be easier just to let this thing go now, before it gets any worse.'

'I'm not going to stand by and watch one more girl have to give up on her future because she didn't have access to good information and adequate contraception. This may not be the city but the kids here deserve the same choices.'

'So your advice to them is to go get an abortion?'

'I'm not talking about abortion. What aren't you understanding about this?'

'Any of it. I never thought you'd be this irresponsible, Rilee,' Dan said, his voice raised.

'Irresponsible?' Rilee searched her husband's furious expression, suddenly realising that his outrage was completely out of proportion to the argument. 'I can't believe you're so ready to take your mother's side on all of this.'

'She's actually right, though. You're stirring up trouble and it has to stop.'

'It has to stop?' Rilee repeated in disbelief.

She saw Dan straighten his shoulders as he levelled a serious look at her. 'It ends now, Rilee. All of it. I don't want you involved in any of this damn crusade you and Lisa have started in town.'

Rilee stared at her husband, desperately trying to force some kind of coherent sentence from her mouth, but she was consumed by shock and outrage. He was *forbidding* her?

'I'm serious, Rilee. This is getting out of hand. The phone calls, the threats. It's over.'

'Oh,' Rilee shook her head adamantly as she glared at her husband, 'this is far from over. It's only just begun. If this town thinks it can shut me up by bullying me then it's seriously underestimating me.'

'I said, no more!' Dan yelled and Rilee's heart lunged in fright. The fact that he sounded exactly like his father was the bucket of cold water Rilee needed to snap her out of shock.

'I am not your mother, Dan. And you are not your father. If you think for one moment you can raise your voice and bully me into something, you're setting yourself up for a big disappointment. I *will* continue to fight for the kids in this town and I'll continue to say whatever needs to be said to get the message through to those narrow-minded, self-righteous locals who refuse to admit the town has got a problem. If that makes you and your parents uncomfortable then I'd suggest you turn a blind eye to it . . . . Shouldn't be hard—after all, that's what everyone seems to do out here.'

Dan's face was a mask of unyielding anger. 'It wasn't a request.'

'You're assuming I was ever asking for your permission to start with,' she shot back.

He glared at her, fists clenched by his sides, shoulders rigid with tension, then turned away, snatching his hat from the hook.

The door slammed and Rilee winced as the nearby window rattled in its frame.

She sunk into the closest chair and let out a breath. Her hands were shaking. Who was that man? He sure as hell wasn't the Dan she thought she knew. *You married him after three months, what did you expect?* a little voice reminded her piously, but she pushed it away. No, she hadn't made a mistake marrying him. She did know Dan; this was not who he was. But for one moment he'd sounded exactly like Jacob, and that thought horrified her. She felt ill. Confrontation had always made her uneasy, but there was no way she was backing down from this. Disappointment rose inside her. How could Dan demand she give up this fight when she knew with every fibre of her being that this was the right thing to do? These kids needed help. She couldn't turn her back on them. She wouldn't.

She pushed away the sadness that lingered after their fight. She couldn't dwell on that, she needed to hold on to the outrage. Anger could fuel her determination far more effectively than sadness, and she was going to need every ounce of determination if she was going to continue this fight without any support from her husband.

Thirty-seven

Rilee sat, feet tucked under her, in the corner of the lounge where she'd watched the sun rise only an hour or so before. Dan hadn't come home.

A soft knock sounded at the front door and she saw Shae waiting expectantly on the top step.

'I guess I don't have to ask how you're doing,' she said, placing a parcel wrapped in a tea towel on the kitchen bench. 'You've heard all about it then?'

'I don't know the details, I just know that Dan spent the night at his parents' house and I figured it had to be something pretty darn drastic,' she said, taking a seat across from her.

'I don't know what's happening to us, Shae. I never imagined we'd ever fight like that, let alone to the point where Dan'd leave and not come home.'

'Every couple fights, you guys aren't any exception to the rule,' she said gently.

'Lately it's like he's putting up a wall between us,' she said, feeling her lip begin to tremble. 'I'm scared he's realised he made a huge mistake marrying me.'

'Rubbish. That man loves you, trust me.'

'Then why are we moving apart?'

'Are you? I mean really? Are you sure that's what's happening? Look, let's just put things into perspective, okay?' Shae said. 'Firstly, you guys got married fast—and that's not a bad thing,' she said, holding up a hand before Rilee could protest. 'I'm just saying, most couples go through their first fight while they're still dating. You guys skipped that part, so this is completely normal. Secondly, he's just found out his dad's sick and he's had to take on a lot more responsibility—that's probably why he's been distracted. Thirdly, his parents . . . need I elaborate on that? They're both control freaks—the poor bastard can't get a moment's peace. He's bound to snap at some point.'

'I know,' Rilee groaned, 'and I have taken all that into consideration, but it's just . . . he wants me to stop everything I'm doing for the community centre. He was so . . . furious. How can I do that after all the work we've done?'

Shae studied Rilee silently for a few moments. 'Maybe he just needed to cool off. He was worried about you, that's all. Come on,' she said, standing up to head into the kitchen. 'We need coffee and freshly baked bacon and cheese muffins.'

Rilee gave a small smile of gratitude. 'By the way, how did you know Dan spent the night at the main house?'

'Mark sent me a text. He said the boss was in a bad mood and that he'd picked him up from the big house. I figured you might be in need of a shoulder to cry on . . . or at the very least, hot breakfast muffins,' she said, holding up a steaming muffin she'd just lifted from the tea towel.

'These are so good,' Rilee said between mouthfuls.

'Good for what ails ya. So are my chewy, gooey chocolate brownies, but it's a bit early in the morning for them. They're more of a remedy for late-night catastrophes.'

It hurt that Dan had left last night, but considering neither of them had been in the right frame of mind to actually listen to each other, it had probably been for the best. Now, though, with a clearer head and some food in her stomach, Rilee knew she needed to find him.

Armed with the remaining muffins and a thermos of coffee, Rilee borrowed the farm ute to go in search of her husband, carefully following Shae's directions.

As she spotted the other vehicle in the distance, her nerves got decidedly more active. What if he ignored her? What if he were still too angry to talk? She brushed her fears away and continued to head in the direction of the two workers. They seemed to be doing something with the fence—she wasn't sure what, but it looked pretty intense, and she braced herself as Dan glanced up at her approach.

Rilee took a deep breath as she gathered her ammunition of food. She sent a friendly wave to Mark, who suddenly needed to get something from the toolbox, and steeled her nerves to look up at her husband.

He took his time removing his gloves and wiping his forehead before making eye contact, and when he did it wasn't with his usual warm, tender look. This was coolly impersonal and it hurt.

'Thought you might be hungry,' she said, putting the wrapped muffins down on a nearby stump.

'Thanks.'

She frowned a little at his unhelpful mood. 'How did you sleep?' she offered.

'Fine. You?'

'I didn't. Not much anyway.'

She thought she caught the barest hint of something cross his face, but it was gone when he bent down to take a muffin.

'I came to see if we could talk about last night.'

'I'm a bit busy right now,' he said between mouthfuls.

Rilee glanced over her shoulder and saw Mark was discreetly checking his phone. 'All right then. I guess we'll talk when you get home.'

'Have you decided to stop pushing with this whole teen pregnancy thing?'

Rilee's heart sank. So much for him cooling down. 'You know I can't. It's important to me, Dan.'

'Then we have nothing to talk about.'

Something inside her broke at his calm dismissal. The Dan she thought she had married wouldn't ever give her an ultimatum like this. 'I guess we don't,' she said quietly, turning away before he could see the glisten of tears she was trying so hard to blink away.

⁂

Dan still hadn't come back to the house at lunchtime, so Rilee decided to head into the clinic and distract herself with work.

The door opened and Rilee looked up, surprised when she saw who it was. 'Edna? Hello.'

'Hello, Rilee,' the older woman said, taking off her large orange sunhat as she sat down heavily. 'It's warming up out there.'

'Would you like a glass of water?' Rilee offered, moving to get one from the dispenser.

'Thank you, dear,' Edna said, gulping the contents of the cup down gratefully.

'You really should be taking a taxi into town, Edna,' Rilee said gently.

'Yes, I know, but you know what they say: use it or lose it. If I don't keep this old hip of mine moving I'm worried it'll seize up and I'll be done for. It's that damn osteoarthritis. I see the doctor about it, but I'm not getting much relief from his suggestions.'

'Well, you're right in thinking that you still need exercise, but I can make you up something that can help with the inflammation and pain.'

'I'm willing to give anything a try at this stage,' she said, and Rilee smiled as she began collecting some of the

318

ingredients she'd need. 'Actually, I just wanted to pop in to let you know that I've heard about all the trouble you've been having lately and I think it's terrible.'

Rilee gave a weary smile at the heartfelt look on the woman's face. 'I seem to have a knack for upsetting people.'

'Don't you listen to them, dear. I heard what that new community whatchamacallit place was going to offer and I think it would be wonderful for the town. It's not just the young'uns around here who are at a disadvantage being so far away from a doctor. Us oldies who don't drive any more find it hard to get to places like Centrelink when we need to sort out our payments. I heard you might be able to get government agencies to come out to town now and again. Those are the kinds of services we need out here. Don't you let a few bad eggs stop you from making this happen. We need you.'

'Oh, Edna,' Rilee said, her voice sounding husky as she fought to control the emotions hovering just beneath the surface. 'It just feels like an uphill battle, you know? The harder I push for change, the harder everyone fights me.'

'Maybe you just have to fight smarter,' Edna said, patting her hand and getting to her feet awkwardly.

Walking her to the door, Rilee held the door open. 'Stop in on your way home and I'll have the mixture ready for you.'

Mixing herbs was always relaxing. She loved working the pestle and mortar, grinding and crushing ingredients into pastes and powders and breathing in the earthy scents as she created the medicines she used to help heal and relieve pain. The strenuous, repetitive grinding was a good way to release frustration, and she often found the process therapeutic.

After a while she felt considerably better; if not a hundred percent, at least a lot more optimistic. Edna's talk had renewed her determination. If she just laid out all the facts for Dan in a calm, rational way, she was certain he'd understand why she couldn't give up on this. This morning's exchange hadn't been exactly encouraging, but she'd regrouped. She'd had to; she wasn't ready to accept the alternative. She didn't even know *what* the alternative was. What was he planning to do if she didn't give up her cause? No, he was just upset and angry; eventually he'd have to realise they needed to discuss things, and hopefully, after a day stewing about it, he'd be in a better frame of mind to listen. She sent him a text, asking him to be at dinner tonight, and mentally prepared herself. They had to work this out somehow. Dan meant too much to her.

At home Rilee waited impatiently for Dan to arrive for dinner. Hearing the sound of an engine, she glanced outside the window and saw his work ute pull up outside his parents' house. Something inside her snapped. 'Oh hell no,' she muttered as she marched across the clearing and pushed open the garden gate, caring little that it slammed shut behind her. There was no way she was going to be given the cold shoulder two nights in a row. This had gone on long enough.

At the kitchen screen door she saw Ellen stand up from where she sat at the table, her intention no doubt to intercept her and protect her precious son.

'We had plans tonight,' Rilee said, stepping around her mother-in-law and aiming her angry glare at her husband.

'I think you need to give him some space, dear,' Ellen suggested.

'I think he's had plenty of space,' Rilee snapped without taking her eyes from Dan, who sat at the table, watching her with a tightly clenched jaw.

'Rilee,' he began, then sighed when the phone rang and his mother threw her arms in the air.

'I told you! It's been ringing all day. I don't need this on top of everything else,' Ellen cried, leaving the kitchen to head up the hallway.

'What does she mean by "on top of everything else"?'

'Dad's been booked into hospital next week for the first of his radiation treatments.'

With everything that had been happening lately, she'd momentarily forgotten about the last appointment Jacob had returned from. The news took some of the wind out of her sails. 'It's good that they're starting treatment,' Rilee said quietly.

'Yeah. It's shaken them both up a bit though.'

'Understandable,' she agreed. 'Is there anything I can do? Maybe I should see if I can help?'

The sharp look he sent cut through her like a knife. 'I don't think that's a good idea right now.'

Right. Your mother can't stand me. Duly noted.
'Regardless of all this going on, we still need to talk.'

'I'm trying to hold everything together, Ri. Now's not a good time. I've just been dealing with a stressed mother, a father who never normally backs down on anything looking absolutely terrified, and I've lost two of the calves today.'

'What? How?' News of the calves briefly sidetracked her.

'I don't know,' he said tightly.

'Why didn't you call me?'

'You've been too busy righting all the wrongs of the world,' he said coldly.

'Those cattle are my business too, remember? Oh, that's right. I'm supposed to be the silent partner—you know, the one who isn't supposed to tell you that buying a heap of cattle and a bull was probably a bit of a risk this early on in the business.' She knew it was a cheap shot to rub it in like that, but damn it, she was tired of trying to be the peacekeeper.

'Yeah, I figured you'd get a kick out of being right,' he snapped. 'I can't deal with you on top of everything else right now,' Dan told her impatiently, getting to his feet.

'When would be good time then?'

'Later.'

Rilee stared at the man she'd married and felt numb. She knew if she tried to speak now, the fragile hold she had on the tears that threatened would slip. The last thing she wanted was to have his mother come back into the room and witness her humiliation, so Rilee swallowed past the painful lump in her throat and turned away.

She didn't stop at the door when she heard him sigh, she just let the door bang behind her and headed back to the cottage. There she locked the door and shut the blinds, falling onto bed and finally allowing the flood of tears to come, alone in the dark.

and witness her humiliation, so Rilee swallowed past the painful lump in her throat and turned away.

She didn't stop in the door when she heard him sigh, she just let the door bang behind her and headed back to the cottage. There she locked the door and shut the blinds, falling onto bed and finally allowing the flood of tears to come, alone in the dark.

Thirty-eight

The phone was ringing when Rilee looked up to see Shae at the back door later the next day.

'Are you going to answer that?'

'No.'

'Okay . . . What are you doing?' Shae asked as she followed Rilee down the hall and saw the suitcase on the bed.

'Packing.'

'I can see that. Why?'

'I'm going away for a few days.'

'What about Dan? What does he think about it?'

'Dan isn't talking to me at the moment. I'm pretty sure he doesn't much care what I do.'

'I hardly think that's true.'

'I tried to talk to him. He's not interested in hearing what I have to say.'

'He's just under a lot of pressure from everyone at the moment: his dad being sick, his mother leaning on him, not to mention he feels like he's let you down about the cattle.'

Rilee stopped throwing in clothes to look up at her friend. 'So you've talked to him?' Of course she would have. Mark was Dan's friend; he would have known he could go to them and drown his sorrows.

'He's a mess,' Shae said quietly.

'Really?' Rilee snapped sarcastically. 'And I'm not?'

'You just need to give each other some time—' Shae started before Rilee cut her off.

'What we *need* is to get away from his parents breathing down our necks and the whole town judging me.'

'This will blow over. And it's not the whole town, it's just a few troublemakers stirring up gossip. When nothing much happens around town, people tend to blow small things out of proportion . . . This thing with you and Dan is just typical newlyweds settling in to marriage.'

'I didn't expect my husband to turn his back on me at the first sign of trouble. Maybe I misjudged him . . . us . . . Maybe his parents were right and getting married was a big mistake.'

'It wasn't a mistake,' Shae said firmly. 'I've never seen two people more in love or more suited to each other.'

'Yeah, well, maybe love isn't enough in this case.'

'Don't give up on him, Ri. He spent the night at our place and I heard how much pain he's in. That man loves you. He's hurting about a lot of things right now.'

'Then why is he telling everyone else but me? Why won't he come home and talk to *me* about it?'

'Because these men are as stubborn and proud as they are loyal. Last night he just needed to get his head straight—get rid of some of his frustration so he can sit down and have a rational discussion. He needed a night drinking with his mate. Fellas do that.'

'Well, I don't understand that at all,' Rilee snapped. Just one more thing about people out here that she didn't get. Her list was growing with each passing day. 'It doesn't matter,' she dismissed, getting back to her packing. 'I still need a break from all of this. I'm tired of being the one who has to adapt to everything, and I swear if I hear "That's just the way we do things here" one more time, I'm going to freakin' lose it.'

She saw Shae's lips twitch slightly.

'I'm serious, Shae. I've been trying so hard, from day one, to fit in, but nothing I do is ever enough. They're never going to accept me and I'm always going to be that city woman who keeps trying to change things.'

'They will accept you, it just takes—'

'*Time.* Yes, I know. That's what I keep hearing,' Rilee said with a frustrated sigh.

'Maybe you're right. Maybe going away for a few days is a good idea,' Shae said after a moment of silence. 'Just don't throw away everything you've worked so hard for, okay?'

She needed to get some perspective and she couldn't do that here with Kincaids glaring at her everywhere she went. There was only one place she could go where she knew she wouldn't be judged.

It was time to go home again.

Thirty-nine

The long road stretched out before her as she drove, the endless kilometres that passed beneath her tyres became a soothing balm to the turmoil of the last few days. As she crossed the range and headed up the coast the landscape changed dramatically. Gone was the endless sea of whiskey-coloured paddocks, replaced by the dramatic mountain slopes of emerald green. She could have flown, she supposed, but the drive gave her the solace she craved and she loved being able to see the vast changes in scenery as she travelled through the different regions. Australia really was a huge country full of contrasts.

As she got closer to her parents' farm, she began to recognise familiar landmarks. The highway had changed since the last time she'd driven home. It bypassed a lot of the smaller towns now and she was glad when she could get off the highway and back onto the quieter roads that would take her past Nimbin and further inland to her parents' place.

A simple sign hung on the front gate with *Rainbow Farm, Organic Herbs* painted across it. Rilee smiled as she remembered the photo her parents had sent her the day they hung the sign. They'd stood beside it, arms around each other, with huge smiles plastered across their faces. The fact they had managed to make a successful business out of organic herbs was just an added bonus to them; it was the growing they loved. She was incredibly proud of them.

She stopped the car on the other side of the gate and got out, drawing a deep breath of the cool, fresh air. It was very different to Thumb Creek. For starters, everything was so green. The subtropical vegetation was thick and luscious, quite the opposite of the wide open plains of crops and cattle at Thumb Creek.

A moist, earthy scent filled her lungs as she pulled up outside the house, built entirely by hand by her parents. It was a combination of straw and mudbricks and had a cosy cottage appearance. She opened the front door and called out but was met with silence. She hadn't really expected them to be here to greet her, despite the fact she'd called to say she was coming—they spent the majority of their day either in the gardens or in the large sheds used for packing and processing the multitude of herbs they grew to supply the naturopathy industry.

As Rilee walked down the path to the sheds, her phone beeped and she pulled it from her pocket, giving it a quick glance before replying to the text message and putting it back. She'd promised Shae she'd let her know she'd arrived safely, and no doubt the message would then be passed on to Dan, if he even cared. She was still hurt that he'd refused to talk to her. He had to know she'd left Thumb Creek—Shae would have told him, probably nagged him to go and do something to stop her leaving, but clearly he hadn't. She'd left him a note on the kitchen table telling him she'd gone to visit her parents for a few days, but she hadn't heard from him.

She smelled the packing shed before she even walked through the doors. A multitude of scents swirled around her; the combination was overwhelming at first, but it was a good overwhelming, full of rich, robust, pungent smells.

'Look who we have here,' a familiar voice called out.

Rilee looked up to see her father at a table sorting through plants and a grin stretched her face as she headed towards him. His grey-streaked hair was pulled back in its familiar ponytail, and he was wearing his usual uniform of baggy board shorts and a worn T-shirt. As he wrapped her tightly in his hug, Rilee felt a sudden wave of emotion envelop her. It felt so good to be welcomed . . . wanted. She'd missed this so much.

'Where's Mum?' she asked after her father finally released her.

'She went into town to pick up some supplies. She should be home any minute. She was over the moon when she heard you were coming. Where's Dan?' he asked, looking behind her.

'He didn't come. It's just me.'

Her father studied her silently for a few moments. 'Oh well, maybe next visit then.'

And there it was, the gaping difference between her family and the Kincaids. No judgement, no pressure. Just acceptance that when she wanted to tell him more, he'd be there to listen. How could she have ever hoped to get used to the disapproving, criticising ways of her husband's family?

'Come on, let's see if Mum's back yet,' her dad said, leading her from the shed. 'I could use a break.'

They were just boiling the kettle for a cup of tea when Rilee heard her mother's car pull up outside.

'My baby's home,' Shelly said as Rilee met her at the front door.

'Hi, Mum,' she said, muffled against her mother's long hair.

'I'm so happy you're here. Where's Dan?'

'He isn't here.'

'Oh.' Her mother glanced across at Rilee's father briefly.

'It's just me . . . I wanted to come home for a visit. It's been so busy with the clinic and . . .' A sob cut off further conversation, and she saw her parents exchange worried frowns. 'I'm okay, really. Everything's fine.'

'Well, that's a relief,' her father said drolly. 'Usually when someone bursts into tears, it's a bad sign.'

Rilee waved a hand in front of her face and fought to regain her composure.

'How about you tell us what's happened? You'll feel better once you get it off your chest. David,' her mother said, looking up, 'make up a pot of chamomile, passionflower and skullcap and maybe throw in some holy basil.'

Rilee began crying harder. It was so nice to be home and be taken care of.

'Better double the usual dose,' her mother added over her shoulder, rubbing Rilee's back reassuringly.

With a steaming cup between her hands, Rilee began to relax as she started talking about everything that had happened over the last two days, beginning with the cattle and ending with the phone calls about the school presentation. 'I know this community centre would be a good thing for the town. Those kids need help, but everything I do gets met with resistance. Why can they see I'm trying to help?'

'It sounds like they're afraid of change. Maybe you just went at it a little too fast for their comfort,' her father suggested.

'Too fast? I'm supposed to sit on my hands and patiently wait until they're all comfortable with the idea, while in the meantime, kids are putting their health and futures at risk?'

'No, of course not, but small towns are tricky places to navigate when you first move to one. You think we haven't had our fair share of moments? Admittedly in this area we're not that unusual, but we were still outsiders for a long time.'

'What does Dan say about all of this?' her mother asked.

'Dan's not saying much of anything. He's angry and I can't work out if it's because he's sick of being in the middle of his mother and his wife, or if he regrets marrying me. He wants me to give up on it all, just sit at home and be the perfect little wife who does as she's told and stays out of trouble.'

'Are you sure we're talking about the same Dan here? I highly doubt he'd have ever mistaken you for the docile type,' her mother said dryly.

'He refuses to talk about it. Which shouldn't surprise me considering the entire family spends most of their lives not discussing anything.'

'People handle things in different ways,' her father said.

'That's just it,' she said, looking at her parents. 'They're so different to anything I've ever had to deal with. They're like another species.'

Rilee's mother laughed and shook her head. 'Come on now, we raised a more open-minded daughter than this.'

'I've tried, Mum. I really have.'

'Well, you're not a quitter either, so it looks like you're going to have to keep trying. Dan's going through a lot right now and he's going to need you.'

'How am I supposed to help him if he won't even listen to me?'

'There are some things you can't force, Rilee,' her mother said gently. 'You're just going to have to be patient and let him find the time and words to explain it. But it's going to be hard to do while you're all the way over here and he's back there.'

'I know,' she sighed miserably. 'I'm not running away from it.' She saw her parents' knowing smiles and gave a grimace of one back. 'Okay, so maybe a little bit, but it feels like they're all pushing me away. I'm hurt too and it doesn't seem to count for anything. It gets lonely when people keep telling you that you don't fit into their world.'

'I suspect Dan's stubbornness isn't really about your cause. I think he was worried about you, and he reacted out of fear. And you don't have to fit into their world,' her mother said. 'You have to *find your place* in it. And yes, it takes time and patience to become accepted, but it *will* come.'

'I don't know, Mum,' she said, fighting the return of tears. 'No one wants me there and I'm not sure Dan and I are strong enough to survive this. How can he ask me to give up on something that's become so important to me?'

'A man who wanted to marry you as badly as Dan did is not the kind of man who would throw it all away over something like this. His family's going through a tough time right now, he just needs some time to think things through,' her mother said calmly as she topped up Rilee's mug.

Rilee let out a long, slow breath. It was so good to be in a place where she felt only love and acceptance, rather than cool hostility. She knew she'd made the right decision in coming back.

∽

It was funny how sometimes it took going home to put things back into perspective. All the next day Rilee and her mother worked side by side out in the fields tending the herbs, and the combination of physical labour and sunshine did wonders to restore her spirit. She filled her mother in on life at Thumb Creek and her clinic, as well as the fallout from the high school talk.

'The people don't sound very welcoming. Maybe you're right. Maybe it's better you left,' her mother commented after Rilee had exhausted herself, relaying practically every bad experience she'd had in town, but her mother's comment made Rilee hesitate.

'Well . . . at first they were a little standoffish,' she said, remembering back to her first encounters with Pru and Shaz, but then other people came to mind. Edna and Shae; the mailman was always friendly when he dropped in the mail to the usually empty clinic. Actually, there were lots of friendly faces, the more she thought on it; she didn't always know their names, but they smiled or gave her a wave when she passed them down the street. 'Not all of them are like that. I mean, the abusive phone calls and vandalism weren't exactly welcoming, but that was just a knee-jerk reaction.' Not to mention having a ringleader like Priscilla making trouble.

'Really? Hmm,' her mother said, patting the soil firmly back around the base of a plant. 'I guess I must have got the wrong impression then,' she said, looking up and smiling at her daughter.

Rilee had a feeling she'd just been the subject of reverse psychology. *Well played, Mother,* she thought as she watched her stand up and dust off her hands.

When she'd left Pallaburra, she'd felt like an outsider, relieved to escape a place where she clearly didn't fit in. But after talking about it, she began to realise just how much she missed not only Dan but her life at Thumb Creek in general. When had *that* happened?

Forty

Late that afternoon Rilee waved her mother off, happy to finish weeding the remaining rows of figwort. The tranquillity of the afternoon shadows falling across the paddocks was her favourite part of the day. There was something incredibly soul-cleansing about having her hands in the cool, fertile soil and listening to the stillness that surrounded her. Even so, she missed the noisy kookaburras that sent out a riotous chorus in the tall gum trees behind the cottage each afternoon. A wave of longing washed over her.

By the time she'd reached the end of the row, the shadows had crept across the valley and it was growing cool. Rilee sighed as she got to her feet, taking one last long breath before turning away from the sun as it sank behind the mountains.

When she reached the house, her mother looked up and smiled. 'You had a phone call a few minutes ago.'

'Oh?' She tried to remain nonchalant but, judging from her mother's knowing look, she didn't think she was too successful.

'Go call your husband.'

Rilee picked up the phone and closed her eyes. Her stomach was doing flipflops and her hands had begun to sweat. 'This is ridiculous,' she muttered, quickly scrolling through her numbers and pressing call before she could talk herself out of it. On the fourth ring she heard Dan's familiar deep voice and her mouth went dry.

'Hi . . . it's me. Mum said you called,' she added, hating the way she sounded so stilted when all she wanted was to throw her arms around him and bury her head against his chest.

'She said you were outside.'

'How have you been?' Rilee asked, and felt like groaning. Had it really come to them having to resort to small talk as a substitute for actual conversation?

'Pretty crappy actually. You left without telling me.'

'You weren't exactly in the mood to talk, if you recall.'

'I didn't expect you to just pack up and leave.'

'I left a note telling you where I was going.'

She could imagine how that strong jaw she'd caressed countless times would be clenched tightly now, and she ached to be there to reach up and caress it now.

'I came home and you'd gone,' he said finally. 'Do you have any idea how worried I was?'

His abrupt tone made her feel like a five year old getting a lecture and the brief moment of tenderness was gone. 'It took you two days to realise I was gone? Maybe if you'd stopped sulking and come home earlier, you'd have found out sooner.'

'I did come home, the day you left, I just haven't known what I was going to say when I called you.'

'So I take it this is you ready to talk now?' she asked, with a hint of snarkiness in her tone.

'I didn't expect you to hightail it back to your parents' place.'

'I didn't expect you to do that either. And I certainly didn't expect you to take your mother's side over mine. I guess we've both learned to live with disappointment.'

There was an angry silence on the end of the phone and Rilee felt the fight leave her in a rush. She hated this. Why couldn't they go back to the way they were before? How did they end up here? 'I needed a few days away to clear my head. I said I'd be back in a day or two, it was all there in the note,' she finally said, feeling miserable.

'I wasn't sure you were. I wasn't sure of anything.'

Rilee was fed up with going in circles. 'I know you've been under a lot of stress lately with the business, your dad being sick and trying to handle the property alone, but that's no excuse for the way you treated me. What happened to the man who supported my career and wanted me as a partner in his business? Was it all an act? I mean, you clearly didn't want to listen to anything I had to say about buying the bull, and then you practically forbade me to continue with the community centre and showed no interest in my floundering business. Just how much did you think I could take before I'd had enough?'

She heard a harsh breath being let out on the other end of the phone. 'I know I acted like a jerk. I didn't mean to take it out on you, but you've got to understand, Ri. All this stuff about encouraging kids to get abortions—'

'I never did that! That's what your mother and the rest of the ignorant troublemakers in town said I was doing. I tried to tell you this before, the morning-after pill is not the same as an abortion! It stops the pregnancy from ever happening. It's got nothing to do with getting rid of a baby that's already conceived.'

'Yeah,' he sighed. 'I know. I had a visit from Lisa and she explained it . . . with a few more swear words than you. I realise now that it's not the same thing.'

She could imagine the small twist of his lips that usually accompanied the rueful tone he was using now.

'This whole crusade you've been on,' he said as the silence stretched. 'It scared me, Ri. You're stirring up people and I was worried. Someone smashed your window—what if things got really out of hand, what if something happened to you? Is your safety worth the risk?'

'I seriously don't think my safety is at risk. Not compared to the risk kids will continue to take if something isn't done. No fifteen-year-old is ready for the responsibility of a baby. Access to contraception and keeping them in school has to be better than living with the consequences of an unwanted child. And if they make the choice to keep the baby, they need support to parent and help to continue their education.'

She heard his small grunt of acknowledgement on the other end. 'It's just going to take some time for people to come to terms with.'

There it was again. *Time*. 'How much *time* are they going to need? How long before you can be proud of what your wife is trying to do to help the community you and your parents value so damn much?' she snapped. 'I understand why you were upset, but what I don't understand is how you could just shut me out and listen to everyone except me. I'm *supposed* to be your wife, Dan!'

'You *are* my wife, Rilee,' he said tightly.

'Then why the hell do you continue to take your family's side on everything?'

'Because you know what my mother's like—she can be a pain in the arse when she wants to be,' he sighed.

'Then it's time you showed her that being a pain in the arse is not acceptable. I appreciate that you love your family and I can even learn to accept living right next door, to them, I really can. But until we all reach some kind of understanding, and set some boundaries, I'm not sure I want to go back there. It's not fair that I'm expected to be the one who has to compromise all the time. You and I need to be able to live our own lives, Dan, without her approval or interference.'

'My parents and I work together, Ri,' he said irritably. 'You can't just shut them out of everything we do.'

'I'm not asking you to, all I'm asking is that there are boundaries. She doesn't get to walk into our home as though it's hers. She doesn't get to command us to dinner. She needs to let go of the reins a little bit. She's suffocating me.'

'Fine,' he sighed.

'Don't do that,' Rilee said sadly.

'Do what?'

'Treat me like I'm an obnoxious child. I *want* to fit in with your family; I've tried so hard to do just that. I understood your mother had a right to be a bit annoyed by us getting married without telling anyone, but at some point she needs to let go of that. You and your father give in to her behaviour because it's easier, but all it's doing is driving a wedge between you and me. Do you always want to be stuck in the middle of your mother and your wife? That's no way to live, Dan. We need to find a way to all coexist or we won't make it.'

'So you're ready to give up?'

'No. I want to fight for our marriage, but you have to be willing to back me up, not pat me on the head and side with your mother. I want them to love me, Dan, I want that so badly, but I won't allow them to treat me like I don't belong with you, that I'm not part of your family. And you shouldn't let them.'

She heard Dan let out a long, weary sigh on the other end of the phone and closed her eyes. She was emotionally drained and heartsick. She missed him.

'I guess I've been hoping things would just sort themselves out. I should have been paying more attention, but

I got distracted with the cattle and then Dad's illness . . . I know I let you down. I didn't mean to, Ri. I'm sorry.'

Rilee bit the inside of her lip to stop the sting of tears falling. 'I guess this is the hard part of marriage everyone keeps going on about.'

'Guess so,' Dan agreed.

'I want this to work, Dan. I love you so much.'

'I love you too, Ri. Will you please come home?' he asked and she heard his voice break slightly.

It took a moment for Rilee to swallow past the tightening of her throat. 'I'll leave first thing in the morning,' she said quietly.

'Okay.'

For a moment she thought he was going to say more, but when only silence followed, Rilee swallowed back her disappointment and said goodbye. It wasn't a hallelujah moment, but it was the most promising conversation they'd managed in weeks. It was a start.

Forty-one

Later that night, Rilee lay in her bed, staring up at the ceiling. It was no use, she had to resign herself to the fact she wouldn't be getting any sleep. Her mind kept replaying Dan's call. She missed him so much. She was optimistic that she'd been able to get across her concerns. Well, she amended dryly, some of her concerns, Ellen was still a problem that needed to be sorted.

Her phone sprang to life on the bedside table, the loud ringtone piercing the stillness of the quiet night. She snatched it up quickly before it could wake her parents down the hall.

'Rilee?'

For a moment Rilee was confused. She'd expected it to be Dan's voice on the end of the line.

'It's Mark. There's been an accident. It's Dan.'

The flight to Sydney from Lismore had seemed to drag on forever, even though it had been only a little over an hour and a half. Her father had patted her hand and said plenty of reassuring words during the drive to the airport, but she'd barely been able to hear him. Her parents had offered to go with her, but there was only one seat remaining on the first flight out in the morning and she'd assured them she would be fine. She just needed to get to Dan's side.

He'd rolled his ute over an embankment on his way back from town, only minutes after they'd spoken on the phone, and no one had found him until later that night when he hadn't returned home. His father had gone out looking for him and stumbled upon Dan's lights in the ditch before calling an ambulance. He'd been flown to Sydney by helicopter, his injuries too extensive for the regional hospital.

Rilee sat in the taxi, anxiously counting the minutes until they reached the hospital. Paying the driver, she ran into the front lobby, heading for the first nursing station she could find.

Inside the elevator she struggled to keep her breathing even. Her heart seemed to be beating too hard; she felt the pain of it against her chest. She took a deep breath and closed her eyes to steady herself. She would be no good to Dan if she collapsed in a heap. She needed to stay calm, which was easier said than done when her mind kept drifting to worst-case scenarios.

When the doors finally opened, Rilee stepped out onto the ICU floor and immediately saw Jacob and Ellen seated at the end of the hall.

They looked up as she approached. Rilee opened her mouth to calmly ask how Dan was, but instead of a rational question, a gigantic sob escaped, followed by uncontrollable tears. There was only the slightest of hesitations before Rilee found herself wrapped in two surprisingly strong arms and Jacob's gruff voice comforted her as she wept. 'Come on now, girl. That boy of mine's a Kincaid. He's tough as they come. He'll be fine.'

Rilee sat down unsteadily and wiped her eyes, accepting a tissue from Ellen who had come to sit down on the other side of her. 'Have you seen the doctor yet?'

'Briefly, but he's coming out to talk with us once he's finished examining Dan. There's been some kind of rupture to his liver and damage to his lungs,' Jacob told her, and Rilee was worried about how shaken Dan's father looked. 'They've got him intubated so they can monitor him closely. He'll be in ICU until he's more stable. We'll know more as soon as the doc gets out here.'

The information floated through the air. Rilee was only vaguely aware of what he'd been saying; for some reason she couldn't seem to hold on to any of the words and make sense of them. Still, it was good that he'd had his parents here with him . . . even if his wife had abandoned him. Guilt raked her soul. She should never have left . . . her inward berating was interrupted by a young man in a white coat heading down the hall towards them.

'Mr and Mrs Kincaid?' he asked, looking between Dan's parents.

'Yes, and this is our daughter-in-law, Rilee. Dan's wife,' Ellen said, touching Rilee's shoulder lightly. Despite her shock, Rilee was still able to appreciate the uncharacteristic treatment from her in-laws. She would have liked a moment or two to enjoy it, but the doctor was already speaking and she needed to focus on Dan right now.

The doctor turned to Rilee and nodded. 'As I briefly explained to your husband's parents earlier, your husband has a number of injuries. When he presented to the emergency room he was conscious, but the bruising to his lungs was restricting the depth of his breathing so we decided to intubate and sedate him to maintain his airway and assist his breathing. He has three fractured ribs as well as extensive bruising and grazes, but we're most concerned about the contusions to the lungs and a small rupture to the liver, which has been contained at this stage. However, we need to keep a strict watch on it to make sure there's no further bleeding.'

'Can we see him?' Ellen asked.

'Yes, but only for a few minutes.' He indicated they should follow him.

Rilee had never been in an ICU before. For some reason she expected it to be deathly quiet, but it wasn't. Machines beeped and buzzed, and there was a rhythmic sound of life-support machines regulating patients' breathing.

The doctor led them through the room, stopping at the end of a bed. Rilee's eyes were already roaming the familiar face, her chest tight. He was so still. So pale. Her eyes followed the path of numerous tubes and leads from his body connecting to monitors and multiple bags of fluid, but the worst by far was the tube down his throat. His stubble looked dark against the backdrop of white sheets. There were numerous grazes covering his face and arms. Beneath his eye was a row of stitches, and the whole area was swollen and red.

Beside her, Rilee heard Ellen give a small whimper, turning her face into her husband's chest.

Clearly none of them could remember him ever looking so vulnerable before, and it was an unsettling and confronting moment.

'We've done a CT and X-ray and he's cleared of spinal injuries, but to be satisfied that the haemorrhage in his liver isn't going to bleed further we need to monitor him closely for another twenty-four hours. He's not out of the woods yet.'

They thanked the doctor as he left them and Rilee leaned down and kissed her husband's forehead. 'I love you,' she whispered, before they were gently reminded by the nurse that time was up and led from the room.

Rilee accepted a ride back to the motel Jacob and Ellen were staying at and booked herself a room. They were expecting Natalie and Megan to arrive later that night. She had no idea how long she would be staying, but she knew there was nowhere else on earth she wanted to be right now. Everything they'd been worried about seemed so unimportant, and all she cared about was Dan waking up and getting back on his feet again.

Rilee opened the door of her room and dumped her suitcase and bag on the spare bed, then headed across to the sliding door to let some fresh air inside. The smell of the motel room was making her feel slightly nauseous, which reminded her that she hadn't eaten anything since dinner last night.

As she stepped outside onto the small balcony later that evening, she took in the long lines of tail-lights trailing a path from the city and breathed in the once-familiar smell of exhaust and air pollution. It was so different to the clean, fresh air of Thumb Creek.

A soft knock on her door drew her back inside, and she hoped the astonishment she was feeling didn't show on her face as she opened the door to reveal Megan standing there. She didn't look quite as together as she had the last time they'd met. Her eyes were a little bloodshot from the late flight and there was a strain around her eyes that gave away her vulnerability.

'I know it's late, but can I come in for a minute?'

'Of course,' Rilee said. 'Have your parents filled you in on everything?' she asked as they took a seat at the small table.

'Yes. It's sounding a lot more positive than it was initially,' she said, and Rilee heard her voice break a little as she lowered her head slightly to compose herself.

Rilee reached out and gently touched her sister-in-law's arm, her own eyes stinging with tears. 'He's going to be fine. He won't give up.'

She nodded briskly before straightening her shoulders, and Rilee slowly withdrew her hand, feeling as though she was overstepping the mark again.

'I wanted to apologise to you,' she said, holding Rilee's surprised gaze. 'I acted dreadfully when I was home last. I guess you worked out that Priscilla was my friend,' she said with a twist of her lips that was exactly like her brother's. 'I had no right to treat you the way I did. I should have been happy that my brother found someone he really loved. I was being jealous and petty, just because I couldn't have the kind of relationship you two seemed to have.'

'I can understand that,' Rilee said, willing to let bygones be bygones if it meant they could start over. 'Let's just forget it.'

'I don't really deserve your understanding, but I want you to know that you don't have to worry about Priscilla making any more trouble. I heard what she's been doing and I assure you that I had no idea about the vendetta she's been carrying out against you and your business. As soon as I heard about it, I put a stop to it.'

Rilee couldn't help gaping.

'I threatened her with legal action and told her to make some public amends or I'd tell everyone what she'd done. I can't believe she would go to such despicable lengths out of jealousy. I'm truly sorry.'

'No, that's okay. I mean, it wasn't your fault,' Rilee stammered, trying to take in the sudden U-turn of events. 'Thank you for helping.'

350

'If I were you, I wouldn't dismiss the possibility of legal action against her.'

As damaging as Priscilla's hate campaign had been, Rilee really couldn't think of anything worse than dragging everyone through something like that, and at the moment she had more important things to worry about than some spoilt brat's temper tantrum. She said goodnight to Megan and then leaned her back against the closed door, suddenly feeling a lot more optimistic. The thought of being surrounded by Dan's family without him would once have filled her with dread, but now she felt their support and care. It was true what they said: times of crisis really did make people realise what was important in life.

∽

As Rilee sat on a bench outside the hospital the next morning, Ellen appeared carrying a cup of coffee and asked if she could join her. It should have felt awkward sitting beside the woman who had made her disapproval so obvious, but the silence between them didn't feel strained. Dan's condition hadn't changed, but the doctor was pleased there'd been no bleeding from his liver or lungs, and that was certainly a huge weight off everyone's minds.

'I feel responsible, Ellen,' Rilee finally said, staring down into her almost empty cup. 'I shouldn't have left.'

'If anyone should feel responsible then it's me. I know I helped drive you away. If you hadn't felt as though you needed to leave Thumb Creek then none of this would have happened.'

Rilee couldn't help the surprise that followed that little admission. 'I know I'm not the daughter-in-law you wanted, and I'm sorry we started off on the wrong foot.'

Ellen let out a short breath. 'No, dear, I should be apologising. It had always been expected,' she shrugged helplessly, 'Dan and Priscilla. I was too focused on what a marriage between them would mean for the two families and I ignored the fact that you can't force love. Dan had been trying to tell me that he wasn't interested, but I just figured eventually he'd realise Priscilla was the perfect choice for him. It turns out he was a lot smarter than I was.'

Ellen leaned towards Rilee slightly. 'I recently discovered Priscilla has been spreading terrible rumours and making a general nuisance of herself where your business is concerned. I am extremely disappointed. I expected a lot more from that girl. I know I can't take back the damage she's done, but I can help fix it. I've made sure everyone knows the truth,' she said earnestly, and Rilee had to swallow through an unexpectedly tightening throat. 'The truth is that I felt threatened by you and I reacted badly.'

'Threatened? How?'

'You were so confident and . . . cheerful,' she smiled dryly. 'In case you hadn't noticed, there hasn't been a great deal of happiness in our house for quite some time.'

Rilee bit the inside of her lip as she sat quietly to give Ellen time to collect her thoughts.

'You were this bright, optimistic young thing bouncing into our lives and you reminded me of things I'd forgotten we'd once had. I can't even recall when all the joy left our family,' she said wistfully. 'I remember when the children were little there was laughter and smiles, but at some point over the years, as they left home, it just grew quiet . . . until there was only Jacob and I in that big old house and we'd somehow become two strangers.'

Rilee saw the woman search in her handbag and pull out a handkerchief, dabbing at the corner of her eyes delicately.

'You were so determined to bring light back into our lives, and I fought against it because it scared me.'

'Why?' Rilee asked, searching the older woman's damp eyes.

'Because I was afraid to get my hopes up. What if Jacob couldn't change? What if, despite everything you were trying to do, he simply didn't love me any more?'

'Oh, Ellen.' Rilee wrapped an arm around her mother-in-law's shoulders and comforted her. Ellen had spent such a long time perfecting that tough exterior in order to protect the tiny ember of hope that remained inside. Fear and insecurity had been the driving forces behind her cold attitude this entire time.

'I hope you can forgive me for the way I've been acting. If you come back, I promise things will be different,' she said, straightening her hair and composing herself once more. 'Dan had already laid down the law after you left. He was so upset. I think he thought he'd lost you, and I know that was in large part because of me. I'd like to start over.'

Rilee blinked back the tears. 'I'd like that too.'

A relieved smile crossed Ellen's face and she gave a small nod. They sat in silence, finishing their coffee, and Rilee felt a strange sort of peace settle between them.

When they went back inside the hospital, Megan and Natalie gave them the news that the doctor had just been and they were making a decision about taking Dan off the ventilator following the results of the CT scan. Rilee tried to contain her impatience, but she couldn't seem to sit still and gave up trying, instead pacing the floor of the waiting room. When the doctor finally appeared, he was smiling, a stark contrast to their previous meeting, and Rilee instantly felt relief wash through her.

'It's looking very good,' he said as he came out to see them. 'We've done another scan and there's no further bleeding noted.'

'What happens now?' Rilee asked.

'We'll start weaning him off the medication we've been giving him and see how he responds. If he's coping all right we'll extubate. He'll remain in ICU for another twenty-four hours, and then he'll be transferred to a monitored bed where we can keep an eye on him.

'When do you think he'll be able to go home, doctor?' Ellen asked.

'He'll need to be here for at least a week. Make no mistake, your son was extremely lucky. Had his liver ruptured at the scene, he wouldn't have even made it to hospital. He'll have a lengthy recovery.'

The mood, while not buoyant after the doctor's solemn words, was at least more positive than earlier.

At the nursing staff's suggestion, they returned to the motel after lunch, with the hospital not anticipating there would be anything happening until the next morning.

The family spent the rest of the day in Ellen and Jacob's suite, and despite the worry that hung over their heads, it gave Rilee a chance to spend some quality time with her new sisters. Her parents were driving down in the morning, and Rilee couldn't ever remember a time where she felt surrounded by so much love. She wished Dan were here to see it. If only she could rewind the last few weeks. If only they hadn't fought. *If only, if only.* She gave a sigh as she tipped her head back against the leather sofa. There was no point wishing for things she couldn't change, they just had to focus on the here and now, and getting through the next twenty-four hours.

∽

Rilee grasped Natalie and Megan's hands tightly as they sat waiting to be allowed in to see Dan late the next day. He was now free and clear of the ventilator and breathing on his own. While he was still not up to a proper visit, seeing him without a tube down his throat would be a huge relief.

When a nurse came to tell them they could come in, Rilee hung back, allowing his parents and siblings to walk into the room first. From her position near the door she could see he'd lost the vulnerable look he'd had in past visits, but the memory of how helpless he had seemed still brought a tear to her eye.

His sisters and parents hovered near the bed and he managed a faint smile at them, but Rilee could see he was fighting to remain awake.

Ellen gently patted his hand before leaning over to kiss his cheek. 'We'll come back tomorrow,' she said, before stepping aside to make room for Rilee.

For a long while Rilee simply sat and took in his battered face, before gingerly taking his hand in hers. His eyelids fluttered open and she quickly blinked away the tears that began to blur her vision.

'Hi,' she said quietly.

She saw his throat working a little as he tried to speak and she winced at how sore everything must be feeling after all he'd been through.

'Don't try to talk yet,' she said. 'Just rest.' She summoned a smile to reassure him as his eyes got heavy and closed once more. Rilee lowered her head to their joined hands and squeezed her eyes tightly shut. She'd come so close to losing him and relief ebbed through her now that he looked like making a good recovery.

The next day her parents arrived and Dan was deemed fit enough to move to a different ward where he would continue to be monitored. He was still weak though, so visits remained short and, after the second day, Ellen convinced Megan and Natalie to go home. Their brother was out of danger and there was little they could do for the next week while he remained in the city, so a visit was planned once he was back home.

Rilee lifted her head and gave a small groan, rubbing her stiff neck before her eyes shot open and she found herself looking into two sleepy eyes, watching her through slightly lowered lids. She must have fallen asleep. She eased back from where she'd been leaning against the bed, still in her chair, and ignored her body protesting at having been contorted into some weird human form of a pretzel. 'Sorry, I didn't mean to fall asleep,' she said, brushing her hair from her face and hoping she didn't look as bad as she felt.

'You didn't have to stay,' he said, his voice still croaky.

'Where else would I be?' She moved her hand to on top of his.

'I'm sorry,' he said, breaking the quiet of the room.

'Don't worry about all that now.'

'I love you, Ri.'

'I know,' she said softly. 'I love you too.' But he was already asleep.

A nurse came in and smiled at her. 'He's still on a lot of pain medication. I think you better go and get some rest. I didn't have the heart to wake you when I came in earlier, but you're not going to thank me when you're all stiff and sore later.'

Rilee had reluctantly dragged herself back to the motel. It was quiet without her parents there; they'd been happy to stay longer, but Rilee couldn't see the point. She was spending most of her time at the hospital and there was really nothing they could do. Still, it had been nice to have them

around and she felt a little teary about how great everyone
had been throughout the whole ordeal.

Rilee had also noticed the subtle change in Ellen and
Jacob since the accident; it hadn't been lost on the girls
either. She hadn't had a chance to really think about it
with everything going on, but Natalie's comment a few
days earlier that her parents were stuck in a two-bedroom
suite and hadn't killed each other now floated back to mind.
Ellen and Jacob *had* been different.

As she watched them over dinner that evening, it was like
looking at her in-laws in some kind of alternate universe—
having the kind of relationship they *could* have been having.
While they weren't acting like a pair of newlyweds, there
was a subtle shift in their body language. They sat closer
on the lounge—she couldn't even remember them ever
sitting on the same lounge at home before. She'd even overheard them discussing stories from the newspaper; maybe
it wasn't some huge romantic gesture but it *was* interaction
and communication, and Rilee hoped this was the start of
a new beginning for the couple. After all, if she and Ellen
could forge a new friendship, surely there was hope for
their marriage.

Rilee met up with Janice and Sid at a nearby café the
next morning, allowing Jacob and Ellen to have some
time alone with their son. It had been great to see them
both—the visit wasn't anywhere near as long as she'd have
liked, but it had done her the world of good to see her old
friends again. They'd surprised her with news that they
were planning to retire within the next few years and do

some travelling, and Rilee made them promise to head out to Pallaburra and stay with them. It was hard to imagine Sid caravanning instead of standing behind a bar, but the thought gave her something happy to think about as she headed back to the hospital.

As she entered Dan's room, Ellen and Jacob were just about to leave.

'We'll let you two spend some time together. I think your father and I will stay in the city for a few days. We're actually looking at some properties down here,' Ellen said.

'Properties?' Dan's voice still had a hoarse sound to it.

'Your mother's always wanted a place in the city, son. If I'm going to be spending all this flamin' time down here, it makes sense to have somewhere to stay. All going well, we're thinking after my treatment we'll probably start spending a few months of the year in the city. The doc reckons I need to start taking things a bit easier,' his father shrugged. 'But don't go getting any ideas about taking over the place. I'll still be hangin' around to make sure everything's running right,' he added, just so they didn't think he was going completely soft.

She could see Dan doing a double-take at his parents.

'Come on, I'm hungry. Let's find a place to eat,' Jacob said, getting to his feet and holding his arm out to his wife.

'Oh for goodness sake, Jacob. Have you been drinking or something?' Ellen said, although there was no sting to the words and she slid her arm into his willingly.

Jacob sent them a wink as they walked out the door and this time Rilee couldn't hold back her giggle.

'What the hell was that?' he croaked.

'I think *that* was your parents reconnecting.'

'What did you do to them?'

'Don't look at me. They did it all by themselves.'

'Just *how long* was I out for?' he asked with a befuddled frown.

She did chuckle at that. 'Sometimes it takes almost losing something to give you a kick up the pants,' she said softly.

Rilee felt her throat tighten as Dan's gaze settled on her. She'd almost lost him. He could have died. She saw his eyelids droop slightly and gave his hand a gentle squeeze. 'You get some rest. I'll come back later.'

'Don't go,' he said, and his hand tightened on hers.

'I'm not going anywhere,' she promised, kissing his cheek softly as she watched him lose the battle to stay awake.

Forty-two

Six weeks later and life had settled back into a new kind of normal back at home. After his last check-up and the doctor's approval, Dan was allowed on light duties, under Rilee's strict instructions that if he did anything more than supervise, she would hogtie him to the bed. Unfortunately, Rilee suspected he considered this an incentive, so for good measure she warned Mark that he would be in trouble as well if she caught Dan doing anything strenuous.

Rilee's return to the clinic, having left town during the fallout from the high school education session, was one of nervous anticipation. Her heart sank a little as she saw the number of messages waiting for her on the phone. Surely they'd given up on the nasty calls by now? She almost deleted them without listening, but relented at the last minute. She cautiously pressed the button and played the first one. It was a request for an appointment. Rilee hit the second message after taking the details of the first call and to her surprise it was another appointment request. Within a few minutes she was up to message eight and she'd already filled most of the columns on the next few days in her appointment book. '*I'm calling for an appointment. Edna said you were a miracle worker and she feels better than she has in years. She said I should give you a call,*' the woman on the answering machine was saying. It wasn't the first one who had mentioned Edna as the referring source and Rilee caught her lower lip between her teeth as gratitude washed over her. The last message was from Teal asking if she could call him back.

The sound of the door opening made Rilee glance up from her paperwork. 'This is a nice surprise,' Rilee smiled as Shae walked in and sat down. Her smile quickly faded when she saw how pale her friend was. 'What's wrong?'

Shae lifted her red-rimmed eyes and Rilee immediately moved to her friend's side and took her hand. 'Shae?'

'I took a test this morning,' Shae said.

For a moment Rilee frowned. A test? 'A *pregnancy* test?' she finally realised, eyeing Shae intently.

'It was positive,' Shae whispered, squeezing Rilee's hand tightly.

Rilee stared at her for a moment and then beamed, overcome with relief that it was good news and not bad as she'd been anticipating. 'That's wonderful,' she said, and they shared a hug. Soon, though, the practitioner in her kicked in and she started checking on Shae's diet and asking general health questions, reaching for her pen to start writing out a list of supplements. It was early days and there was always the risk of another miscarriage, but Rilee was confident that her treatments had helped and things would be different this time around.

She'd been so busy with Dan and his recovery that she'd barely had time to catch up with Shae since they'd been home. Now that she thought back on it, Shae had seemed a little quieter than usual, but she hadn't thought too much about it at the time. She felt like a crappy friend and an even worse practitioner.

'I'm so sorry I haven't dropped around since we've been back.'

'You've kind of had a bit on your plate,' Shae said dryly.

Rilee had to agree. She was happy to consign the last few weeks to the past and leave them there.

No sooner had she waved goodbye to Shae than the door opened again and someone else walked in.

'You're back!' Lisa said and threw her arms around Rilee.

Rilee gave a surprised chuckle. 'I guess you missed me,' she said when they broke apart.

'I did. I'm so glad Dan's home and on the mend.'

'It takes more than a near-death experience to keep my husband away from his beloved cattle,' Rilee said dryly. 'He makes a lousy patient.'

'It's never easy when we try to treat loved ones. But anyway,' she said briskly, 'I take it you haven't heard from Teal yet?'

'I had a message asking me to get back to him. I haven't had a chance yet . . . Why?'

Lisa rolled her eyes theatrically. 'Oh, nothing major, just that they've managed to secure funding for our community centre and the whole thing's got the green light!'

For the second time that day, Rilee was dumbfounded. 'They're going to do it?'

'Yep!' Lisa's grin almost split her face. 'There'll be computers which can be used to access online programs or Skype for face-to-face appointments and therapy sessions. We'll have fortnightly visits by a doctor, counsellor and youth worker. They'll be assisting with career information and job training for young people. Down the track they hope to bring in wider community-based programs that will cover all sorts of things—the elderly, young mums, childcare . . . The possibilities are endless, and the community centre itself will provide new local jobs.'

'This is amazing,' Rilee said, unable to do more little than stare at her friend and shake her head.

'You did it,' Lisa said proudly.

'We did it. Until you came on board, I wasn't getting anywhere.'

'You started it. And this town had better be damn grateful.'

Rilee's lips twisted slightly. 'I'm sure there'll be someone unhappy about something, but you know what?' she said, tilting her head slightly. 'That's okay. It's what they do here. Change scares them. We just have to ride out that initial knee-jerk response until things settle down. I'm not going to take it personally any more.'

'You've come a long way, grasshopper,' Lisa said drolly.

'Thank you, master, I learned from the best.'

'Well, I have to get back. I left Mum alone in the store, she's probably dismantling my display of novelty condoms while I'm gone.'

'I heard about that,' Rilee grinned. 'You wouldn't be *trying* to provoke the good people of Pallaburra, would you?'

'Who? *Me?*' Lisa asked as she waved over her shoulder.

Rilee sank into her chair and closed her eyes, a contented smile on her face.

The sound of the door opening had Rilee dropping her head and giving a silent chuckle. There seemed little point in trying to get anything done today after all. As she looked up, her smile faltered a little. 'Talissa,' she said warmly, covering her surprise.

'I thought you'd left town.'

'Nope. I just had some family business to take care of.' Rilee wasn't sure if there was a purpose to the visit, but she'd gotten used to the roundabout way the young girl broached whatever was on her mind, so she waited calmly.

'I was thinkin' about what you said about studying.'

Rilee felt a shot of excitement spike through her, but fought hard to mask it. Too much enthusiasm would send Talissa retreating back inside her shell faster than flies through an open screen door.

'I want a better life for my daughter. I wanna finish school and be a teacher.'

Rilee did try but she just couldn't remain cool about it; instead she gave a small squeak of excitement. 'That's really great news. I'm so pleased for you.'

'Yeah, well, I don't know what to do next. I thought maybe you might know.'

Right at that very minute, Rilee knew that everything it had taken to see the community centre come to fruition had been worth it. 'Let's make some phone calls and see what we can find out.'

No matter how much red tape and community adversity she had to face, she'd do it gladly, because this was what it was all for—to give kids like Talissa a fighting chance in the world.

This wasn't the dream she'd had before she met Dan; her city practice hadn't happened, and her country one was only now starting to pick up, but maybe life had a different plan for her. Maybe instead of fighting to hold on to the dream she'd always carried, she needed to see where this path was leading her.

Outside a car pulled up and Rilee spotted Dan gingerly climbing out. He pushed his hat back off his forehead slightly, taking his sunglasses off and hooking them onto the front of his shirt. She let her eyes follow the width of his shoulders and down over the denim of his dusty work jeans. He was her knight in . . . well, denim. He'd stormed into her life and set her on a path that was leading her towards a very different future to the one she'd been planning.

Maybe they *had* rushed into this marriage, and maybe they had missed a few of the preliminary steps, but in her heart she knew the most important thing: she loved this man more than life itself. The rest they'd figure out later.

Together.

Acknowledgements

Huge thanks to Tamara McWillams for a conversation one day that started with 'You should do a book with a naturopath in it . . .' and all her follow-up help with the technical details (that'll teach you to come up with a really good idea, Tamara!).

Thank you so much to the various people who helped with research, questions and early reading: Lyn Mattick, Netti Lane, Kirstin Knight, Kristy Watson, Glenda Grey, Sonya Popowycz Comiskey and Natalie Young. And thanks as always to supernurse Leanne Jarvis for giving me all the big words I need to make me sound so much smarter than I actually am. Big shout-out to my agent, Jo Butler; I'm still so impressed with your city driving skills—give me a corrugated dirt road any day!

To my fantastic publisher and all the crew at Allen & Unwin, thank you for continuing to allow me to write these stories and all your help to make them shine.

Earlier this year I was honoured to be an Australia Day ambassador. While writing my Australia Day speech I realised that writing rural fiction is so much more than simply a genre I like to write in. Rural Australia is my passion. The communities I write about and the issues that they face could apply to any rural community anywhere in Australia. I feel privileged to be able to share these stories with you, and I hope in some small way we can help raise awareness for rural Australia and the obstacles that distance, population and lack of funding pose to so many of our smaller communities.